I0452746

THE
HOLLOW
CITY

A Network Tale
by
Sean B. Casey

First Edition

Cover Design: James Ryan

Book Design: Eva Kuczynski

ISBN 978-0-9996734-0-9

This book is dedicated to my Parents.

Without them and the teachings they bestowed on me, I wouldn't be the person I am today to create the book before you now.

I know I don't visit as much as I should, or call as often as I could, but let these words be written here forever,

I love you both.

Acknowledgement

This self-published work, despite that name, could not be completed without a tremendous effort on the part of others. In my first ever experience working with an editor, I couldn't have known what I got when I hired Paul Fairbairn. His coaching and insight truly helped shape the work and deepened my understanding of writing. I can't wait to finish the next project to get the chance to work with him again.

For my second hire, this time for the cover, I came across James Ryan. James was a pleasure to work with. His quick communications and adjustments made the cover even better than I first imagined.

The books wouldn't have been started without my friends and family. A billion thanks to them. Your continued interest and checkups on the progress of the book helped me focus on a long path to the book's completion. Words will never express how much you all mean to me.

To the online communities out there, from the casual acquaintances to the few that I have grown personally close to; Thank you all so much. Your support over the last year and a half gave me the final push I needed to start down the road of moving the pages from the screen to a published book.

Day 1

RICHARD SULLIVAN SLOWLY closed the window shades inside the hospital room. He could still smell the foul stench of medical waste clinging to his custodian's uniform.

He looked over at the young girl lying on the bed. Various tubes snaked around her, and fluid-filled bags hung from metal stands above her head. Her hair was tightly braided, carefully woven by her worried mother earlier that day. The girl's face was pale, her eyes ringed with dark smudges. She was nine years old.

A pang of sadness pierced Richard's chest. His hands trembled and his head was pounding, but he refused to give into the urge. He had work to do before he could indulge himself. He grabbed the medical chart that hung from the bed's footboard. She was only one of many unfortunate souls on this level of the intensive care ward, but Richard knew her case intimately.

"They say it's terminal," the girl said. "I've got a cloned heart, but my body doesn't like it. They say my body's rejecting the . . ." She trailed off, lost in medical jargon.

Richard smiled sadly at her. He was confident in his decision—this was the one he'd been looking for. No matter the cost.

"Sally, how long did they say you'll have to wait before a . . ." He paused a moment to compose himself, ". . . before a donor is found?"

"They don't know," she said quietly. "They said, at my age, donors are rare for CHD. That stands for Connery Heart Disease, you know."

Richard smiled again. "Is that right?" he said. "*Connery* heart disease?"

"Sure," she said. "But my mommy says not to think about that. I should think about getting better." Though her words were strong, Richard could see the fear that gripped her.

He crossed to her bedside. The incessant chirping of monitoring machines filled the room. He took her tiny hand in his, noting her underdeveloped bone structure. He gently stroked her hair. She started to weep, almost silently.

"Don't cry, Sally. What if I told you I had a secret? But if I reveal it to you, you can never tell another living soul." Richard grinned broadly.

"My mommy doesn't like me keeping secrets from her," she said. Richard's grin widened.

"Well your mommy sounds like a very smart lady. You should listen to her. What does your mommy say about half-truths?"

"What's a half-truth?"

"It's when you tell the truth, but you leave out the unnecessary pieces."

She scrunched up her face. "Unnecessary pieces, like what?"

"Like when the doctors come in later and ask you all sorts of questions, you leave out the part where I visited you. When they ask how you're all better." Richard was practically glowing. He was about to perform a miracle, his one true source of happiness in a tormented existence.

"But I'm not all better. If I was all better, I'd be home."

Richard felt power accumulating in his chest. "Not yet," he told both her and himself as he drew in more energy from an invisible force.

Placing the girl's left hand on top of his sweaty palm, he took a deep, steadying breath. The tips of her fingers rested gently on top of his own. He placed his right hand on the opposite side of her head, directly touching her temple. He grunted as stored energy seeped down his arms. The tips of his fingers, where they touched the girl, glowed faintly blue.

Sally's back arched as the opening surge of energy rushed into her body. Wisps of blue diffused into her veins and arteries, racing towards her heart where they gathered around the failing organ. With each heartbeat, the energy was absorbed into the cell walls.

Breaking contact, Richard staggered back a few steps. He collapsed into the chair beside the bed and sighed loudly. He felt as if he'd run a marathon. His stomach grumbled, and he realized he was ravenous.

The girl suddenly sprang up in her bed. "It doesn't hurt when I breathe anymore!" she cried.

"That's very good to hear."

Richard was struggling to keep his eyes open. He managed a weak smile in her direction, but this episode had drawn more vitality out of him than he'd expected. More than he had ever used in one sitting before tonight.

A sudden look of realization washed over the girl's face.

"You!" she cried, bouncing to her knees on the bed, pulling at the tubes and wires that were still attached to her. "You're Saint Michael! The one who helps all the people here. They say it's the good care, but no one can explain how they get better. You're the reason why, aren't you?"

Richard eyed the girl. Her face was flushed with excitement; she was no longer the same pale and sickly kid she had been just moments ago.

"Most of the time it is those great doctors and nurses who save the people," Richard said. "Every once in a while though, something extra is needed. That's where I try to help." He suppressed his smile. "But remember, for me to continue, you can't tell anyone I was here. Even if they pepper you with questions, you can't say a word."

"I promise." She placed a small hand over her newly-healed heart, sealing her vow. "Your secret is safe with me." She beamed at him, and he grinned back.

Groaning with exhaustion, Richard climbed to his feet. Every joint ached. He gave the girl a short wink and a half-smile and headed for the open doorway. As he stepped into the corridor, she said, "I know what I can tell everyone about tonight."

Richard turned back to face her. "Oh, and what's that?"

"I can tell them it was an angel who came and healed me. That way I won't have to leave anything out if someone asks what happened."

Her innocent smile cut through to Richard's core. He felt the hard lump of sadness reform in his chest. Returning her smile as best he could, he stepped into the corridor and closed the door behind him. Once out of the room, he let out a sigh of resignation. If Richard were an angel, he was a fallen one, cursed by God Almighty himself.

He shuffled down the halls of the hospital, stopping periodically to rest, using his hand against the whitewashed walls for support. This "Saint Michael" talk couldn't go on for much longer before someone started to seriously investigate the hospital's growing number of rumors. And then where would he be? He wasn't yet ready to abandon Boston for a new home. He truly believed he had a shot at breaking the cycle this time.

It seemed to take an age for Richard to reach the closed-down East Wing. Within, dustcovers shrouded the bits of medical equipment slated for auction to raise revenue; layers of dust had coated the walls and the surfaces of the old wooden desks ever since the custodial crew had been ordered to ignore the area—another golden idea from the hospital administrators' plan to cut overheads and resist the replacement of human workers with budget-saving robots. There were no patients here now; this wing's patients were in the care of the robotic doctors of the newly opened AutoHospital No. 17.

Richard walked to a large supply closet and unlocked it with one of the many keys on his keyring. Mike Patel, Richard's immediate supervisor, had set up a cot in there. Richard had told Mike about the terrible nightmares that he suffered on an almost nightly basis. Mike, who was well aware that Richard put in more hours than any of his coworkers, had placed the cot in the room to allow Richard short breaks to re-energize himself.

Richard flopped onto the old military-style cot. He set the alarm on his cell phone for thirty minutes. That would be long enough for him to get some of his strength back, but, he hoped, not long enough for his visions to manifest. They were always most intense when he slept for long periods after exerting his power. Closing his eyes, he was immediately embraced by slumber.

AN HOUR LATER Richard found himself down in the lowest level of the hospital, inside one of the many custodial supply rooms. This particular room was filled with cleaning supplies and had a sink with running water. Richard's back was cramped painfully as he bent over to reposition the mop bucket under the hot stream pouring from the water spigot. There was an oil spill down here requiring his attention.

Darkness clung to the room. In its corners hid any number of potential perils. The only light was from a single dusty bulb on a metal chain attached to the ceiling. In the gloom, Richard felt as if a heavy weight was pressing down on his chest, making it hard for him to draw in breath. Pain was part of the agreement in healing others.

As he watched the water pour into the yellow mop bucket, his thoughts drifted off. He recalled a news program about the therapeutic effects of a jacuzzi bath, and the thought of submerging his aching muscles in such soothing waters elicited a moan from his lips. He dismissed the thought quickly, reminding himself that he did not have the spare money to enjoy luxuries like that.

Once the mop bucket was sufficiently full, Richard shut off the spigot. He caught sight of his reflection in the still-rippling water.

Where did the years go?

His face had grown gaunt and the circles under his eyes darkened with each passing year. He ran his hand through his messy brown hair and figured that he needed a haircut. He had for weeks.

The aging pipes of the supply room began to shake and rattle against one another. Richard looked around the dusty, cramped room. He could sense unseen eyes watching his every movement. Attempting to ignore the uneasy feeling, he mentally recited his mantra:

There is nothing to fear. There is nothing to fear.

He put the bucket on the floor and used the mop to propel it to the door. He was reaching for the knob when it suddenly turned of its own accord. The door jerked open. Both Richard and the person on the other side let out a startled yelp before either recognized the other.

"Dammit Richard, you scared me."

Richard stared at Julie. "I scared you?" She was frowning at him, her pretty face red, though he couldn't tell if it was from embarrassment or irritation. "What are you doing down here?"

"We ran out of gauze upstairs and no one has restocked the supply cupboard yet. I can see you have your hands full." She shot Richard a disarming grin. "We missed you last night. I thought you were going to have a few drinks with us after work."

The mention of booze made Richard's stomach tighten, despite Julie's grin. "I'm sorry. I had a long shift and I was wiped out after. I just went home to sleep." It sounded like a lie even to himself.

"Well, we're going out again tonight," Julie said, eyes twinkling.

"I don't know," Richard said, looking away. "I'm still pretty tired."

Julie pouted. "Oh Richard, you have to come," she said. "You know Sally in the intensive care ward, right?"

"I've cleaned her room a few times. Seems like a nice family." Richard tried not to stiffen at the mention of Sally.

"Her body is finally accepting the cloned heart. We're going out to celebrate."

"That's awesome, Julie, it really is," Richard said, desperate to get out of this. "But it's for you and the doctors to celebrate. You all save so many lives each day. I just push a broom."

"Funny thing that," she said and peered at him. "The medical records will say that the immunosuppressant finally started working. But me and a few others, we think it was Saint Michael."

"Not that talk again. How many times do I have to explain to you, I just don't believe in all that nonsense?"

"Saint Michael is real, Richard. I know it. There are too many unexplainable things. I know you don't believe me but I have proof that there are people out there with supernatural powers. *Others*, that's what the bloggers call them. They even have video evidence. People flying or disappearing with no camera cuts or anything. Stuff like that."

"That can be easily faked." Richard and Julie had had this conversation a few times before. "Wouldn't we see it on the news if these people really did these things?"

"I know it makes me sound crazy, but what if they are being told not to report it?"

"Julie, come on. Conspiracy theories? Please. Give yourself and the doctors more credit." He hefted his bucket, slopping the water. "Enjoy tonight. I'm going to call it an early one."

He really didn't know if there were people like him out there. He'd never thought to seek them out. Even if he did find someone, would they be cursed like him? Then what, be curse-buddies together?

"Next time," she wagged a finger playfully in front of Richard's nose, "I'm dragging your ass with me so you can't sneak out on us." She demonstrated her intent by firmly grabbing his wrist.

"I wouldn't, I mean I—," Richard stammered, his heart suddenly racing.

"Jeez Richard, don't have a heart attack over it," she said and released him. "You need to relax more."

With that, she bounded into the room and grabbed a large box of gauze packets. She paused only briefly to give Richard a small peck on the cheek before hurrying off.

He stared after her as she strode down the long corridor and turned the corner to the elevator.

"Do you need any help carrying that?" he called out to the empty corridor when his senses finally returned to him. He began pushing the mop bucket in the opposite direction down the hallway.

Richard knew he needed to push Julie away. She was too smart and was convinced of the existence of these *Others* ever since her sister's accident. Julie had come to him shortly after it happened.

Her sister Claire had worked for a large video hosting site that scrubbed marked content for manual takedown when it was missed by the company's algorithms. One night while she was working, a massive power surge had wiped all the hard drives in the whole facility. But worse, the huge current had leapt from the servers and into Claire as it raced to the ground, throwing her body across the room. The official record left the cause of the surge unknown and Claire remained in a coma that she still hadn't recovered from.

The boiler room was twice the size of the supply room and the smell of burnt oil tickled Richard's nostrils as he entered. The room buzzed with HVAC equipment and air handlers. A small wall-lamp next to the door provided the solitary source of light. Underneath, mounted to the wall on a metal plate, was a row of switches that controlled the rest of the lighting in the room. Richard tried each switch with no results, and grumbling to himself, he wandered into the gloom.

At least the oil spill was in the patch of light. Richard knew he should take that as a good sign, but tonight had too many ill omens surrounding it. He shoved the sloshing bucket closer to Boiler Number Two, and rubbed his eyes, trying to wipe the weariness from them.

A creak from the door behind him started Richard's heart pounding again. He whipped around, holding his mop firmly in both hands like a major league slugger, his weight on his front foot.

"Whoa!" The slightly-graying Indian man who had just entered held up both hands. "Take it easy, man."

Richard lowered his mop, and Mike Patel lowered his hands.

"I left you two hours ago. You didn't look half as bad then as you do now," Mike said.

"Sorry, boss. I barely slept a wink last night. It's kind of got me on edge."

"The night terrors again?"

"It's been getting worse lately."

"You know what you need?" Mike said, not waiting for an answer. "A vacation. Just get away from this place. I mean, you haven't used a single day of vacation to go away in the two years you've worked here."

Richard mustered a weak smile. "What's a vacation without relaxation? I just don't see the point."

Mike shook his head. "You need to loosen up, buddy. You have too much stress. My temple has always been there for me. Maybe you should find something you can put your faith in. When me and Pana first moved here, we didn't know anyone and the stress from moving halfway across the world, it was just too much. But my faith was always there for me and the temple's community helped us out a lot. It really can help you to put your faith and trust in a higher power."

He gave Richard a light pat on the shoulder before turning to leave. At the doorway, Mike paused and wagged an index finger in the air as he turned back to face Richard. "Right, almost forgot," he said. "The whole reason I came down here. An electrician should be here soon to fix the lighting issue."

"Thanks," Richard muttered as his boss left, and he got to work cleaning up the spill.

He began by shoveling the sawdust he had laid down earlier into a large trash bucket. The sawdust had absorbed most of the excess oil, leaving behind a dark stain. To combat this, Richard mixed up a cleaning paste in a small metal bucket. Using a wooden stick, he stirred his concoction until it became a loose paste. Satisfied with its consistency, he smothered the paste over the stain.

As he knelt with his back to the boiler room door, he failed to notice the smoke that had begun flowing through the gap at the bottom. The smoke was thick, denser than that produced by a normal fire, and it rose quickly to the ceiling, where it coalesced in a shadowed corner. Richard shuddered involuntarily, but ignored the sensation and returned to his work.

Once the blemish was liberally coated with his gooey paste, Richard grabbed a wire brush and scrubbed the stain. The lone light flickered briefly. Richard tried unsuccessfully to convince himself that it was his imagination, and putting all thoughts out of his mind, he focused his nervous energy into his strokes.

The opaque fog rolled on unnoticed, farther into the gloom of the boiler room. Once completely shrouded in the darkness above the light, tendrils of smoke snaked down towards the cement floor. The flickering light roused Richard as he applied another coat of paste. He jumped to his feet.

That wasn't my imagination.

He squinted straight ahead, where momentary movement had caught his attention. Focusing on that area, Richard could see the faint outline of a man. He opened his mouth to call out, but before he could speak, he was engulfed by darkness as the single light winked out.

"Mike, are you there?" Richard called. He turned in slow circles, and realized that he'd begun to tremble. Red and blue LEDs on the machinery winked in the dark. He heard footsteps from deeper inside the boiler room.

The sole light sparked back to life, and Richard gasped, taking an involuntary backwards step. A man, seemingly composed of shadows, stood five feet in front of him. The outline of the figure appeared to blur and dissipate into the darkness behind it. It was a little taller than Richard with no discernible facial features. It tilted its wispy head sideways, lowered its shoulder, and suddenly charged.

The shadow struck Richard in the center of his ribcage. As the air was forced out of his lungs, the lightbulb exploded in a cascade of sparks, sending glass shards flying in all directions. The figure lifted Richard off his feet and drove him into the wall below the light fixture, slamming his head into the row of inoperative switches.

The back of Richard's head immediately felt warm and damp. His lungs seemed incapable of drawing breath. A misty tendril reached out and grasped Richard by the throat, ripping him away from the wall. He clawed at the unfinished basement floor and the cement clawed back, tearing his elbows and fingers open.

The arm of shadow released its grip as Richard drew level with the mop bucket. Clumps of his hair clung to the wispy hand. With a quick flick of its wrist, the hand of swirling shadows fizzled to nothingness. The clumps of hair twirled to the ground.

Richard lay there, gasping, his vision filled with the yellow bucket. There was momentary silence. Richard blinked.

And suddenly his breath was cut off. A reformed tendril coiled around his neck, constricting like a deadly serpent. It effortlessly lifted Richard from the floor. His head hovered above the mop bucket as he clawed at the ephemeral limb. The shadow plunged Richard head first into the dirty water.

The alkaline liquid stung his eyes. He choked frothy water into his lungs and dirt milled his gums. He fought the urge to breathe in more of the filthy water, as darkness began creeping in from the edges of his vision. Dread was being steadily replaced by a calm acceptance.

Somewhere in the world beyond the water, Richard heard the creak of a door opening.

"Richard? The electrician called to say he was going to be . . ." Mike's voice trailed off.

The unplanned interruption seemed to distract the shadow. The momentary lapse allowed Richard to firmly clutch both sides of the mop bucket. Using the last of his strength, he tipped the bucket over, sending the gray water racing across the patchwork floor. His head fell forwards, striking the cement, and his burning lungs spasmodically ejected the water he'd inhaled. Violent tremors wracked his body.

"Who—who are you?" Mike said.

The shadowy being rose from its crouched position next to the overturned mop bucket. With its attention firmly on Mike, it straightened its back and then collapsed in on itself, forming a floating sphere.

Mike backed up, eyes wide. "*What* are you?"

A leg the same hue as oxygenated blood emerged from the sphere and stepped softly to the floor. A second leg pierced the outer layer of the sphere, followed by a glistening torso and two pairs of arms. The sphere shrunk as each appendage slid out. As the torso righted itself, the sphere rolled vertically, exposing a sinewy neck. A final rotation revealed a demonic face with long canine teeth curving over its lower lip. The sphere silently evaporated into darkness.

Mike raised his hands, shaking his head. "No," he said. "Impossible. You can't be Yama. You can't be. It's just not possible. Not possible."

Mike backed into the boiler room door, which had closed behind him. His face was coated in sweat. Beads of it dripped from his chin.

Yama, who stood over eight feet tall, took a couple of strides to cross the boiler room.

"The time of your judgment has dawned," Yama said. "You will succumb."

The demon's voice was difficult to discern, as if a chorus of voices was speaking in unison. With his back still pressed against the door, Mike blindly fumbled with the knob, gaping at the glistening, scarlet being that towered over him.

"Please," Mike said, panting for breath. "I have a wife and two children. My oldest just started college. This can't be my time."

Yama, using two of his four arms, grabbed Mike by the wrists and pinned them against the top of the doorframe. Leaning in close, Yama stared deep into Mike's eyes and began to breathe in deeply, on the verge of sucking in the breath that escaped Mike's lips.

"So fresh, and so much fear," Yama said quietly.

Watching this, Richard had managed to discharge the last of the water from his chest. He struggled to his feet and grabbed the empty bucket with both hands. He lunged at the demon, adrenaline fueling his swing. Richard's aim was good, but Yama phased in and out of existence when the bucket should have collided with him.

The attack left Richard off balance. He lost his grip and the mop bucket went tumbling end over end across the floor. Yama phased back into reality, facing Richard, while Mike, now released, crumpled to the ground behind the demon.

"I should have ended your existence when I had the chance," Yama said in his roaring swirl of voices. He took a step toward Richard and his body phased in and out again. With each step, his existence flickered exponentially.

"No, not now. Not when I am so close." Yama's body was nearly transparent. With each phasing, less of his body re-materialized.

"This is not the end!" he roared. "I will find you again." The finger pointing at Richard was the final appendage to dematerialize from the boiler room.

Dragging in huge gulps of air, Richard glanced towards Mike, who was still huddled on the floor trembling, his eyes clamped tightly shut. Richard closed his own eyes, and gently massaged his eyelids with his thumbs. When he looked again, Mike was staring intently at him.

"Maybe I should try to explain what little I can," Richard said. "But you wouldn't happen to have a drink nearby, would you?"

Mike's mouth moved but no words came out. Eventually, he weakly said, "Night terrors?"

TWO DAYS EARLIER, James Parker stood on the shoulder of I-95 with a backpack slung over his shoulder and his thumb extended.

He'd finally decided to leave his abusive father's home in a large apartment complex just outside of Providence, Rhode Island. James's plan was to escape to a life with his mother and younger brother in Maine, one of the only states left that hadn't been overloaded by a flood of people in the last decade. He'd carried out his own small retribution on his father by swiping the few hundred dollars that his father kept in a dresser drawer, though James wondered which his father would miss first: his seventeen-year-old son or the cash. He figured the stolen money would last him the whole journey to Maine.

It was overcast and cold, and James hadn't had so much as a sniff of a ride in hours. He was contemplating giving up altogether and tramping back the way he'd come, when a late model driverless Mustang roared past, and then slowed, its brake lights glowing. James trotted after the car as it stopped, and stooped to the open passenger window when he drew level. The driver was a young, well-dressed man in his late twenties. He had an easy smile and honey-blond hair.

"Need a lift?" he asked while brushing back a lock of hair that had fallen over his eye.

"Yes, sir. Thanks."

"Hop in. The name's Jared."

The passenger door of the Mustang popped open. James felt uneasy under the watchful eye of the driver, but the excitement of the new car and the prospect of getting out of Massachusetts was too much for him to resist. He slipped into the plush leather seat.

"Comfortable?" Jared said.

"You bet." It was probably the most comfortable seat James had ever sat in.

"Where're you headed?"

"Maine," James said, and the car leapt back onto the road, smoothly and rapidly accelerating. Within the car, the engine was almost silent. "I'm going to my mom's."

"Oh yes?"

James glanced at Jared, who looked away, back at the road, even though the car was driving itself.

"Yeah," James said.

"And you've come from where?"

"Providence."

"You live there alone?"

This guy was asking way too many questions for James's liking. Why was he so interested anyway? The drivers of the other couple of rides he'd had so far had been much more terse. So he said, "Sure, alone," because he suddenly felt like he shouldn't give too much away.

As I-95 merged with Route 128, Jared said, "You're a long way from Providence. I never expected to find such a cute boy walking all by his lonesome." Jared's stares were really making James uneasy.

"I'm just trying to get to my mom's."

"Aren't you just so sweet," Jared said and licked his lips.

He placed his right hand on James's upper thigh. As James tried to move his hand away, his fingers dug in painfully deep. The car suddenly swerved off the road and entered a rest area. The car parked itself towards the back of the deserted space.

Jared flung open his door, reached across the center console, and dragged a panicking James from the car by his arm. It was the middle of the day but the parking lot was empty. Driverless cars had rendered rest areas all but obsolete. Jared wrestled James away from the car, and stood behind him, his forearm around James's neck. When the switchblade pressed against his throat, James had no idea what to do.

"Take your pants off."

James couldn't comprehend the situation. The switchblade made it impossible for him to think, so he simply did as he was commanded and tugged his jeans down. The back corner of the rest area was hidden by dense trees. The chances of any passing motorist seeing what was happening were minimal.

With the knife at his throat, James was unable to get his jeans over his sneakers to take them off. They bunched up around his shins. "Forget it," Jared said, the knife pressing even closer. "Just empty your pockets."

James dug his hands into his front pocket and pulled out his father's stolen money along with a picture of his little brother, Taylor. Jared snatched them both, then pushed James forward.

James fell to his hands and knees, his jeans effectively tying his legs together. "Stand up," Jared said, moving around to face James.

James got unsteadily to his feet. He saw that Jared's easy smile had been replaced with a devious, lustful grin. He moved like a predator, eyeing James up and down. James understood what was to happen next, but he was prepared to spill his own blood before he gave in to it. He bared his teeth at the rapist.

"Don't fight me. I'd hate to have to cut that pretty face of yours."

"Screw you. I'm not just gonna let you do whatever you want to me."

Jared snorted, but James stood dumbfounded, his body unable to respond as he watched what happened before him.

A hand appeared, seemingly out of nowhere, and closed around Jared's neck. His snort turned into a gurgle as his windpipe was crushed. James heard the sick crack of bones breaking. With a quick flick of the wrist, Jared went careening into the edge of the surrounding forest.

James could do nothing but gawk at the man who now stood in front of him. His savior stood just over six feet tall and wore a long, black leather jacket that contrasted starkly with his sickly pale skin. James guessed the man's age as maybe mid-thirties, no older than early-forties.

James tried to form some sort of thanks, but shock kept him silent. Jared, whom James had assumed was already dead, hacked blood onto the ground and dragged himself upright, clutching his wounded throat. The new guy fixed Jared with a long stare, and the would-be rapist suddenly screamed and turned away, scrambling off into the woods. Along with James's cash.

The newcomer bent down and picked up the picture of Taylor, which Jared had discarded. He examined it carefully.

"Nice looking fellow. Your brother, I take it?" The man spoke in a deep, almost lifeless monotone.

"Yes. Thank you, sir." James's gratitude sounded weak, even to his own ears, but his suspicion of this savior was growing with each second.

"Don't call me 'sir,'" the man snapped. He stared at Taylor's picture for a while longer, then looked up at James and said, "I saved your life. You are now indebted to me."

"What do you mean?"

"Don't get hysterical. It's nothing much. I need a driver for a few days. After that, you can keep my van and I will replace the cash that has just been stolen from you." James stared at the man with his mouth agape. "Of course, if you refuse, I will have to make a trip up to Saco, Maine and task Taylor with fulfilling your debt."

James's mind was reeling. This stranger knew things he had no way of knowing. It was possible he'd seen Jared take the money. He could have guessed that the picture was of his younger brother. But to know his name was Taylor and that he lived near Saco . . .

James considered how far this man had thrown Jared. It was impossibly far for two hands, let alone one. Muscle-bound strong-men, pumped up on now-legal steroids, couldn't even do that, and the man before James was little more than a bag of skin and bones.

The lifeless voice echoed in James's thoughts. There was a power in that voice that James could not resist. He had no choice but to feebly nod his acceptance.

"I'm James Parker," James said and offered his hand.

"You can call me Raef Deos. It is a pleasure to meet you, James." Raef's hand was cold to the touch and seemed to lack any semblance of color. "Let me take you to my van."

IN THE HOURS following his rescue, James learnt nothing more about Raef.

They stopped at various gas stations throughout downtown Boston, James driving the van and Raef giving directions. Raef's van had a cheap paint job and seemed like it was held together by rust; flecks of white paint flaked off every time they stopped. The interior was bare except for the two captain's chairs in the front. The metal floor was scuffed and threadbare with rust. James filled up propane tanks and gas canisters, well over a dozen. It must have cost Raef more than a thousand dollars for the fuel. Raef then directed him to an abandoned warehouse in a rundown part of the harbor district, far away from the working robotic docks.

This part of the dockside region hadn't seen much use as of late. Raef told James that in the past few decades, Boston had been forced to consolidate most of its export industries, and layoffs had forced the workers into government-subsidized housing. Eventually, these buildings would be turned into high-rent condos and hotels for the exclusive few across the harbor in East Boston.

James unloaded the tanks of fuel and brought them into the warehouse, where Raef placed them into a configuration James couldn't decipher. It took him a while to get all the canisters out from the back of the black van. He felt as if his arms could detach from his body at any moment.

Raef was adjusting the last canister into its proper place when a stranger arrived at the warehouse. He wore a black hood that obscured his face from James's view. His trench coat was so dark it seemed to absorb the surrounding light. Raef led the man to a back office. James could hear them arguing but he couldn't make out any words except for *midnight*. A few minutes later, the man in the trench coat made of black holes walked out, carrying a metal briefcase.

Raef stayed inside the rundown office that was attached to the back wall of the warehouse. Left alone, his natural curiosity forced James to follow the man outside, lingering a few steps behind the swirling coattails. James stuck his head out of the steel-shuttered loading dock, but couldn't locate the man in the trench coat. He saw no car lights, heard no engine start up. It was as if the man had simply vanished into thin air.

"James!" Raef called out from within the warehouse. "Close the shutters. We need to rest before our big day tomorrow. You have a lot of driving to do."

Bewildered, James took one last look at the empty parking lot outside, and did as instructed.

THE FOLLOWING DAY, James parked the van outside a ratty apartment building that looked both uninhabited and derelict. The other houses in this part of the city seemed mostly abandoned. Many had *Condemned* signs displayed on the small front lawns. The vagrants in the area paid little heed to the posted warnings.

James and Raef climbed out of the van, and made their way into the small apartment building, heading along the dingy hallway that led off the front door. The smell of mildew was overpowering. James sat on the floor and slumped against the stained wall to wait for the higher-ups to call them in. Raef went into one of the abandoned apartments to meditate. He'd experienced an intense migraine in the van, a little over an hour ago, and meditation, he'd told James, was the only way to help himself to recover.

Raef's migraines were a source of great curiosity to James. James's own mother suffered from migraines but whenever she had one, she took prescription medication. Raef, on the other hand, would retreat to a dark quiet area and meditate. James had spied on Raef during a meditation session the previous night, and found the man in a bizarre trance, mumbling to himself.

The people who surrounded James dealt in drugs, that was clear to him. He didn't know what other illegal activities they were involved in, but underworld groups seemed to be Raef's main clientele. The briefcase and the man in the swirling trench coat certainly fit the criminal scenario, but that experience had come with a different sense of dread.

The gang occupying this building called themselves "Niners" and they all dressed in red attire. The young man who appeared in front of James wore a red T-shirt a few sizes too big, tucked partly into oversized jeans that revealed a large red belt with a crossed-guns belt buckle. He walked past James and halted at the entrance to the apartment halfway down the hall. Raef had been in there for only a half-hour or so, while he waited for the gang's boss to receive them. The Niner raised a hand to rap on the door.

"I wouldn't do that if I were you," James said. "He doesn't like being disturbed during his meditation sessions." James had learned this the hard way on his first day with Raef. He rubbed the bruise on his cheek distractedly.

The Niner glanced at James and dismissed him with a grimace. He knocked loudly on the door and called, "Mr. Jones is ready for you."

"No, not now." The voice on the other side of the door was low and brooding.

"Yeah, now. The boss doesn't like to be kept waiting, and neither do I." The Niner knocked again, this time louder and longer. He was clearly trying to assert his dominance, displaying a youthful arrogance in the process.

A few moments of silence passed. James coiled himself into a tight ball. There was movement behind the door, then a click as it was unlocked.

"I warned you," James said, turning his bruised cheek to the Niner.

The door was flung open from within. One hinge gave way, spinning off down the hallway. Raef stormed out, and even from where James was sitting, he could plainly see the fire burning behind Raef's eyes. Raef grabbed the Niner by the throat, lifting him off his feet, and pinned him against the wall. James noticed that Raef's eyes had shifted color, matching the red diamond that adorned the back of his long leather jacket.

"If you ever, *ever* disturb my meditation again," Raef hissed into the Niner's face, "I will rip the windpipe from your throat. Do I make myself clear?"

The Niner, whose oxygen supply had been completely cut off, could only manage a pitiful nod. His pale face was rapidly turning purple. Raef released his grip and the Niner fell to his knees coughing and retching.

"Come on then," Raef said with a sneer, before the Niner could fully recover. "Let's not keep Mr. Jones waiting."

The Niner struggled to his feet, still taking in deep lungfuls of air, and led Raef down the hallway past James to a staircase. He managed to look over his shoulder only once. James smiled triumphantly at the Niner, but dropped the expression immediately when he looked at Raef.

"I tried to stop him," James said, even before the question was asked.

"I take it you were never a hall monitor at your high school."

"No, sir. It won't happen again." James had said those same words so many times throughout his life. They were normally followed by a beating from his father.

"You are correct. Next time will be different. I will make sure of that." Raef's blazing eyes bore a hole through James's being. "And stop calling me 'sir.'"

James swallowed hard. He couldn't comprehend Raef's inane objection to being called "sir." James wanted to know why but lacked the courage to vocalize the question. It was one of Raef's many weird characteristics.

"Come along, James. Your correction will have to wait. We have an appointment to which we must attend."

The Niner, whose flushed cheeks now complemented his attire, led the duo to the top floor of the building. Colorless wallpaper hung from the walls in peeling flags, and there were holes in the lath walls that looked as if they'd been kicked or punched in. James crushed long-dead insect husks under his feet. He cautiously picked his steps on the creaking boards of the stairs.

Unlike the missing or boarded-up windows of the lower floors, the top level had intact glass windows that were clean enough for James to see out of. He also noticed that the old wooden floor was swept clean, as if they'd entered a whole different building.

The top floor consisted of a solitary hallway that ended abruptly at a set of double doors. Two doorways, one to the left, the other slightly offset on the opposite side, were covered by particle board. The work must've been done fairly recently because the board didn't have the same aged-quality as the wood covering the windows downstairs.

The Niner paused at the double doors. He glanced back at Raef, who revealed a half-grin. The Niner looked away and knocked on the door.

THE SMALL APARTMENT had been converted into an office. Tek thought it was in utter contrast to the rest of the building. The wall that separated the kitchen from the living room had been removed, opening up the space, and it was lavishly furnished. In front of a bay window sat a large oak desk with an immense leather chair behind it and two plain wooden chairs out front. The carpet was of a plush red knotted design. To the right of the desk an expensive flat-screen TV was mounted on the wall. Opposite the TV there was a movie theater-style couch with fitted cup holders, which was where Tek sat with his companion.

The other, larger man was chatting on his cell phone. He wore a sleeveless shirt, and his exposed muscles popped without flexing. His head was shaved close to the scalp. Thomas Walker was his given name but most people in the organization did not know his real name, referring to him only as "Bricks."

"How'd it go down?" Bricks asked the person on the other end of the line. After a pause, he said, "All right, continue as planned and keep your eyes open."

Tek sat at the opposite end of the couch and regarded the big guy. Bricks had been a football star in his younger days, a linebacker at a school for the children of the elite, until a blown knee had ended his dreams. He'd drifted into the Niners shortly after.

"Well?" Tek asked the third man in the room, who sat in the oversized chair behind the desk.

Scott "Bones" Jones was the *de facto* CEO of their clan, a position he'd attained when the previous leader had done a long stint in jail on a murder charge. Organization and delegation were Jones's strong points. He always wore a business suit and looked as if he belonged in Government Center rather than in the makeshift headquarters of a criminal gang. His hair was neatly trimmed. He spared no expense in getting it cut twice a week. He was a true believer in the "dress for success" motto, even though most other people in the game had a different idea of how dressing for success should be done.

Mr. Jones, as the lowest of his underlings referred to him, was the main reason for the clan's rise to prominence over the last two decades. He'd made a connection with the supplier of the highest-quality heroin and cocaine available. He'd bought wholesale and instead of fighting over territory, he'd negotiated with the other clans to push his product, offering a better deal than the gangs had been paying at the time. The product was of such high quality that those who refused his offer soon saw their customer base dwindle.

Mr. Jones straightened his tie. "Let's hear it then, Bricks."

"We smacked those corner boys hard," Bricks said. "They'll be out of the game for a minute."

"What were the losses?"

"Nothing major. One of our boys took a slug to the shoulder. They took him to a hospital a couple of counties away. We got our people together now. The numbers advantage should be enough to end this quick."

"Good." Jones leaned back in his chair, satisfied with the report. "I want Johnny guarding the main stash house tomorrow night again. I don't want him working a corner or even hanging out on the street. If—excuse me—*when* they retaliate, I want him protected. People constantly around him."

"Got it," Tek said. He felt he needed to add something to the conversation. He was the skinniest man in the room, but he commanded the most fear from the low-level Niners. Mr. Jones had assigned him as the gang's domestic enforcer. He was responsible for doling out punishment for indiscretions by other Niners. It was a role that suited Tek perfectly. He had no reservations regarding broken bones. Or worse.

A knock at the door interrupted their conversation. "Who is it?" Tek called out, running a hand over his short-cropped hair.

A strained voice came through the door. "Boss, I have Mr. Deos here as you asked. And also an associate of his."

"Send them in," Jones called.

Tek was nervous, an unusual event in itself, and one which spoke volumes about the tension that suddenly grew in the room. It had been almost ten years since he'd last seen Raef Deos, but Tek would never forget the deathly chill that shot through him every time their paths crossed. Mr. Jones outsourced specific jobs to Raef, jobs that required immediate attention, and Raef always completed his jobs in record time, without attracting any extra police attention.

As Raef strode into the room, Tek's heart stuttered. Raef looked exactly the same as when Tek had first met him, over twenty years ago. He even wore the same out-of-style black leather jacket that hung to just below his knees, with a red diamond on the back.

Tek glanced at Jones. If the boss noticed anything strange about Raef's appearance, he did a good job of concealing it.

"Hello, Scott. It's good to see you again," Raef said and casually strolled over to the desk and extended his hand across it. Raef's associate was a young boy, and Tek guessed that the kid was probably in the right age range to maybe be Raef's son. The boy wore an apprehensive expression and his face was pale, though he still had more color than Raef, who reminded Tek of a vampire. Tek pitied any boy who had that man as a father.

Standing to shake Raef's hand, Mr. Jones grinned and said, "It's been too long, Raef. You look well." He sat back down and motioned for Raef and the skinny boy to do the same.

"Thank you," Raef said. "You too look very well."

It amazed Tek how a cold-blooded killer could so easily wear the mask of a civilized man and dispense pleasantries so readily. He recalled hearing a story of how Raef had wiped out a whole family during one job.

It had happened early in Mr. Jones's reign over the group. A rival gang had refused Mr. Jones's wholesale offer and had gone on to attack the few corners that the Niners had controlled at the time. The leader of the rival gang had taken refuge in his grandparents' house. Raef found the house and murdered everyone inside, grandparents, mother, father, two sisters and the gang leader's newborn baby boy. Tek was a hard man, but he was nothing when stacked against Raef.

"Looks like you boys have been busy since last we met." Raef paused, scanning the room and its occupants. "I don't see Stacks. I figured his bid would be done by now."

Tek felt the couch shift as Bricks flinched. His own stomach balled up at the mention of the turncoat. Through it all, Jones's expression remained frozen.

"Stacks is no longer with us." Mr. Jones's statement was neutral, hiding any anger behind a mask of indifference. "I assume you were informed of the situation."

Raef seemed content to leave the issue settled. "It seems you have a problem with Russians, once again." Raef had been the one who'd originally forced the Russians out of the drug game in South Boston, over twenty years ago. Scott and Tek were only teenagers then, waging a war in which they'd never intended to become involved.

"Exactly. Unfortunately, a homegrown threat has moved on me earlier than I anticipated. Most of my resources are tied up with that problem. I can't spare the manpower to wage a war against the Russians." Tek knew what Raef didn't: that the homegrown threat was in fact Stacks—the one-time leader of the Niners, and the man Jones had replaced.

Tek also knew the story of how Raef had become involved with the Niners. Scott Jones and Stacks—or Alvin Robinson as he was known back then—were walking home one humid night in the summer of '06, when a group of Russian hard heads came upon them. Stacks had just begun to crew-up and work the corners of his neighborhood, quickly earning himself a reputation and his apt nickname. The Russians were the established dealers of the time, and didn't take kindly to anyone muscling in on their business.

Ambushing the pair, the Russians laid into Stacks and Jones with metal pipes. They weren't instructed to kill, just to send a final, stern warning. The beating went on for a few minutes before Raef arrived. He already harbored ill will towards the Russians for reasons no one in the clan ever understood, and he made short work of the muscle. He'd helped the boys grow their empire ever since.

Raef nodded. "A two-front war sounds like the kind of problem that's taken many great leaders to an early grave."

"That's what I'm up against. I'd like you to take out the three Czars. With the local leaders out of the picture, and the chain of command disrupted, the Russians won't be able to exploit my vulnerabilities while I take out some trash."

"A sound strategy. Considering that you talked with Mr. Anderson, you must know my current fee."

"Funny guy that Mr. Anderson," Jones said. "Bit of an accent on him. British? I guess I never realized you worked globally."

"The organization I represent is indeed far-reaching. But the less said about it, the better for all involved. I believe we were discussing the fee?"

Jones nodded to Bricks, who stood and reached around the back of the couch. Tek knew what was hidden there: a leather briefcase containing one hundred thousand dollars, half of Raef's standard fee for the three VIP targets. Bricks gently placed the briefcase on the table in front of Raef. He clicked open the latches and propped the lid open. The money was neatly stacked and bundled, making an impressive sight.

"This is the half you requested." Jones motioned to the briefcase between them. "Would you like to count it?"

Raef gave a dismissive shake of his head. "No need. It should take no more than a few days to complete everything. Keep watching the headlines, and I'll contact you to arrange for the second half of my payment."

Raef slid the chair back as he stood up. He closed the briefcase and swiped it off the desk in one fluid motion. His young associate followed right after, head hung low. Tek could only wonder at the horrors the boy had been subjected to.

Bricks slipped behind the desk, his head close to Jones's ear. Tek, still seated on the couch, could barely hear him whisper. "I know we used him a ton in the past, but that's a lot of cash to let someone—anyone—walk away with." Tek couldn't blame Bricks for his mistrust, especially with the big man's history of betrayal.

Jones shot Bricks a look of contempt, reminding the lieutenant of his place in the pecking order.

At the doorway, Racf stopped, his assistant nearly bumping into him. With his back to the room, he said, "You will see a return from this investment. Trust me."

He took a step forward and crossed the threshold. As he did, he turned his head and smiled the coldest smile Tek had ever seen. Swallowing hard, Tek realized he was relieved that the meeting was over.

Day 2

T HE MBTA BUS rolled along to its pick-up zone, where Richard stood nervously waiting. The rising sun had just crested the horizon, which gave him some small sense of relief. He had survived another night of terrors, albeit with a few stitches to his scalp. And the need for a long explanation, full of lies.

The visions sometimes assaulted Richard in the daylight, but they never seemed as severe then. That didn't stop Richard's stomach from flipping over as he fretted about the implications of the physical assault. Normally it was only hallucinations that plagued him, and that hardly involved others.

Richard climbed the steep steps onto the bus. He tapped his Charlie Card, a monthly prepaid bus pass, against the RF reader. This early in the morning, the bus was three-quarters full of other third-shift workers shuffling home, grateful to have any job.

Richard flopped into the first vacant seat he came to. With his elbows on his knees, he held his head in his hands. His conversation with his supervisor still lingered in his thoughts. His deepest secret had been laid bare. If it hadn't been for the supernatural being that attacked them, Richard wasn't sure if Mike would have believed the story.

Richard dozed, drifting into a memory-filled twilight. He remembered a sunny summer day and the sound of smashing glass. And blood, so much blood . . .

He jerked awake, halfway home. He scanned his fellow occupants on the bus. Most had their eyes closed or heads down. Richard gulped as an icy chill ran down the back of his spine.

A tan SUV pulled alongside the bus on the outer lane of the busy three-lane avenue. Richard's window lined up with the front passenger window of the SUV while both vehicles slowed to a stop and waited for the traffic light to change to green. A mother and her young daughter were riding in the car.

The girl, upon seeing Richard, beamed an innocent smile that Richard weakly returned. Her innocence reminded Richard of Sally. The girl's smile widened, and the hairs on the back of Richard's neck started to rise. Her grin spread impossibly wide, from ear to ear. Long canine teeth slid out from her upper gums, curving down over her lower lip. Her eyes rolled up, revealing vertical, bloodshot pupils. Richard found he couldn't break the demonic gaze.

The light changed to green and the bus and SUV pulled away separately, breaking the line of sight. Richard's heart was racing, and once the SUV was fully out of his view, he reached into his inner jacket pocket and retrieved his flask. Without even bothering to see if anyone was watching, Richard drained the contents in one large gulp.

"Please, let it end," he mumbled to himself, closing his eyes and letting his forehead rest against the seat in front of him. He must have slept a little more, for when he next opened his eyes, the bus's air brakes were squealing as it pulled up to Richard's stop.

THE MID-SPRING SUNLIGHT bathed the street in a soft glow. Richard walked from the bus stop to his apartment building, passing the countless homeless people who had colonized the sidewalks and alleyways.

The early-morning warmth did nothing to thaw the fear that clutched at Richard's heart. These streets were usually bustling with children scurrying to their school buses. This morning, he hadn't seen a single one of the long, yellow vehicles with their ridiculous tin-men behind the steering wheel.

He turned onto his street. Two buildings before his apartment block was an old-style analog liquor store which he frequented too often. He knew that getting blackout drunk was his best chance at stopping the visions. He also knew that the amount of alcohol he was ingesting was sure to shut down his liver sooner rather than later. But knowledge is not the alcoholic's friend, and so he turned and entered the store.

A few minutes later, he emerged with a plastic bag full of bottles of liquor: whiskey, vodka, and brandy, things he could drink straight without delaying the onset of their effects. The store owner knew Richard by sight and always gave him a disapproving look at the checkout.

Richard briefly paused in front of his four-story apartment complex, taking in the dilapidated sight. Bacteria grew on the exterior walls, discoloring the small amount of paint that hadn't chipped off. Richard pressed his thumb to the reader on the weathered steel door to gain access into the building. The elevator still had an out-of-order tag stuck to its malfunctioning doors. Richard peeked through the gap and saw the interior light flickering. Tired and bruised, he climbed the steep steps. At the third floor a slightly overweight fifteen-year-old boy halted his progress.

"Hey Sully!" the pimply-faced teen called out.

Richard hid his bag behind him. "Hi Greg. Shouldn't you be in school by now?"

"Don't you pay attention to the calendar? It's a three-day weekend, no school today."

"Is there ever a month when you don't have a holiday?" The thirst for more alcohol left Richard's mouth full of cotton.

"I don't think so, I'll have to check into that one." Greg shook his head. "Say, you look like crap. Is everything okay?"

"Yeah," Richard said. "Just had a long night of work." He did his best not to recall the details and shifted his scarred skull away from Greg.

"I take it you won't be joining Mom and me for dinner tonight then? It's the two-year anniversary of Mom's cancer going into remission. You moved into the building a few months before that, so we could celebrate both. I just got a fully-immersive VR rig and we could try that out, too. The haptic feedback on it is amazing."

Richard remembered the subtlety of the situation. He'd worked his power when Greg's mother was admitted to his hospital. He'd snuck into her room the first night after the doctors had administered a sleep-inducing painkiller. The cancer had taken four more visits and a hefty amount of energy to send into remission. It was Richard's greatest accomplishment to date, the only time he'd successfully battled cancer. He tried not to dwell on those times when the battle had been lost.

He hesitated, fumbling for a response that wouldn't hurt Greg's feelings. "I can't believe it's been that long," he said. "Maybe we can do it another night. I have to work graveyard shift again tomorrow night. I need to realign my sleep schedule. Sorry, buddy."

Greg's face dropped, but he quickly masked his disappointment. "Okay, but if you change your mind, you're welcome to join us. I got this awesome Samurai game you need to check out."

"Thanks," was all Richard could muster before continuing the climb to his apartment on the top floor. When he reached it, he stopped in front of the plain brown door and stole a glance over his shoulder at Julie's identical door.

He'd worked with Julie for more than a year when he realized he had something more than a fleeting crush on her. He wasn't sure if it was her golden hair, azure eyes, or feisty, funny personality, but whenever Richard thought of her, his body became weightless. The troubles of his life melted away whenever he was under her calming influence. But those feelings couldn't mean anything, could they?

Richard had been afraid of getting too close to anyone since his "Awakening," as he liked to call it. He was never nervous around girls, although his self-imposed isolation now made him cognizant of each word he spoke, and he didn't want to lead Julie on. He was concerned that his condition would ruin anything he started, but, more than that, he feared that it would put the people he cared for in jeopardy.

His last girlfriend had been Stacey, a decade ago when he was still in high school, before he briefly joined the Army. It had been a boring high school romance until one eventful night. One of his visions had scared him so much that he'd fled Stacey's house in only his boxers. A week later, a much more physical manifestation had occurred, similar to the incident in the boiler room. He'd left town the next morning, eventually enlisting in the Army in a failed attempt to escape, fearing that any contact with loved ones could cost them their lives. He'd become a nomad for many years, moving from place to place, never staying too long.

The sound of Julie's bolt unlocking brought him out of his hazy fog. Quickly, he turned around and attempted to insert his key in his lock. He fumbled the keys and dropped them on the floor as Julie slid out from behind her door.

"What's up, butterfingers?"

He bent to retrieve his keys and took a deep breath before turning to face her.

"Julie," he said, smiling despite everything. "I, um, I didn't see you there."

"Wow, you look terrible," she said, crossing the hallway to him.

"Thanks. You look good, too."

"No, I'm serious. Is everything all right?" Richard heard honest concern in her tone. "You didn't look nearly this bad last night." Her eyes briefly hovered over the plastic bag that lay where Richard had dropped his keys.

"It was a long night after you left, that's all. Thanks for asking." Richard found it hard to look her in the eye with the taste of cheap liquor on his tongue.

Julie placed her hand on his shoulder. The touch confused all of Richard's senses. His heart was racing again.

"Are you sure?" she said and met his eyes openly.

The horrors of last night receded in his memory. Under her intense gaze, all of Richard's problems evaporated. He gave her a genuine smile.

"Yes. Trust me." It was a lie, but one that Richard had perfected after the first hundred times he'd told it.

"Good." Julie's face flooded with warmth. "You know, I noticed a funny thing. The last few times a Saint Michael report's come in, you've been working on the same floor."

Richard didn't know what to say. He wasn't prepared for this situation. "Julie . . ."

"I know, I know," Julie said. "You don't believe in that stuff. I just thought it was funny and you looked like you could use a laugh."

He let out a breath he hadn't realized he was holding, now that he knew she was only joking, but it was only a matter of time before he slipped up. "I'll be in a better mood once I get some rest. Sorry for being a wet blanket."

"Well at least tell me we're still on for a movie tomorrow night. I got two text messages about you in the last twelve hours. Mike *and* Greg."

Richard was caught off guard by the extent of the concern shown by his friends. Movie night must have been another Greg initiative. Richard's schedule was the usual excuse to get out of these things.

"Damn it, Greg," Richard muttered under his breath. "Movie night is tomorrow night?" At least his usual excuse wasn't a lie this time.

"Don't worry about work," Julie said. "I talked with Mike earlier and he agreed to give you the night off. He said you really need it." She hesitated briefly, eying the dressing on the back of Richard's head. "I hope I'm not crossing any boundaries here."

Richard wondered about the timing and contents of her conversation with Mike. The exchange Mike and Richard had shared after the attack had done nothing to calm Mike's nerves. Richard wouldn't blame his boss if he found some grounds for firing Richard. The idea of getting out permanently was already rattling around in his brain, but it would mean losing the chance to help those who desperately needed his healing touch.

"Sounds like you guys have a conspiracy going on here, but I guess watching a movie isn't the worst you could conspire to do. Tomorrow would be great."

Julie leaned in, and gave Richard a peck on the cheek. "Good, I can't wait." She eyed the bandage one more time. "You sure you're all right?"

Richard nodded and smiled. Julie bounded down the hall and into the stairwell. Once he knew she was out of earshot, he sighed loudly. *Too close*, he thought to himself. *Too close*. He unlocked his door and stepped inside.

His one-bedroom apartment was littered with drained liquor bottles. They covered his kitchen countertop and lay on the carpet around his sofa. Most of his apartment was bare, save for the sofa with a coffee table in front of it. There was a thirty-inch TV on a stand, which Richard had purchased from a flea market in the suburbs for pennies on the dollar. His hospital salary after taxes, healthcare, and other deductions barely covered the cost of his rent, bills, and drinking habit. Especially his drinking habit.

His little kitchen held little more than an oversized sink, a tiny dining table, and a couple of mostly-empty cupboards. Richard dumped his bag on the table and looked out the sliding glass door leading to the small ledge outside that had been advertised as a "balcony." He'd recently bought a used weight-bench and free weights, which cluttered the tiny area. He hadn't even used them yet, and his battered body scoffed at the idea of using them right now.

Tomorrow maybe.

Now that Julie's calming influence was gone, a habitual depression clambered back into his mind. He found a half-full plastic bottle of whiskey on top of his refrigerator, and flipped off the cap, which skipped across the threadbare carpet.

He carried the bottle into his bathroom where he took a large swig. The liquid burned his throat as it made its way to his rolling stomach. The bathroom was little more than a closet really, crammed with a minuscule vanity, mirror, toilet, and standing shower. He balanced the whiskey bottle on top of the vanity, and stared at the reflection of his dark-ringed eyes. Gently, he touched the wound on the back of his head. He remembered a similar wound from more than a decade ago. Strange how he was thinking so much today about the awful event that had led up to his Awakening.

Richard downed two more swigs of whiskey before firmly grabbing an old Cuban cigar box that lay under the sink, behind a stack of towels. It had belonged to his father David, and to his grandfather before that. David had given it to Richard when he first signed up for the Army. He placed the box on top of the small counter beside the sink.

Flipping open the worn cardboard lid, Richard stared at the revolver within. A woody cognac and nutmeg scent tickled his nose. Fortifying himself with the last of the whiskey, he plucked the gun from the box. He pressed the barrel firmly against his temple and watched the mirror reflect his actions as the cold metal dug into his flesh.

"*Just do it!*" Richard yelled at his reflection, shattering the silence. The muscles in his trigger finger began to tense. Tears sprang to his eyes and streamed down his face as the hammer crept back. His finger relaxed, and the hammer gently closed.

"Fucking coward!" he spat and slammed the gun down on the counter.

He stalked out of the bathroom and retrieved a new bottle from the plastic bag. He returned to the bathroom with the bottle already at his lips. Liquid fire burned in his throat as he pounded the new bottle down next to the cigar box.

He grabbed the gun and jammed it back against his temple.

"Do it, before you get someone killed," he hissed.

His finger was back on the trigger but he found it even harder to squeeze. He gazed into the mirror but didn't see his own reflection. Instead, he saw Sally, and she stared back at him, eyes full of innocence.

He looked away and placed the revolver back in the cigar box. He closed the lid and put it back behind the towels underneath the sink. Walking out of the bathroom with the liquor bottle in hand, Richard surveyed his homestead. He lacked the resolve to finish the deed quickly but found comfort in the slow death assured by the bottle.

"If you're going to be a coward, you should at least be one in a cleaner apartment."

THE SUN HAD yet to reach its zenith in the cloudless sky as a bright red Ferrari took a sharp right down a crowded city street near Route 28. Matt Nader sat behind the wheel. Riding with him was his partner and close friend Jake Talbot, whose pale complexion and jet-black hair always struck Matt as the complete opposite of his own tanned skin and blond hair, like a photographic negative.

"Why did you take this route? Today of all days," Jake said as he turned up the car's air conditioner.

Matt glanced at Jake, and was astonished again by how lean Jake had grown since his incarceration a few years ago. While skinny, Jake's muscle tone was well-defined. Matt believed he could beat his friend in a test of strength, but wondered if he could beat him in a test of endurance.

"It's the quickest way," Matt said. "Besides, it's really not that bad of an area."

"Not that bad? Did you even read the paper today? Last night, three people were gunned down less than two blocks from here."

"Come on, Jake, it's a little different during the afternoon. I don't think anyone is stupid or brazen enough to go on a shooting spree in broad daylight."

"Policing is fractured in this city," Jake said. "Any neighborhood that isn't in the North End or East Boston is hopelessly underfunded, and the rest is spread paper-thin. I don't see any reason why someone couldn't get away with it. Especially with the workers' protest later."

"What about witnesses or cameras?" Matt asked. He could see Jake was winding into another one of his trademark tirades.

"Half these cameras are disconnected by the masses the day after they're installed. Also, who stands around and looks at faces after they hear gunshots? Witnesses? I don't think so. These communities have seriously bought into the whole 'non-cooperation' thing. People think they're looking after one another by not talking to the police. Example: Dave shoots this kid a few nights ago—"

"Who's Dave?" Matt asked, lost already in Jake's train of thought.

"No one. I mean, just someone I made up, speaking hypothetically." Jake rolled his eyes as if this should have been obvious. "Dave lives in the community and is considered one of the community's own. When the police come sniffing around after the shooting, no one helps with the investigation because illegal activity might have been involved. A week goes by and—oh yeah, the kid who got shot is also in a gang.

"That gang then comes looking for Dave. They shoot and miss, because none of these gangbangers have guns legally, so they can't go to a range and practice. Anyway, they miss and the bullet hits some small, innocent child. Now we have a headline for the seven o'clock news. All because no one stepped up and told the truth about one of their own."

Matt blinked at Jake. "Been thinking about that one for some time?" he said.

"Not really. It pretty much rolls off the top of my head."

"Yeah, I guess it does," Matt said. "Anyway, all that considered, doesn't it only take one eyewitness to make the case?"

"Maybe," Jake said.

"Still, none of it matters to us. No one has any clue about the deposit riding in the back seat." Matt nodded at the two black duffel bags. "We aren't a target."

"It's not whether you're a target or not, it's about being in the wrong place at the wrong time," Jake corrected.

Matt's patience with the conversation had grown thin. "A huge majority of that shit happens at night, which isn't right now. We'll be fine. We're only a few blocks away from the bank."

Matt rolled the wheel to the right and abruptly stomped on the brake. Both lanes of the narrow road ahead were clogged with stationary traffic.

"Isn't this some bullshit?" Matt moaned.

"This route is quicker, says the guy who doesn't check the news."

"Look at these assholes," Matt muttered as three teenage boys crossed in front of the immobile car.

Jake counted the cars in front of them. "One . . . two . . . three car lengths away from a crosswalk," he said. "Apparently they're too badass to follow the rules."

Matt saw that one youth wore a sweatshirt despite the heat, while the other two wore Celtics basketball jerseys. The hooded sweatshirt matched the green of the jerseys. All three boys wore green hats turned at various angles. Matt spotted a firearm poking out from the slack jeans of the hooded one as the group hopped over the guardrail that divided the street. They were approaching a group of four teens of around the same age, hanging on the street corner wearing mostly red clothes with matching Red Sox hats.

"This doesn't look good," Matt said.

"What doesn't look—" Jake was cut off by the sound of three simultaneous gunshots.

Across the street, the green-clad trio had opened fire at the closest of the youths loitering in front of a vacant corner store's display window. A bullet hit the tallest of them in the temple and the contents of his skull splashed over the grimy window behind him.

The young man immediately to his left was shot in the chest. He slumped back against the brick wall behind him as he reached into his waistband. He coughed up a thick clot of blood.

The third bullet missed its mark. Its intended target scampered a few feet to his right, taking refuge behind a metal refuse container. Once behind cover, he drew his own pistol and took aim.

In front of Matt's Ferrari, tires squealed as multiple cars raced to get through the intersection and away from the gunfire. The ensuing crashes muted the return fire from the injured party. His shots were wild and one errant projectile shattered the rear window of the Ferrari. There was a dull *thunk* and a hole appeared in the dashboard where the bullet remained lodged.

"We need to get out of here now!" Jake yelled above the chaos of screams and horn blasts.

"Where do you want me to go? We're boxed in." Matt was hunched down in his seat. Particles of glass coated the back seat like frost.

In the street, one of the green-clad assailants lay motionless, shot in the head. The other two had retreated behind a black suburban parked at a meter in front of the store's boarded-up entrance. A bullet sunk deep into the front bumper of the car, then another shattered the windshield.

"We need to grab the money and bail!" Jake yelled.

Matt nodded and watched Jake draw out his .45 caliber pistol from its holster, pulling the slide back and chambering a round. Matt followed suit, making sure his gun was loaded and armed. He grabbed the first duffel bag from the back seat and handed it to Jake, who scrambled out of the passenger door on the side opposite the chaos. Matt grasped the second bag and had to climb over the shift stick to leave through the same door.

"This takes me back to live-fire training at Fort Bragg," Jake said, crouching alongside the front passenger tire. He had a grin on his face that Matt had seen too many times throughout their military career—the slightly-crazed smile of a man who knows that a single shot could end his life at any second. But that adrenaline seemed to give Jake a high that no drug could match, and it was at times like these that Matt was glad Jake was his friend and not his enemy.

"I should shoot them all," Matt said. "They shot my fucking Ferrari."

"I was just thinking," Jake said, eyeing his friend. "Since you love this route and all, maybe it's a good place to open that classic-auto body shop you're always going on about. If you open it up quick enough, I'm sure you could capitalize on today. The property tax will be ridiculously cheap."

"Jake, don't start. I'm just trying to remember if we put my car on the company insurance." Matt peeked through the window and saw the lookout for the Niners, who was stationed farther down the road, discharging three rounds from behind the back of an SUV. A bullet felled one of the invading group, who sprawled on the pavement shrieking.

"You know this is your fault," Matt said, drawing a blank look from Jake. "You jinxed us."

"Jinxed us? What are you talking about?"

"Your whole bullshit soapbox speech about shootings."

"Don't pin your bad decisions on me, just because you failed to listen to the fountain of all knowledge. Let's just get to the bank and deposit the money."

Matt looked mournfully at the Ferrari. "Baby, I'm sorry. I have to leave you, and you may get towed. I promise I won't leave you impounded for long." He ran his hand along the outer shell of the expensive car.

"That's healthy," Jake said. "Real healthy. Now, can we start with the fleeing please?"

The pair darted away from the carnage as the Niner lookout unloaded the rest of his clip at the one remaining assailant left standing.

A FEW BLOCKS AWAY, Johnny Roberts was exiting a convenience store with his two babysitters and his best friend Nick. Johnny thought about Scott Jones's commands from yesterday—no corner work, no hanging on the stoops. The orders were devastating to Johnny's status among his peers. Guard duty on the main stash house was the only role Johnny could perform over the next few days. But Scott was like a father to him now, and so Johnny did what he was told. He'd never really known his true father and Scott had become Johnny's very definition of what a man should be. The only memory he had left of his father was the image of him driving away from him and his mother in the old beat-up Accord.

"Damn man, I know you heard *that*," Nick said, turning towards the sound of gunfire and biting into an extra-long Slim Jim. Even though Nick's diet was loaded with unhealthy fattening food, he never seemed to gain a pound. "How can we stand here and do nothing while our soldiers get murdered a few blocks away?"

"It's not your issue," Ray-Ray, the bigger of the two bodyguards, warned. "If you wanted to play the game today, you shouldn't have volunteered to hang with Johnny."

Johnny knew that Ray-Ray had pulled this inglorious guard detail by letting one of his young corner boys run off with the corner's daily count. He also knew that Ray-Ray would rather be doing almost anything else. As far as Johnny was concerned, the feeling was mutual.

"Those shots got to have come from Long View," Nick said. "Listen Ray-Ray, that's Little Moe's corner. I know you came up with him."

"And what if I did?"

"So you're just going to let them get slaughtered?"

"And if we violate Jones's orders, what do you think happens to us?" Ray-Ray stepped up to Nick, forcing the smaller boy to back down.

"You want a visit from Uncle Tek?" the other babysitter, Ice, said. He wore two rings on his right hand, and across the bridge between them his name was picked out in diamonds.

"Jones didn't say nothing about walking in that direction," Nick said. "If we happen on some of Stacks's crew fleeing the scene, our orders don't say nothing about what we do with them."

Ray-Ray's eyes widened at that. Johnny had listened to many of Scott's anecdotes, and he knew that Ray-Ray had suffered at the hands of Stacks. Getting revenge on Stacks and his so-called Young Gunz crew had been at the top of his priority list for a while.

"I don't like it," Ice said firmly.

"Why don't we leave it up to Johnny?" Nick said. "He's the top dog here."

Johnny hated Nick at that moment. He knew if he backed down from the fight, he would look weak. He felt all eyes focused on him.

"Let's do it," he said at last.

The four Niners crossed the street, leaving their vehicle parked at the charge station next to the convenience store, and headed in the direction of the gunshots.

MATT AND JAKE ducked into the shadows of a narrow alley between two tall apartment buildings. Matt, breathing heavily, tossed the bag of money onto the pavement. He was getting too old for this shit.

"Jesus Christ, this has to be an all-out war," Jake said between labored breaths.

"They kept coming out of the woodwork. There was no end to them. I saw at least two other corners being assaulted."

"I kept hearing sirens, but I didn't see any police."

"Neither did I," Matt said absently. "I hope my baby is okay."

"You saw the crowds gathering," Jake said. "A car like that? It'll most likely get torched in the inevitable riot that's coming. The police cars couldn't even get to the main streets."

"Don't even joke about it," Matt said, shoving Jake and knocking him off balance.

At that moment four Niners barreled into the alley's opposite entrance.

"Look at what we got here, Ray-Ray!" the skinny kid in the lead yelled at Matt upon seeing the two well-dressed, slightly older men at the end of the alleyway.

Matt stood up, as did Jake beside him. He reached towards his gun, ready to draw.

"Careful, they're armed," the youngest of the group said to his companions. "They could be cops. Why else would two clean-cut boys be in this part of town right now?" The skinny kid grinned but seemed to dismiss the notion with a shake of his head.

"You boys must not know the rules around here," Skinny said. "To pass through, you gotta pay the toll."

Matt felt his anger rising. "Oh yeah asshole? What's your toll?"

"Depends on how much you got." Skinny drew the weapon stashed in his belt.

Matt and Jake instinctively responded in kind while the other three Niners exposed their weapons but didn't draw them. The widest member of the group pulled the youngest back a step, so that he was behind the tallest guy at the back.

"It seems we've arrived at an impasse," Jake called out to no one in particular.

"Let's be smart about this," Skinny said. "You're outgunned and outnumbered. Just give up what you got and walk away."

"Outgunned?" Matt said, annoyed. He flashed a knowing smile at Jake. "Not from where I'm standing."

Skinny took two aggressive steps forward. "What are you, a hard ass or something?"

Jake said, "What you fail to realize is that we are two highly trained individuals. I know the shots we fire will find their mark. Can you say the same?" His voice was a flat monotone, which Matt knew was a dangerous sign.

"Is that supposed to scare me?" Skinny stepped forward again, almost snarling.

"Merely stating the facts."

"Enough bullshit," Skinny said.

He squeezed out a round that hit Jake in the shoulder, spinning him off balance. But the Niners had started drawing their weapons a moment too late. Matt crouched and fired back immediately, hitting Skinny in the abdomen. The youth folded up and dropped to the ground.

As Jake fell backwards, he squeezed off a single round, hitting the youngest guy, who had drawn his pistol but was desperately trying to flip the safety off. The bullet penetrated his skull below the eye, shattering the orbital bone. He fell into the shadows of the alleyway and lay there, motionless.

Matt leveled his gun at the two standing Niners. *Wideboy and Tallboy*, he thought wildly, aware that his adrenaline was peaking. They both looked dumbfounded that the battle had been decided before they'd had the chance to fire.

"Drop your weapons and kick them over here!" Matt commanded.

The Niners reluctantly did as they were instructed, dropping both nine-millimeters and kicking them across the concrete. They skidded halfway to Matt. "Now, get the hell out of here."

Hesitantly, the two guys backed away. Once they'd made enough distance, Matt turned to see that Jake was slumped against the brick wall. He clutched his shoulder, grimacing.

"Shit, you're bleeding," Matt said and rushed to his partner.

"You never remember exactly how much it hurts when you get shot," Jake grunted.

"Did it pierce your vest?" Matt ripped the sleeve from his collared shirt and prepped it to be used as a tourniquet.

"No," Jake said. "It missed the vest completely. My shoulder. The bastard shot me in the shoulder." He pushed back against the wall and tried to rise.

"Need some help there?"

Jake nodded and Matt placed his arm around Jake's good side and lifted. Jake moaned as he straightened out. Once on his own feet, he gently pushed himself away from Matt.

"I've had enough of this petty violence," Jake said.

Across the alley, Skinny was coughing up a lot of blood, and gargling like a drain, clearly aspirating it. Jake limped over to the felled Niner and stood over him, leering down. Matt felt like looking away, but kept watching anyway.

"You're going to find out what happens to people who mess up my day," Jake said. He took a knee and slapped Skinny across the face. "Wake up. I know you're not dead." When no response came, Jake slapped him again harder. "Look at me."

The boy's eyes fluttered open. He rolled over against Jake's leg. Blood dripped from him.

"I'm only going to ask this once, then the pain comes." He leaned in, inches from the boy's pale, sweaty face. "Where is the main resupply spot for the drugs?"

"Go . . . fuck . . . yourself."

"Remember, I asked nicely first," Jake said quietly. He slowly and deliberately shoved his thumb into the gunshot wound, twisting it back and forth. The young Niner screamed like a little girl.

Matt did finally look away. He realized that he could hear no sirens in the aftermath of the firefight, which sent a chill down his spine. The police must've been out in force dealing with the corner wars and the planned protests. The fact that multiple gunshots in an alleyway didn't warrant a passing patrol car response clued him in on the true gravity of the situation.

Jake had completed his interrogation. He'd produced more information than was needed, but the questioning had drained the last of the boy's energy and he lay immobile now, glassy eyes unblinking. Jake had programmed all the addresses he'd coaxed out of the boy into his cell phone. Matt looked on, disconnected from the horror. He'd seen Jake do similar before now. Similar and worse.

"For a second there, I didn't think he would talk," Jake said as he wiped the remnants of his questioning from his hands onto the pavement.

"Just take it easy," Matt said. "You're still losing quite a lot of blood." He motioned in the direction of the Niner. "You killed him?"

"No. He was dead before I started working him over. His body just didn't know it yet."

Matt wouldn't judge his friend. He had done things during his time in the military that he was not proud of, and Jake had almost lost his life to one of these thugs; his wife Andrea *had* lost hers.

Matt took off his torn shirt, and fashioned a sling with its remains. He slipped Jake's arm into it. "You going to be able to huff it out of here?" he asked his partner. "We've stayed too long as it is."

T HE LATE AFTERNOON sun had begun its lazy descent across the city's skyline. Its rays weakly penetrated the window behind Scott Jones as he sat uneasily in his office chair. Tek was exhausted, having spent most of the day scurrying up and down the stairs, receiving face to face updates of the day's battles.

Stacks—Scott's former partner and now chief rival—had attacked multiple corners in a desperate last stand. The morning had seen heavy losses for the Niners, but as the day had progressed and allied clans from the surrounding suburbs had arrived, the tide had turned. The last reported assault was hours ago.

"All things considered, not a terrible day." Tek stretched across the plush cushions of the couch.

"Not a terrible day?" Jones was on edge. "We got half of our corners unmanned. The other half are crime scenes. Crackheads are too scared to buy from our dealers. This kind of heat ain't going to split anytime soon. We're fucked." He slammed his fist on the desk.

"The losses we can replace," Tek said. "If the junkies go elsewhere to buy, it's still our product at wholesale. The heat has always been on us." He fixed Jones with a level stare. "When is the last time you were near any drugs, or handled weapons, or touched any part of the escort business?" The question was entirely rhetorical—Jones had been hands-off the day-to-day for years. He had his men to do the dirty work, and Jones spent his time settling disputes between the clans. "What does the police have on you, or me, for that matter?"

"This is different," Jones said wearily. "It's on a bigger scale. The police are going to backlash hard. This wasn't the way we were going to play the game." He rubbed his temples, trying to relieve the tension. "Everything else in the world advances yet we still play the same game."

"This is the way the game is played. It won't ever change. This is just a bump in the road." Jones shot Tek a fierce stare but Tek refused to back down. "You tried your best with Stacks, did more for the guy than you should've. Hell, we took a huge hit to our rep letting him walk a year ago."

"I didn't hear you say shit a year ago," Jones said.

"That's not what I'm saying. What's done is done. We have to move forward." Tek sat back up. "You know the police are going to use this to get wires and surveillance going against us again."

"Lock-down protocol. No re-ups on cell phones. No talking shop in the car, and a rotating location for our group meets. We have to sweep our own fronts for bugs, and soon." Jones shook his head bitterly.

Jesus, Tek thought. *I was trying to cheer the guy up.*

"I'll personally make sure that no money or drugs are exchanged," Tek said, still trying to boost Jones's morale. "And I'll make sure that there are enough vacancies in the area to move the stash twice a day if need be. We won't lose too much business."

Still shaking his head, Jones said, "Seems like we've been losing little by little for almost a year now."

"We're almost through this, Bones," Tek said, using Jones's old nickname. Jones had cut his teeth selling marijuana and cigarettes under the radar of the already established hard drug dealers in his neighborhood, earning him the nickname "Bones Jones." "Just a little bit longer, and we can reclaim all our lost turf. Hell, if we can manage to take out Stacks, the rest of *his* turf is easy to reclaim." Tek stood up and walked over to Jones, standing next to his chair. He gazed out the window, looking at nothing in particular. Grimy tenements were stacked into the distance.

"How did it all come to this?" Jones said, mostly to himself, Tek thought.

Tek circled around, placing a hand on Jones's shoulder. "Not your fault; Stacks got greedy. We had a great thing going but he wanted more. He wasn't made to wear the crown of a prince."

"Where's Bricks?" Jones asked.

"You know him," Tek said. "He wants to lead the hunt for Stacks himself. Doesn't trust anyone else to get the job done. We got word that Stacks was operating out of a spot in Roxbury."

"Roxbury? That is ballsy." A twenty-minute drive would take Bricks into the heart of the enemy. "To think, a year ago we almost thought we could pacify him."

"We didn't sever the ties. Stacks owns that."

"You remember what happened?" Jones said.

Tek sighed. "Yeah, I remember," he said. He crossed back to the couch and sat, and remembered.

TWENTY YEARS AGO, Stacks controlled the Niners, until he was convicted of murder. He had attracted a lot of police attention by muscling rival dealers out of the surrounding neighborhoods, but the prosecution had only one murder charge that they could progress beyond pretrial hearings. By taking a plea bargain, Stacks avoided a life sentence.

In Stacks's time as leader he'd chosen to target the highest-level rivals and eliminate them. This tactic created additional heat in the newly-gained territory, effectively limiting the potential gain. Jones, who had been Stacks's right hand man, took over the reins when Stacks was incarcerated, and he had a different vision for the clan: instead of running rivals out of the game, he proposed flipping them, making enemies of their former suppliers rather than of the dealers. They could run their corners with their crew; the only difference would be in where they bought their product. Jones and his Niners moved up to wholesalers, dealing a purer grade of product, meaning those on the corners could cut it a few times and still have the best product in the area. It was a win-win situation that most of the opposition immediately recognized.

This new strategy worked well for the clan. By using economic means instead of brute force to take over the corners, there was no added pressure around the organization from criminal investigators. By the mid-'30s, Jones and his version of the Niners controlled most of the drug trade from South Boston to Brockton. In some places, Jones's drugs could be found as far south as the border of Rhode Island.

This drew the attention of the other clans' former suppliers, members of the Russian crime syndicate. Jones's move had cut deeply into their profits. A few minor altercations broke out, but a pact between the Niners and the Russians was made before a full-scale war erupted. There were nearly two decades of tentative peace until Stacks was released from prison.

Upon his release, Stacks assumed a high-ranking role in the Niners, a kind of Vice Presidential position. He took personal oversight of all judgments and punishments for violations of the crew's rules committed by its own members. Stacks's violent behavior and pent-up rage found homicidal release in the role.

It was a tense but workable relationship between Captain and First Mate. Jones tried his best not to force the issue, never giving Stacks a direct command, keeping strictly to suggestions. Unfortunately, after a low-level Russian gangster moved in on a Niner-supplied corner, Stacks sought retribution on his own terms.

Stacks staked out the corner in question and waited patiently as the Russian crew sold and resupplied throughout the day. Stacks tailed the moneyman when he left the corner, following him to his boss. With a few carefully-chosen Niners, Stacks conducted an unsanctioned raid, wiping out most of the Russians in the building.

To rectify the situation, Jones called a meeting at one of the local parks with Stacks, Tek, Bricks, and Leon, another high-ranking member tied to the group by Bricks. They were to conduct a sort of intervention, hoping the presence of only those who'd known Stacks the longest would help curb his defensive tendencies. The plan was for all in attendance to remind Stacks of the rules and to show how his actions affected the organization on multiple levels.

It was an unusually cold early-spring evening when the group gathered in Southwest Corridor Park. Scott was walking along one of the linear park's two pathways. A single line of trees separated this part of the park from the noise of Columbus Avenue. He was too busy simulating the coming exchange over and over in his mind to listen to the buzzing words of those around him.

They took a left at a fork in the pathway, going deeper into the park. Bricks and Leon were walking together a few feet ahead of Scott, discussing last-minute ideas. Scott had asked them along, as both had been personally recruited by Stacks. The benefit of the words coming from them far outweighed the risk of them turning on Scott, which was currently his worst-case scenario. Tek, Scott's most trusted friend, silently walked in step beside him as always. The trees grew denser the deeper they ventured into the park, as if nature were reclaiming it from the inside out.

Stacks had already beaten them to the meeting point. He paced back and forth along the length of a square patch of concrete while staring at his watch. The group spread out as they arrived.

"What the fuck's up, Jones? Why we meeting way the hell out here? What do you got cooking in that mind of yours?" Stacks advanced towards Scott with an accusatory finger jutting at him.

"We think you need some time off, away from the clan. Think of it as a vacation," Scott said.

Stacks stopped his advance with a snort. He stood only a few feet from Scott. His smaller frame did not stop Scott from taking a half step backwards.

"So, you want control of the Niners? You want my life's work. My baby. And you expect me to just walk away while you steal it from me?"

Bricks stepped forward. "It's not like that, Stacks," he said. "It's just a short break is all. We need to settle shit with the Russians before things get worse."

"Don't tell me you are Jones's boy now." Stacks's eyes narrowed as they shifted to Bricks.

"He ain't Jones's boy and neither am I," Leon spoke up. "You brought me and Bricks into this family. You gave us something when the whole world gave up on us. And you told us always do what's best for the clan. You know me, I ain't looking to run shit. I do my job and keep my mouth shut like a proper soldier. Right now, in this soldier's opinion, what's best for the clan is if you lay low. Just for a bit, then you can come back and start up right where you left off."

"Don't tell me Jones poisoned you with his words as well." Stacks had fallen still. He shifted his feet, squaring his shoulders, and stared at each of them in turn. "Listen boys, I hear your concerns. I think I know an easy solution to *all* our problems."

Stacks pulled the gun hidden in his pants and leveled it at Scott.

Scott's heart froze in his chest. His closest friend, a guy he'd grown up with, could end his life with a simple squeeze of a trigger. Time slowed for Scott as Stacks pulled the trigger. A sudden blur of motion rushed in from Scott's side as the gunshot rang out, and the bullet intended for Jones struck Leon in the chest, dropping him instantly.

Tek leapt on top of Stacks, bringing him down in the dirt. Stacks's weapon flew from his hands, coming to a stop next to Leon's foot. Bricks rushed over to try and aid his friend. Leon's wound was making a wet, sucking noise like sludge in a pipe, and Bricks pressed into the bubbling blood with both hands, as hard as he could.

Tek and Stacks rolled on the ground interlocked like lovers, wrestling for control. Neither man could gain the upper hand. Stacks outweighed Tek by a good margin, but Tek was wiry and able to slip out of Stacks's grip. Meanwhile, Jones stood dumbfounded, his gaze fixed on the wounded man bleeding on the ground. A man who had sacrificed his life for Jones's ideal.

Leon exhaled for the last time and the hideous sucking wound fell silent. Bricks roared with rage. Jones saw him spot the murder weapon at the feet of his deceased friend. He grabbed it and aimed at the pair rolling around on the ground. Stacks had his hands around Tek's neck, squeezing the life out of him. Tek desperately poked his thumb at Stacks's left eye. As Jones watched, Tek's thumb disappeared into the socket, and Stacks screamed and rolled away.

The wail of city surveillance equipment suddenly blared out. Jones hadn't ordered the disabling of the government watch system because he hadn't even considered this turn of events.

Bricks fired a round into the night sky and everyone froze. Bricks's venom was focused squarely on Stacks. "Get the hell out of here," he hissed.

Stacks was on his knees, head hanging, hand pressed to his left eye socket. He stood shakily and looked at Leon lying dead next to Bricks's shoes. "Bro, I didn't mean to," he whispered.

"The only reason you are alive is because without you, Leon and I would both be dead by now. If you ever show your face to me again . . ." He left the threat incomplete as patrol sirens rose in the distance.

"Bricks," Stacks said.

Bricks fired once more into the air. Stacks shuffled a couple of steps backwards. He stood there for a moment, then dropped the hand covering his eye. Jones gasped.

Stacks's cheek was smeared with watery blood and viscous fluid. His eye socket was raw and puckered, and as Jones looked on, it seemed to be folding itself inwards, like a raw mouth closing. Beside him, Tek was staring fixedly at the bloody jelly in his hand, rubbing it between his fingers as if testing its texture.

Finally, Stacks turned and hurried away, head down and shoulders hunched.

BACK IN THE office, Jones said, "I could've stepped down when Stacks was released. Let him resume his reign."

"It wouldn't have worked," Tek said. "Leon, Bricks, me, we all agreed on that. We would all be in prison or in the dirt. Stacks is a man who constantly wants more. He can only see what he's missing, not what he has."

"Possibly, but there are too many factors to know for sure," Jones said, preoccupied. He was thinking about Johnny. He had to assume that Johnny was dead. He hadn't heard from the young man, or his babysitters, all day.

"What if we walked away from it all?" he said to Tek. "We're getting too old to still be doing this shit."

Tek nodded. "True. But what are you going to do and still make bank like we do?"

"Is it worth jumping at the sight of every cop car, or making sure we got backup when some thugs we don't recognize walk down our streets? Or how about the three a.m. phone calls when one clan has a petty beef with another?"

"I sleep comfortably at night, but then again, I don't worry as much as you do. Unlike Stacks, I actually enjoy being Player Two." Tek paused, clearly looking for the right words. "Speaking about possibilities," he said. "Should we have contacted Raef about the Russians? Stacks could've worked out a deal with the Russians and Raef already. You know Stacks is pushing their package somehow."

The thought of Stacks working with the Russians was a deadly enough proposition, but adding Raef into the mix was something else entirely. Jones had thought of the possibility, but he couldn't come up with a contingency plan for the scenario.

"Raef, if nothing else, is a man who honors contracts. He will do the job, quicker than he said, and collect the second half of his payment. We're betting on his personal hatred of the Russians and our mutually-beneficial past. Stacks is our problem and we will deal with him as soon as we can track him down." Or so he hoped.

"Listen Bones, I respect the guy's work. I'm just playing devil's advocate."

"You sat in on the meeting. Raef is a strange man who does things I don't necessarily approve of. I swear, if you wanted to kill him, you'd probably have to put a stake through his heart. But with the situation as it is, we need him. Stacks was locked up a long time and he never met Raef. Stacks has no way of knowing that Raef is even in the city."

"The thought of those two working together though," Tek said. He involuntarily wiped his hand on his shirt, as if reliving that night in the park. "You think Bricks has it in him to do it?"

"Bricks will get the job done."

"That history is pretty deep, Bones. He didn't shoot him a year ago."

"I don't know if *I* was ready to shoot him a year ago. But Bricks is a Niner." Jones's usual authoritative tone crept back into his voice. "We got enough shit piling up between Stacks and the Russians. We don't need to start questioning loyal soldiers. You're going to lose your mind if you start imagining threats where they don't exist."

Jones had had enough of the conversation. He pushed his chair back and crossed to the couch. His anger at Stacks and the Russians chased away his depression.

Tek smiled. "It's not paranoia if it's true. Like I said Bones Jones, you make the decisions. I follow and sleep a lot easier that way."

DETECTIVE DEREK WALCOTT drove his unmarked black Charger to the site of the latest investigation. Walcott was the senior officer in the South Boston District Gang Unit. He'd grown up in this district and he understood the harsh reality of life here. He scratched the back of his head, and smoothed his short, curly hair.

His partner, Ana Dats, the freshest member of the gang unit, rode next to him in the passenger seat. She wasn't the biggest, nor the meanest, detective on the squad, both qualities that came in handy when busting up a corner, but she had smarts and for a detective that was more valuable than brute force.

Ana's big break had come when she'd gained statewide fame running down an attempted assassin who took a shot at the district senator. She'd chased the fugitive for five blocks before catching up to the perpetrator and taking him into custody without firing a shot. Anyone who wanted to make detective couldn't afford a single blemish on their record, and that was simple for Ana, who'd kept that goal in mind throughout her career so far. When the district senator had put in his recommendation, she'd had no red flags holding her back.

Detective Walcott pulled into the intersection and stopped before a yellow line of police evidence tape that read "Do Not Cross" in English and Spanish. He climbed out of the Charger, using the side mirror to adjust his suit jacket and tie. He looked across the

Charger's hood at Dats, who was stretching her legs.

"Two days until the plane ride," Walcott said. "Getting nervous?"

"Are we still on this subject, Walcott?" The young detective rolled her eyes. "I thought you'd given up on the pep talks."

"I hope you got a refundable package for your honeymoon. If today is what I think it is, good chance the captain cancels your request for leave," Walcott said with a playful tone.

"You're the lead detective here. I'm just a snot-nosed runt. At least that's what I *think* the Captain called me earlier. I am the epitome of unnecessary. Nonessential personnel."

Walcott knew Captain Mason Levi didn't like the fact that Dats had been helped along with her rapid promotions and choice appointments. He also knew that Dats knew it too. The district senator had been very gracious towards the woman who had captured his would-be killer. Dats had unwittingly acquired a "rabbi," a boon for her career in law enforcement.

"Don't worry about it," Walcott said, and leaned forward. "But did you hear about the time Internal Affairs thought the Cap was smuggling drugs in his mustache?"

"Are any of these mustache jokes good?" Dats asked.

"Turned out he was only smuggling another mustache," Walcott said as he turned and walked away from Dats and towards a group of his officers.

Walcott's unit had cordoned off the intersection, the front of the store, and a side alleyway. A police photographer was taking close-ups of a corpse, and cops were placing evidence markers around fallen shells and bullet holes in cars. A few patrolmen were reviewing video feeds from the surrounding cameras. Walcott motioned for his men to gather round.

"Gentlemen, the Niners established this corner earlier in the day, and by midday the Young Gunz shut them down. We believe that this incident was an attempt by the Young Gunz to expand their dominance eastwards. This case is linked to multiple cases from today, all of which have similar tools and players. We are going to need hard evidence, so get your thinking caps on and don't fuck with any samples before a tech team can get here. I want blood and fingerprints from the survivors. Build a solid case for a change, so we don't get screwed on a bullshit loophole.

"From what little info we've already gathered, it seems that the Young Gunz hit-squad crossed the street a few feet before the intersection." Walcott pointed to the guardrail that bisected the two-lane street. "The intersection was heavy with traffic, as you can still see. They used the cars for cover as they approached unnoticed. Their primary target was the cashman out front. The return fire is what cracked the driver's side window of the red Ferrari."

That Ferrari stood out in Walcott's mind. You didn't easily forget a car of that quality even in one of the higher-class districts, and this one nagged at him for some reason. He made a mental note to recheck previous cases from the last few years. In Walcott's mind, violence was associated with this car. It was most likely just a coincidence, but a niggling suspicion wouldn't let him drop it.

RICHARD SURVEYED HIS nearly-pristine apartment. There was a bottle of vodka, still containing a mouthful of liquor, on the kitchen counter. He crossed unsteadily to it and downed the contents before throwing it into the overflowing bin, where it bounced off other empty bottles.

In the living room, the blinds were drawn and the TV was tuned to a news program. The screen bathed the darkened room in a soft luminescence.

"Continuing our coverage of the large-scale protest rampaging through downtown," the female newscaster with the perfect smile said. "A riot erupted as police tried to move into the area after responding to a shots-fired call. The police are outnumbered and emergency services are struggling to keep lines open. Viewers are encouraged to avoid the area and to stay indoors. If you see breaking news, snap a photo and share it with us on social media. Your image could appear on our broadcast. Also, post your comments and opinions on our website."

The screen transitioned to a closeup of her male counterpart, who boasted hair as perfect as her smile. "The mayor has scheduled a press conference and as soon as it starts, Newscenter Nine will take you there live."

"The whole city is going to hell," Richard said as he swallowed the last of the vodka. He decided he liked cleaning, probably because he could finish the last few drops left in all the bottles of liquor that he found scattered throughout his apartment.

"Of course people are going to protest when their jobs are replaced by robots," he slurred. "Hell, even the robot-repair field is dominated by bots."

"We now take you live to the mayor's press conference," the perfect TV newscaster said.

The screen showed a podium with the State Seal hanging from its facade. Behind it hung the State flag alongside the flag of the United States. A blue curtain covered the wall, obscuring any indication of where the speech was taking place.

"Everyone thought automation would save everything," Richard muttered. "But all it did was lead to layoffs and the obliteration of the middle class." He dropped a pair of socks into his laundry bin and made a mental note to do a load of laundry in the morning, since he now had time off from work. "And don't forget a housing authority with the power to seize land and relocate the poor."

On the TV, the mayor stepped up to the podium, doing his best to hide his bulging gut. No amount of makeup could cover his red, lumpy nose. Richard could almost feel the clamminess of the mayor's skin through the HD screen.

"We have asked the governor for help in lieu of the crisis facing our city," the mayor said. "Starting tonight, state troopers will be joining our municipal and district law enforcement officers, allowing for increased patrols of our city streets to help enforce the peace. You will also notice a drone presence in the sky. These are unarmed drones used only for surveilling public streets. I implore our citizens to leave the streets and the riots behind and to return to their homes."

"With unemployment over forty percent, adding more police won't solve any of the underlying problems," Richard said to the screen. "We need to learn to be a society again instead of a group of individuals."

Richard's apartment had morphed into something presentable. He was satisfied with his efforts. He shook his head, trying to rid himself of his thoughts. "I must be losing my mind, talking to myself."

He walked around his apartment, checking the bathroom that he had wiped clean earlier. He fluffed up the throw pillows resting on his couch. He stretched his body, cracking his neck satisfyingly, then lay down on the couch. His world spun momentarily before a liquor-induced black haze descended over him.

AND HE WAS suddenly back in that sunny day, ten years earlier.

The burnt orange Dodge Neon rolled down a side street towards an intersection in an idyllic suburban town. Richard's family didn't have the money to purchase a driverless car, and the only car Richard could afford was a used, turn-of-the-millennium relic. The four teenage occupants were chatting excitedly about the latest virtual reality system they had purchased by pooling their money together.

An eighteen-year-old Richard sat behind the steering wheel. Next to him, in the front passenger seat, was one of his two best friends, Matt. Behind them was the other, Jake. Sitting next to Jake was his younger cousin, Justin.

"I can't wait to make some blue alien blood splatter." Matt ran a hand through his dirty blond hair, as he turned to talk to the guys behind him. His good looks and nonchalant attitude had led his friends to nickname him Hook—they would cast Matt into a group of girls and watch as he reeled the lot of them back with him.

Jake, with his raven black hair, grinned at Matt. "Let me see the back of the box." Jake, by far the quietest of the group in social settings, had a few inches on Matt, whereas Matt had a few pounds on Jake.

"I heard the optic field of view is two-seventy degrees," Justin chimed in. He was still in high school.

As the Neon approached the intersection, an old tan Camry zipped down the road to the right. It contained a mother and her two small children. Richard later found out that they had been running late for a doctor's appointment.

As the Camry reached the summit of the hill, the mother let off the accelerator. Gravity took over, propelling the car forward. It increased in speed as it headed for the same intersection as the Neon.

Inside the Neon, Matt looked out the window and saw the mother turning in her seat, scolding the children in the back. And then the Camry collided with the passenger door. Matt opened his mouth to shout out, but the impact stole his voice.

The two cars spun together. The Neon pulled the Camry through the intersection, disengaged from the Camry's passenger-side door briefly, then smashed the rear quarter panel on the same side. The metal crumpled in on itself. The vehicles slewed to a halt, tires screaming. The Neon was facing the way it had come, and the Camry was alongside of it, facing the other way.

The Neon's horn had short-circuited and it blared a loud, warped honk. In the backseat, Jake and Justin looked at each other, almost unscathed. Their only injuries were from their heads colliding with one another after the initial impact.

Richard's head was smashed against the side window. Webbed fractures raced across the glass from a softball-sized crater in the center. Blood ran down from it, filling the cracks.

The passenger-side window, directly above the point of impact, scattered tiny fragments that sparkled in the midday sun like diamonds. Richard was covered in them.

Matt was ejected from his seat into the center console. A razor-sharp shaft of the doorframe pierced the right half of his lower abdomen, spearing him from pancreas to kidney. Blood immediately burst from the wound in a scarlet sheet.

The car's horn suddenly fell silent, and all that remained was the ticking and creaking of the wrecked cars.

"Get me out of here," Matt groaned. His head rested on Richard's shoulder. His eyes were clamped shut.

Jake managed to open his door and tumbled out of the wreck. Justin tried to open his door, but, being on the same side as the impact, the warped frame would not budge. He slithered across the seat and rolled out the same side as Jake.

Richard's door opened easily enough, and Jake helped him to clamber out. Jake's already-pale complexion lost the little color it had when he saw Matt. After making sure Richard could stand under his own power, Jake headed back inside the wreck.

"Wrap your arms around me," Jake said to Matt.

Matt did as he was told, hooking his arms around Jake's neck. He grabbed a hold of Matt's legs, just above his knees. He gingerly lifted Matt across the center console, getting him into the driver's seat. Matt groaned and blood soaked both of the boys' shirts and jeans.

"Justin!" Jake called. "Help me here."

Justin took Matt's legs as Jake grabbed him underneath the armpits. Tenderly, they picked the wounded boy up and carried him to the sloping grass by the side of the road.

Richard glanced at the Camry. The grill was buckled and twisted. Black smoke plumed from underneath the hood. He couldn't see any signs that the airbags had deployed and wondered if the car was so old that it didn't have any. Its three passengers were wandering around the grass on the opposite side of the street, dazed. The smaller of the two boys began wailing in between heavy sobs.

Richard staggered over to where Matt lay bleeding and motionless. Compelled by some foreign force, Richard knelt down beside Matt.

"He needs pressure on the wound to stem the bleeding." Jake's disconnected voice echoed somewhere far off in Richard's ears. His hands found the penetrating wound on Matt's abdomen, while his mind wandered further from conscious thought. Richard was only dimly aware of the torrent of blood staining his hands.

Inside Matt's abdomen, a faltering blue light sparked into existence. The spark gathered tiny metal fragments like a magnet, drawing them out from damaged tissue and disgorging them just beyond the entry wound. A ring of metal particles accumulated then washed down Matt's body, carried by the current of rushing blood.

The spark rapidly accelerated cell reproduction once the wound was clear of obstructions. Torn and burst organs knitted together. The shattered ribs hovered inside the abdomen, held in place by an unseen force while new bone replaced that which had been lost. Matt groaned and writhed as his ribs twisted into the correct alignment. The skin of the wound puckered and drew in, weaving itself together.

Richard was only dimly aware of the events occurring under his hands. His mind ached and his body felt weak. Without warning, the world drained of color and light. He moved his hands close to his eyes but still could not see them. Even the act of moving his arms seemed alien.

Alone in this new realm, bereft of light, Richard's senses were confounded. The concept of up and down flipped irregularly. Richard perceived four distant stars in front of him, distant yet almost within reach. He tried to stand up and walk towards them but such a notion was impossible here.

A mote of golden light fluttered off in the distance like a will-o'-the-wisp. In the presence of the light, Richard felt his soul pried open and all his life secrets revealed. The intrusion left him naked.

As it drew closer, Richard could better see the light and make out the details. It was a small butterfly with golden wings. The golden glow was emitting from those golden wings with each flap. The pulsing glow dominated Richard's vision.

Richard was entranced by the pulsing light until he was startled by something slimy reaching his lower half. Though he could see no part of himself, he certainly could feel the being slide over him. Any calming effect the butterfly brought was wiped out in an instant. Richard was soaked with moisture wherever the thing crawled over him.

The butterfly also sensed the arrival of the third being, halting its indirect progress. Richard tried to move towards the butterfly, to move towards safety, and found he was anchored to the spot. Panic struck as he felt the third being on his back. Its slithering journey culminated at the top of Richard's consciousness, which seemed to somehow rise above his body, trying to squirm free of the beast. He was both inside and outside of his body simultaneously.

The beast's coiling motion led Richard to suspect it was a snake, but it could have easily been a snail or slug. Richard tried to scream but in this other universe, he lacked even a voice.

Unable to shift his focus, he saw only the lone, apprehensive butterfly, which kept its distance. Fear surged through him.

Spurred on by Richard's fear, the snake sprang towards the butterfly. Richard saw it for the first time, and his fears were confirmed. The snake was skinny but impossibly long, with leathery scales. A column of red diamonds was strewn across the snake's back, from its head to its tail.

Richard watched helplessly as the snake unhinged its jaw midflight. It swallowed the butterfly in a single gulp. Soundless, it pivoted its head, and glared at Richard before coiling off into the distance.

As the snake slithered beyond Richard's sight, a vortex slowly emerged from the darkness. Richard felt the substance of the space around him race past as it was drawn into the growing maelstrom. Brief flashes of light spat from the churning matter, accompanied by soundless thunder. Richard felt his presence being lifted higher, drawn into the vortex. He looked into the center of the storm and saw a tunnel expanding deeper into the churning light.

In the material world, Richard had not moved in some time. His body gave off a shudder every few moments. He was bathed in sweat. He'd even soiled himself. His friends shouted at him as sirens wailed in the distance.

Jake, after trying unsuccessfully to shout Richard out of his trance, began violently shaking him. Richard's eyes blinked open and he finally focused on Jake. The already-pale boy was almost translucent with shock. Justin was almost as pale.

"What did you do?" Justin whispered.

Richard stared blankly at him. He pulled his bloodstained hands from Matt's abdomen, peering at them. Justin's question rattled around in his brain.

Matt's eyes snapped open. The fatal damage from moments ago had vanished. The wound had left no scar, only slightly discolored new skin. Some of the blood that had leaked out remained smeared on the surrounding skin and on the ground underneath.

"What was that?" a dazed Matt asked.

Jake ran his hand through his long dark hair. "I just witnessed it, and I don't believe it." He gawked wide-eyed, shifting his gaze between Richard and Matt. Justin backed a few steps away from the scene.

Richard's eyes had not left his hands, which he held mere inches from his face. "How'd that happen?" he said absently.

Blue and red flashing lights swallowed the area as police cruisers and emergency response vehicles approached.

"We shouldn't mention this to them," Jake said in a hushed whisper.

"What do you mean?" said Justin.

"If they don't immediately lock us up in a psyche ward, then who knows what kind of secret government experiments they'll conduct on Sully. They could even dissect him *alive*."

Richard gulped at Jake's words. He began scrubbing his hands on the grass, frantically trying to remove the blood from them.

Matt slowly rose to his feet, and brushed the dirt off his body. Rubbing where the wound had been, he fingered the hole in his shirt left by the broken metal shaft.

Behind Richard, who was still kneeling at the base of the hill, an EMT in a crisp white uniform closed in on the group. A small robotic box rolled behind him. The EMT's face grew more curious as he caught sight of the enormous amount of blood on the ground.

"I don't know how I did that," Richard mumbled to himself. "Or if I could ever do it again. What if it wasn't even me who did anything?" He could not meet Matt's gaze, and returned his attention to his bloodstained hands.

"Would someone care to explain what happened here?"

The authoritative tone snapped Richard's focus away from his hands. He looked up at the medic, who was searching for visible wounds on any of the boys, lingering on Matt's torn and stained shirt.

ETECTIVE DATS PATIENTLY waited outside the interrogation room for the lead detective to be ready. Walcott was receiving the police report for the recently arrested Niner who now sat handcuffed to a chair on the opposite side of the heavy steel door. Two sealed plastic bags dangled from Dats's fists. In one was a firearm that had been recently discharged. The other contained several capsules full of heroin.

Nodding to Dats, Walcott said as he approached, "Let's do this fast and hard. No games with this one."

Walcott carried an oversized set of keys and used one of them to unlock the reinforced door, before taking the bag of heroin capsules from Dats. He stepped into the cold, stale air of the interrogation room.

The Niner was restrained in an old metal chair in front of a steel table. Dats noted the red irritation marks from the cuff on his right wrist. A set of new scratches had appeared where the other end of the cuff was attached to the armrest of the metal chair.

Each leg of the table and chair was bolted to the floor to prevent a suspect from using them as weapons. Behind Dats's left shoulder, mounted to the ceiling, a camera was ready to record any admission of guilt from the accused. Or any indiscretion the detectives might attempt.

Walcott sat in one of the two unrestrained chairs. Dats slammed the unloaded gun onto the table, the noise echoing off the walls. She moved next to the punk, looming over him.

"Strike number one," Dats whispered, inches from the Niner's ear. "Carrying an unregistered firearm without a license to carry."

Walcott held up his plastic bag. The capsules rattled around in it. The brown lumpy substance crumbled to powder inside. Walcott's grin spread.

"Strike number two." Walcott picked up where Dats had left off. "Enough here to get you on a felony intent to distribute charge."

"If we can match one bullet from one of today's bodies," Dats tapped the gun lying on the table, "with your fingerprints all over this, that's strike three, right there. Life behind bars without the possibility for parole."

"I hope you didn't enjoy being a free man," Walcott cut in from across the table.

The Niner shifted awkwardly back in his chair, a nonchalant look upon his face. "I thought you pigs played good-cop, bad-cop in these situations. Which one of ya'll is the good one?"

"We don't have to play games, 'cause unfortunately for you, both of us are really good cops," Walcott said.

The Niner grimaced. "Why in the hell are you talking with me then?"

Walcott pushed his chair back. The legs scraped along the cement floor. "We know Mr. Jones is the one who delivered the orders."

"Sounds like ya'll should've collared him then." The Niner turned and spat on the floor.

Dats shook her head. "That really is a nasty habit you've got there," she said. "Be careful nobody rubs your nose in it."

The Niner sneered at her, and Walcott slammed his fist down in frustration. "Are you really that stupid?" he said. "You have a once-in-a-lifetime opportunity laid out before you. Are you really going to throw it away for that parasite?"

The Niner grunted. "Not stupid enough to get caught snitching to the cops," he said. "I'm not an idiot. I have a family that wouldn't last a week if I turned witness."

Dats knew the likelihood of any plea deal was fast fading. It was time to cut their losses before the Assistant District Attorney arrived. Giving the Niner time alone to weigh the heavy charge over his head was their best chance of regaining the advantage.

"Your loss then." Dats tapped the Niner on the shoulder and walked out slightly ahead of her partner. As far as the Niner was concerned, the case was settled and would go forward unless he reopened negotiations on the detectives' terms.

MATT EXITED THE crowded bank amid curious glances. It was a branch of a high-end institution that operated mainly out of Cambridge and East Boston. The bank's usual clientele was Government Center and financial-district folks, complete with briefcases, suits and egos. Matt, in his plain white undershirt and duffel bag, stood out like an inflamed digit. He stuffed the now-empty duffel bag under one arm as he pushed open the glass and chrome double doors.

Matt spotted Jake across the street, leaning against the corner of an overpriced deli. Jake was doing his best not to put any weight on his injured shoulder, or expose his wound to the passing public. Matt crossed the street and approached Jake while the sounds of people chanting echoed off in the distance.

"That's taken care of," Matt said. "Now, time to call an ambulance, Mr. Tough Guy?"

Jake weakly nodded. He grunted as he pushed himself off the wall and his injured shoulder shifted before the sling took the bulk of the burden. Matt slid his phone from its shell and punched in the emergency number. He heard the denying beep of a busy signal. He pulled the phone away from his ear and looked at the screen incredulously.

"What the hell?"

"Problem?" Jake inquired, with his right hand compressing the makeshift bandage into his shoulder.

"It's a damn busy signal," Matt said, still staring at the screen.

"How can 911 be busy?"

Matt redialed with a fierce intensity. The busy tone still sounded.

"Jesus, is it really that out of hand?" Matt jabbed at the red cancel button then flipped the phone closed.

"This might be bigger than we imagined," Jake said.

"I can feel another one of your rants coming on. I'm thinking the ill-preparedness of government agencies in a changing global ecosystem." Matt raised a hand in defiance. "I don't think I can take listening to that right now."

Jake shook his head. "I could also go off on the fact that you still have a flip phone in this day and age, but I don't have the strength." He let out an exhausted sigh. "Screw it, any hospital in the city is going to be overloaded with people. It'd be hours before I'd be seen by a flesh and blood doctor."

"You still need treatment. There's a gaping hole in your shoulder and infection will definitely set in. Not to mention the bullet still lodged in there."

"True," Jake said. "But who says I have to go to the doctor? We both know of something that's cheaper, faster, and not too far away from here."

"Auto-Docs would log and notify the police of your injury . . ." Matt's eyes suddenly widened. "*Sully?*"

Saying the nickname aloud reminded Matt of all the good Richard had done for them over the years; this feeling was closely followed by the shame of losing touch with him. Richard was not an easy man to get a hold of—if he wasn't at work, he was home and passed out, most likely drunk.

"I haven't talked to him in…I don't know how long," Matt said. "You think we can get a hold of him?"

"It's our only option," Jake said. "If we check in at a hospital, the police could track us down. I don't know about you, but I'm not ready to answer questions about that alleyway yet."

"Fine," Matt said. "But it's too far for you to walk in your condition, especially when we don't know what's around the next corner. We need some wheels. Give me a moment."

A faded yellow taxi cab was parked farther along the road, its engine idling. The taxi's top light was off, but the driver's seat was occupied by an ape of a man consuming a slab of pastrami sandwich. His thick mustache was covered in mustard and crumbs. He scowled as Matt approached.

"We need a ride," Matt said. "Urgently. My friend, he's been shot." Matt relayed his version of the events in the alley. A human driver was better suited to this job than the driverless cabs that flooded the streets with their automatic tracking and multiple cameras pointed at the passengers.

"Ever heard of an ambulance?" the cabbie said with a thick accent. "I hear they are really good with this kind of shit." He had a mouthful of fatty pork between his teeth.

"No dice. 911 is busy. We can't even get a hold of one, let alone wait for one to show."

"Working lunch for me then. And I expect a good tip." The cabbie threw the remains of his sandwich onto the blacktop, happy to just have a fare in a tough time for a dying industry. "Get inside. If I find any blood on the back seat, I am charging you for the cleaning bill." He quickly wiped his mouth with the back of his hand before pressing a few buttons on his dashboard computer.

Matt went back to Jake and helped him to the cab. After carefully easing his friend into the back, Matt jogged to the passenger side and hopped in.

The taxi driver swung his head around, giving Jake a quick nod. "Hospital 17 isn't too far from here."

"Actually, we need to get dropped off on Everclear Boulevard," Matt said.

"Excuse me?"

"Our friend's place, he's a doctor. All the hospitals are backed up from the riots."

"I'm surprised he wasn't called in to work," the cabbie said. "The radio has been flooded with reports coming in about it. The boss suspended all pickup and drop off requests east of Columbus Avenue. Whole area is one riot. The mayor's office is thinking about declaring a state of emergency."

Matt and Jake shared a look as the taxi jerked out into the main street.

DATS AND WALCOTT stood in the observation room, behind the one-way mirror that adjoined the interrogation room. The observation room was bare, not even a chair to sit in. Dats watched the Niner fidgeting in his restraints. He used one hand to eat a chicken salad wrap and sip from a can of Coke that had left a moisture ring on the table.

Dats looked at Walcott's faded reflection in the one-way mirror. He wore his navy-blue suit with a pressed white shirt and tie. He stood a head taller than Dats, whose charcoal suit and button-up shirt completely hid the bulletproof vest underneath.

The doorway to the observation room was suddenly filled by an older man with sparse grey hair scraped across his scalp. Captain Mason Levi wore a multitude of awards and ribbons pinned to his chest.

"Any luck in there?" he asked as he rubbed his temples. The spike in violent crime had clearly made his day miserable.

"Not yet, Captain," Walcott said. "We laid out the charges against him. We're letting him stew for a bit."

"The ADA is another hour out," Dats said. "As soon as she gets here, we'll go back at him for round two."

"Did he invoke his right to counsel?" Levi asked.

"Not yet, sir," Dats answered.

"Good. Too dumb to know better. At least there's that. Contact me if anything new turns up." Levi made to leave the room.

"Cap, a question," Walcott said.

"Go ahead, Walcott." He made no effort to hide the irritation in his voice.

"It's about our overtime," Walcott said. The touchy subject was on all the officers' minds.

Levi threw his hands up in despair. "Derek, don't start with that, not today."

"Come on, Cap. It's been over two months now. I haven't seen a dime of overtime in my check. I have child support and alimony to pay. If you factor in all the overtime we're going to be getting after today, that's going to be a big back-pay check that the city can't cash."

"Go talk to Human Resources. It's their thing. Or better yet, call your union rep." Levi's head shook back and forth, and Dats couldn't tell if it was deliberate or some sort of nervous tic.

"Not my department." He left before Walcott could say anything else.

As Captain Levi was leaving, Dats saw her desk in the pit through the open door. The message indicator on her desk phone was flashing. She pushed by the motionless Walcott, who looked as if steam might start shooting from his ears. She opened the door and headed for her desk.

The message was from the lab. The female forensics officer apologetically explained that the evidence collected at the intersection shooting, and at another shooting in an alleyway a few blocks away, wouldn't be ready for roughly two more weeks.

Walcott wandered out of the observation room, visibly suppressing his anger, and joined Dats at their desk.

"The news keeps improving," Dats said, rolling her eyes at Walcott.

"What now?" Dats knew why Walcott was enraged. Most of the cases today wouldn't be closed. The murder detectives would take a serious clearance-hit unless they could pass off the murders to Walcott's department. The ongoing worker protests were trampling most of the evidence at the scenes. Any evidence they could collect couldn't be processed in a timely fashion. The forensics department had suffered most from the constant budget cuts, which had adversely affected the clearance rates of all departments. This was the statistic that was most important for promotions, and promotions were what mattered most to the officers.

"We can't get a full forensic report on either crime scene for at least two weeks," Dats said and placed the phone back on its cradle.

The second crime scene, in the alleyway, was unlike the others. Two Niners had been left in a pool of their own blood—that much was the same—but one had clearly been tortured before death. The other was now in Hospital No. 17, a small fully-automated clinic that had opened a few years ago.

The torture was something new for the Young Gunz. Perhaps it was something personal. Walcott had run the torture-victim's name through the police database and printed out a rap sheet that was seven pages long. The longer the two detectives had to wait for the forensics report, the less likely they would be able to narrow down their suspects.

"Great. What else is new?"

"They claim they're already swamped with caseloads," Dats said. "The budget cuts removed two positions and that new Sort-ing-Bot is out for repairs again. Add today's fiasco, and they could take a bath in all the extra work."

"No overtime pay, no timely reports, and a turf war ongoing. How the hell are we supposed to get any work done around here?"

JAMES SAT OPPOSITE Raef, beneath the canopy of a crowded outdoor restaurant. They were in a small subsection of Greater Boston known as Little Russia. Raef's plate was devoid of food; only bones and other inedible remains lay on it. James looked down at his own plate of beef stroganoff. Unlike his father's version of the dish, this one contained Dijon mustard. A wave of nausea washed over him.

Inside Jones's briefcase full of cash, there'd been a manila envelope containing three photographs and a few sheets of paper. In the van, after the meeting, Raef had handed James one of the pictures and told him to study it.

"Have you spotted him yet, James?" Raef asked as he picked his teeth clean with a fingernail.

James pushed his plate to the center of the table. His appetite had abandoned him after witnessing Raef's frenzied consumption. At least Raef got his money's worth.

James glanced at a table inside the eatery, next to the large window. "The third table from our left. He turned his back to us a moment ago."

"Very good. How many bodyguards are with him?" Raef seemed impressed. He picked up a bone from his porterhouse steak and gnawed at the marrow.

James hesitated. "Uh, two?" Sweat broke out on his brow, running into his eyes and making them sting.

"Are you telling me or asking me?" Raef said. He grinned.

James continued discreetly scanning the area. He tried not to move his head. Finding nothing new, he chose to keep his mouth shut, fearing retribution if he showed fickleness in his assessment.

"Telling you."

"Wrong," Raef said. "The correct answer is four. You correctly identified the two near the czar, but failed to spot two more waiting outside across the street." Raef lifted his fork and nonchalantly pointed it in the direction of two men standing on the sidewalk across the street. The men were dressed in black and red jumpsuits.

Raef casually dipped his fork into James's full plate. "If you watch closely, you can see how they give themselves away. They are passively watching the streets. They want you to believe they are just waiting for another member of their group, but if that were the case, why are they scanning the windows and rooftops?"

James was surprised at the sharpness of Raef's eyesight. He could barely see the men in the dim light of the streetlamps. James squinted, trying to focus on the Russian mobsters, but could barely make out their outlines.

Suddenly, the right side of James's face felt as if it was aflame. He recoiled and looked across the table at Raef, who didn't appear to have moved an inch. "Don't stare. You will give us away." Raef's sudden change in voice made James shiver. His face burned hot and his jawbone vibrated with pain.

"Yes, sir. I'll remember that for next time." James continued to try and irk Raef, even if it resulted in another beating. He couldn't resist his rebellious tendencies, even in the captivity of a monster like Raef.

"For the last time, drop that 'sir' shit," Raef hissed through clenched teeth. "You continue to disappoint me, James. If you don't improve on your worthlessness, I will have no choice but to dispose of you and recruit your brother, Taylor."

Panic struck James. He had to remember that this extended beyond himself. He was already becoming accustomed to slaps and fists, but the thought of his little brother in Raef's clutches was too much. He swallowed hard as he prepared for whatever was to come next, reminded once again of the supernatural power that sat across from him.

James quickly withered under Raef's stare. "No, I'll do better. Please leave my brother out of this. He never did any wrong to you."

"You say that, but your improvement has been slight at best." Raef shook his head disappointedly.

James leapt from his seat. "Okay, I'll finish this job right now then. And then I'll go home and be out of your hair forever." He managed a step before Raef's arm darted out and crushed his forearm in a steel grip. James winced, his knees nearly giving out on him.

"Foolish boy," Raef said quietly. "You take one czar now, and the remaining two go underground. I would have to work much harder for my cash, and that is not a prospect that pleases me. Return to your seat, James."

The boy looked away. His shoulders slumped as he sat back down. He glanced around the eatery, amazed by the lack of attention their commotion had garnered.

"I commend your spirit though," Raef said. "We have to wait until all three are together. Take them all down with a single blow. I'm positive today's events between the Niners and Young Gunz will force them into a face-to-face meeting. These people aren't the type who like to utilize a conference call."

"I understand . . ." James began, and Raef's eyes rolled back in their sockets. Raef covered his face with his hands and though he remained seated, the threat of tipping out of his chair loomed large. James had seen this happen before, just yesterday evening, before they'd gone to meet with the Niner bosses.

A speck of satisfaction sparked deep within James, although he did his best not to let it show. He drew in a deep breath, then successfully said, "Is it the headaches again?"

Raef's eyes rolled back into place. The trembling of his body slowly died away. Ten minutes passed and neither Raef nor James spoke.

Eventually, Raef said, "Their intensity has grown ever since I entered the city. And I had to turn over a handy tool that helped."

"To that guy in the crazy trenchcoat last night?" James asked.

"Yes, Midnight. He does have a certain style about him." Raef snorted.

"So, is he like your boss?" James couldn't contain his curiosity.

"No," Raef said, scowling. "He is nothing more than a simple errand boy, useful for his unique talents. We both kneel before a higher master, and *he* is the one who demanded the tool. But don't fret, I have a plan to be rid of the headaches once and for all."

James felt sorry for the target of Raef's wrath.

The Russian czar had finished his meal. He signaled to the bodyguard nearest to him, issuing a curt order in Russian. The bodyguard left the restaurant and headed for the parked car around the corner.

"Bring the van around," Raef said. "Our guest is ready to leave."

James did as he was told. He watched Raef drop a few large bills on the table, and rose from his seat at the same moment as the czar inside. He used the side entrance to leave the restaurant ahead of the czar and Raef.

He rushed to Raef's van and fired up the engine. Speeding around the block, he parked two buildings down from Raef, who was waiting outside the restaurant. James sat in the van and observed the two guards in the red and black jumpsuits crossing the street and joining the czar as he waited for his transport. The mobsters glanced at Raef, but they made no move against him. Raef wore a bored and disinterested face, hands passively by his sides. His fingers fidgeted constantly, as if working something between them.

A few seconds later, a white SUV with twenty-two-inch rims and tinted windows pulled up to the curb. James's curiosity peaked when he watched Raef flick his fingers in the direction of the SUV, as if throwing something at it. He couldn't see anything leave Raef's hand, making the whole gesture even more peculiar.

The SUV, loaded with its passengers, sped away down the street. James pulled out into the street and rolled up to Raef in the mobile van of nightmares. Raef opened the door and slid into the passenger seat.

"Should I chase after them?" James asked, frantically staring after the receding SUV.

"They aren't far." Raef flashed a knowing smile that revealed dagger-sharp incisors. "We have some time to spare."

The prospect of violence seemed to increase the size of Raef's grin.

RICHARD'S SPOTLESS APARTMENT echoed with his snores. His arm hung over the side of the couch, his hand wrapped weakly around an almost-empty Jack Daniel's bottle. There was drool on his pillow, under his cheek.

A loud knock on the door sent Richard sprawling to the floor. He dropped the bottle and the last of its contents dribbled into the carpet. His eyelids immediately grew heavy and began to close again, despite the fall. The knocking came again as Richard's eyes shut.

"No one's home, go away," he shouted groggily.

From the other side of the door, a voice boomed, "Come on, Sully. It's an emergency."

The familiar voice roused Richard from his stupor. He struggled through alcohol and exhaustion to his feet and tossed the empty bottle into the trash can. He disengaged the multiple locks bolted to his door before pulling it open. Outside were two grubby men who looked as if they'd just struggled through a war zone.

"Matt? Jake?"

Matt's shirt was torn off and Jake's shoulder was in a sling. Jake was draped in blood, though whose it was, Richard couldn't say.

"What happened?"

"You heard about the riots and the gang war?" Matt said.

"Hard not to. It's been breaking news on TV all day." Richard absently pointed at the television, which was quietly entertaining no one.

"Well, it was breaking Matt's car window earlier." Jake winced as he adjusted the sling holding up his arm. The bandage was soaked through with blood.

Richard moved out of their way. "Come inside." He glanced up and down the hallway as Matt and Jake entered, but none of his neighbors were in sight.

"We booked it out of there. I had to ditch my ride," Matt said sadly.

"Wow," Richard said, wide-eyed. "It must have been serious if you left your Ferrari."

He ushered them to the dining room, which was really just a few square feet of rug with a table on it, between his living room and kitchen.

"'Serious' isn't the word," Matt said. "And that's not even the worst part. Afterwards, we ran down the wrong alley, filled with the wrong people."

"They fired first and we responded in kind," Jake cut in. "We took two down and let the other two go."

"Four on two, and you only suffered a shoulder wound?" Richard said, peering more closely at Jake's injury.

"I don't mean to sound like an ungrateful guest, but my shoulder is on fire," Jake said.

"Climb up on the table here. Be careful though. It's not too steady."

Richard went into the tiny kitchen and got a full bottle of cheap vodka from a cupboard. His head was pounding from the hangover that had laid siege to his brain. There was only one quick fix. And it would keep the visions at bay.

Changing his mind, he replaced the plastic bottle of vodka and took out an expensive, aged brandy. It was a gift from his father when Richard had visited a few years ago. He reserved it for special occasions.

Carrying the brandy back into the dining room, Richard paused. "Did you try a hospital?"

"Have you tried to call 911?" Matt asked.

Jake gingerly climbed onto the table with Matt's help. Jake lay flat on his back and slipped his arm out of the sling and rested it across his chest.

"Not recently," Richard said.

"It was a busy signal. Can you fucking believe that?"

Richard intertwined his fingers before flexing them outwards. The joints cracked in rapid succession. The veins stood out in his arms. His fingertips tingled with energy. Richard carefully removed the wet bandaging stuck to Jake's wound.

"Thanks for the offer," Jake said, eyeing the brandy. "But you know I don't drink. I'll deal with the pain."

Richard shook his head. "That's for me, not for you."

He screwed off the cap and took a generous swig from the bottle, sloshing the liquid around in his mouth before swallowing. He moaned in satisfaction.

"No thanks," Matt said. "I don't want any either."

Richard wiped his mouth with the back of his hand. "Sorry," he said. "I'm not used to entertaining guests. But like you say, it's crazy that all the emergency lines were tied up."

"Yeah. The riots must've overloaded the system." Matt peered closely at Jake's wound, not wanting to miss a second of the miracle that was about to happen.

Richard flexed his fingers twice more, focusing energy at his fingertips. He closed his eyes briefly and opened up his mind's eye—or at least that's what he liked to believe he was doing. Jake's skin became translucent in Richard's sight, revealing the inner workings of his shoulder.

Shards of the bullet had lodged in the head of the humerus. The ligaments of the acromioclavicular joint were torn to shreds and the surrounding tendons didn't look much better. At least the bones of the clavicle and scapula were intact.

Richard opened his eyes and looked down on Jake with a new-found respect for his friend's pain threshold.

"How did you manage to make it here without passing out?" Richard said.

"I'm a tough guy," Jake said, though he was pale and had started sweating profusely.

Richard shook his head again, smiling. He slid one hand underneath Jake's shoulder, who grunted in pain. Richard placed the fingertips of his other hand in a circle around the entry wound, palm positioned above.

Blue light appeared between his fingers, jetting into the still-oozing wound. Matt drew closer still, trying desperately to peer beyond the blinding blue light. Soft *clinks* rang in Richard's hypersensitive ears as fragments of the bullet fell onto the wooden kitchen table. An instant later, the light winked out. Matt laughed quietly.

"What's so funny?" Richard said. He took a moment to steady himself.

"I was just thinking. You healed me when you first discovered your powers, then again after I tore my ACL playing soccer. This is Jake's first time. You popped his cherry."

Even Jake sniggered at this, then carefully tested his arm. He slid off the table and punched Richard lightly in the bicep, knocking him slightly off balance.

"I guess you fixed it," Jake exclaimed. "You bastard!" He grinned. "I expected some pain to linger. It itches a little but it feels better than it has in years." He windmilled his arm to demonstrate.

Richard felt his body sagging and his eyelids drooping. He grabbed the bottle of expensive liquor and walked into the kitchen. All the accumulated energy inside was spent, leaving him drained. He gulped down two more shots before placing the brandy back inside the cabinet above the sink. Then he grabbed the cheap vodka.

BACK IN THE dining room, Matt whispered to Jake, "You idiot."

"What?"

"Have you forgotten high school? Did you forget about Sully's mom and what happened to her outside that bar?"

"What did I say?" Jake said, all innocence. Then, "Oh shit. *Bastard.*"

"Yeah, dumbass," Matt said. "Have you forgotten all the taunts and jibes Richard went through after the paternity test showed his father wasn't really his father?"

Jake smacked his forehead. "Shit, I didn't even realize I said it." He turned from Matt and saw a shaky Richard putting away the bottle of liquor in the kitchen.

"Are you okay, Sully?" he asked sheepishly.

Richard nodded dismissively. "Yeah. Using my gift just leaves me hungry and tired."

"Are you getting better with your powers?" Matt asked as he tried to steer the conversation quickly away from Jake's slip. "That took hardly any time. I think you were hovering over my knee for about fifteen minutes when you fixed it. Not forgetting that you passed out immediately after you were done. Nearly made me shit my pants. I thought I'd killed you."

"Jake's wound was easier to heal," Richard said. "He didn't have any complete tears, so I only had to fill the gaps, not coax two severed ligaments back together." Richard shifted uncomfortably, obviously in pain. "You're right though. It seems the more I use the power, the easier it is to call upon. Although, the toll on my body doesn't lessen one fucking bit." He looked down at his hands as if they were foreign entities.

"Have your powers ever failed you?" It was a question that came to Matt for the first time.

"Yeah, a few times," Richard said. "Usually when it happens, it's because I can't focus the energy I get properly. Other times it's because the problem isn't just simple 'mending.' There was a family I met while traveling. Lily, the mother, such a wonderful person. She had liver cancer. It had spread so far. She was undergoing chemo at the time." Richard began to pace backwards and forwards between kitchen and living room.

Matt thought about his friend. Richard was an *Other*, there was no doubt about it. If Matt hadn't personally seen Richard in action, he'd be like most of the world and never believe the stories on social media, or the unconfirmed reports that popped up on the internet regularly. Matt was happy to have Richard as the only *Other* in his life.

"I think I might have helped kill her," Richard blurted out. "The chemo was doing so much damage to her other tissue. I just wanted to heal her, but I think I healed the cancer itself. I know now what to do but back then . . ."

"Hey, you can't beat yourself up over it. Think of all the people you've helped over the years. No one is perfect."

"Thanks Matt, but I don't need a pep talk right now," Richard said and began working on the vodka.

"It's been a long time," Jake said. He was on the couch watching the news program. He looked around the apartment. "I think this is only my second visit to your place."

"Yeah," Matt said. "Too long."

"Time has a habit of sneaking up on you," Richard said.

Matt wondered if Richard had read that somewhere. Over time, Matt had grown to accept the fact that Richard kept his friends an arm's length away. He'd never understood the reasons behind it. He only knew the change had begun when Richard's powers had awoken in him. It had put a strain on their relationship that neither had chosen to address.

"How are the visions?" Matt and Jake were the only two people Richard had told. He'd told Matt to keep the secret even from his own family.

"Getting worse. Earlier this morning or late last night, I can't remember which, I was attacked at work." Richard fidgeted. "Worse than that, my boss walked in during the attack and became a victim too." Richard sighed.

"Jesus," Matt breathed.

"No, I'm pretty sure it was an Indian deity."

"What?" Matt said, perplexed by the non-sequitur and the wry smile Richard wore.

"The form my vision took. It was some type of four-armed Indian god that attacked us. Tall and red, like Satan himself." Richard smiled at Matt's reaction.

"Has it ever been a physical manifestation before?" Jake said, his face pale.

"Once, shortly after graduation."

"*That's* why you suddenly joined the Army, and hopped on a bus for boot camp," Matt said as he pieced the story together.

Richard stared off at nothing. "I was with Stacey when it happened," he said. "I think the visions grow more intense the longer I stay in one place. I couldn't keep risking the lives of people I cared about, so I split. The visions must be somehow tied in with my powers."

"Why didn't you tell anyone?" Matt asked. "If you'd told us, we could've helped. We could've—"

"Nothing can be done about it. Besides what would I have said? Stacey and I were out by Prospect Point. We were making out when I had to take a piss, so I ran into the woods in my boxers. There I was, having a nice old piss, thinking about my half-naked girlfriend in the car, when a friggin' legit *werewolf* starts chasing me. It slashed me too, across the shoulder, before I got back into the car. Stacey said she didn't get a good look at it; said it might have been a bear."

Matt wondered at the secrets Richard kept from them. He had secrets of his own, but those were wartime operations. He wasn't proud of many of them, but the situations he'd found himself in had left no room for pride.

"With the visions I was having, I couldn't be sure what was real anymore," Richard said. "Point is, I have a gift and I'm not letting it go to waste, no matter the cost." He took a seat next to Jake on the couch. He was clutching the bottle of vodka so tightly that his fingers were white.

"You could have told us. You don't have to face everything in this world alone. You have people that care about you. We'll always be here for you, buddy," Jake said.

Matt walked to Richard and draped an arm over his shoulders. "Although, we do have kind of another big favor to ask."

"We hate to do this to you, but someone has to take a stand," Jake said. "This crap cannot keep going unanswered." As he spoke, Matt could not help but think of Jake's late wife, gunned down by accident. It was during a territorial war between two rival gangs a few years ago. When Matt had found Richard wandering aimlessly around the Midwest, he'd told him about Jake's impending trial.

"What is it? Spit it out already," Richard said.

Jake pulled out his cellphone. Matt watched him open his memo app. The screen filled with a list of addresses. Jake highlighted the most important one before showing it to Richard.

"Take a look at this."

RAEF HAD LEFT James inside the parked van one block away. They had trailed the czar from the eatery to this dilapidated pawnshop, and now Raef was watching from the shadows as the czar and his bodyguards walked to the front door with its *Closed* sign hanging from a small suction cup. The door opened and the czar walked in without breaking stride, followed closely by his cronies. One lookout remained outside.

Raef waited until the last two czars arrived. Each one came with its own contingent of bodyguards and entered by the same door. One member of each group waited outside, forming a three-person lookout party.

Raef had thoughts of his former life in the forefront of his mind. He'd gone by a different name back then, had a different life. It was a quiet existence before the uprising, before the war. That war had led Raef down a long and winding path, changing his life in more ways than he could possibly have imagined.

He teemed with thoughts of vengeance as he approached the back entrance to the pawn shop. The cloudy evening sky helped hide his advance. These were not the exact Russians he truly loathed, but they were adequate substitutes. Though after six long years of torture, no amount of pain and death could compensate Raef for what had been done to him during his time in captivity. Or for what the invading Russians had done to his life.

He straightened his leather jacket as he reached the back door of the squat one-storey brick building. He turned the knob but found it locked. A quick jolt of energy set all the tumblers of the lock in a straight row and seconds later, Raef strode over the threshold.

He quickly scanned the back room. It was an unlit, cluttered mess. Bicycle parts, old DVD players, and other useless things lay in disorganized heaps on metal shelves. To the right, light trickled under the door from an adjoining room. Voices filtered in from the other side. The group of lackeys in there was not privy to the conversation between the czars.

Being careful not to knock anything over, Raef crept closer to the door that blocked the light. He pressed his ear to the wood and heard the higher-ranked underlings chatting about last night's baseball game and how much money they'd lost betting on the home team. Raef knew that beyond this back office, the three czars were talking about their next pivotal moves for the organization.

Raef took a step back, raised his foot, and kicked the door inwards. It bounced against the wall behind it and Raef exploded into the room.

Six well-built Russians turned at the unexpected interruption. Raef pounced on the first immediately and ripped the Russian's Adam's apple from his throat. He tossed the instantly limp body at three of the bodyguards grouped together, bowling them over. In one fluid motion, he snapped the neck of another, moving almost too quickly to see.

Only one Russian remained standing, and he opened fire at Raef, who ducked behind the body of his latest victim. The rounds smacked into the lifeless body in front of Raef or sailed harmlessly into the wall behind him. Raef discarded his meat shield and lunged at the shooter. He struck the Russian in the eyes with two pointed fingers, blinding him. The man howled and fell away.

The three pinned bodyguards scrambled out from under their dead comrade. The odds had been split in half, but they were no longer caught off guard. Raef's index and middle fingers were coated with gore that slowly dripped to the ground. His fingers twitched, and as the mobsters aimed, the single lightbulb above the desk in the middle of the room exploded, sending shards of glass in every direction.

Raef was on the move again before the Russians' eyes could adapt to the dark. He reached the first of the three and grasped the man's lower jaw, fingers in his mouth. Raef wrenched his hand down, separating the jaw from the upper mandible. The Russian's tongue flapped wildly as he screamed.

Raef knew that his time and energy supply were rapidly running thin. He heard raised voices from the next room where the czars were discussing business. The sole underling waiting in the front room would be approaching any second and Raef still had two to deal with here. Not to mention the three guards waiting outside. He slipped the firearm out of Broken Jaw's hand, which was spasming wildly. Raef fired two shots in the darkness. Both hit the armed Russians in their heads.

The door to the meeting room swung open. An older, scar-faced Russian stood in the doorway as Raef stepped in front of him. Surprise registered as the czar took in the mess that had once been part of his personal escort.

Raef slipped into the room and closed the door behind him.

"Gentlemen, please sit back down," he said. "This will only take a moment."

T EK SAT ON the red-bricked steps that led into the abandoned apartment complex. The Niners had been using this place as a base of operation for the last year, all through the tensions with the Young Gunz. Bricks sat next to him, talking on his cell phone in coded words so any unwanted listeners would be none the wiser. Tek found it hard to keep up with the conversation himself at times.

The last rays of sunshine had disappeared behind the tenements some hours ago. Junkies flooded the streets looking for their next fix. Tek was waiting patiently for Bricks to wrap up his conversation. He checked his watch as Bricks rang off.

"That better be good news," Tek said. "It's already dark and today's been filled with enough disappointment."

Bricks put his phone back in his pocket. "The psycho came through," Bricks said incredulously.

"Already?" Tek blinked. "He was in our office only yesterday."

"Our boy on the inside said he hasn't seen the bodies himself. He's driving out there now, but the responding officer called it a 'fucking bloodbath.'"

"Guess we better get the other half of his cash ready," Tek said.

Ice and Ray-Ray, the two Niners charged with Johnny's safety, rounded the corner. Neither looked particularly happy as they dragged their feet along the sidewalk, panting heavily.

"Some good news will be a nice change for Jones," Bricks said as the babysitters approached. "Where you been?" he asked.

Ice twitched and said, "Hey Bricks, Tek."

"Are we glad to see you guys," Bricks said. "We were worried something happened. Where are Johnny and Nick?"

"Well, that's why we're here," Ice said. "You see . . ."

"Out with it." Tek's moment of ease was gone, replaced by budding anger.

Ray-Ray stepped slightly in front of Ice. "Nick's dead. They took Johnny to the hospital, we don't know if he made it." He made no effort to mince words, especially not in front of the enforcer Tek.

Tek and Bricks simultaneously sprang from the steps. Tek grabbed Ray-Ray by the collar with both fists.

"Who did it?" he hissed.

Ice glanced at Ray-Ray and said, "Well, it could have been—"

"Two white boys, no idea who they run with." Ray-Ray cut Ice off abruptly before he could get them in more trouble.

"What happened?" Bricks asked Ray-Ray. Ice cowered behind him.

"We stopped to grab a quick charge and a bite to eat when we heard gunshots," Ray-Ray said as Tek finally released his hold. "We were by Little Moe's corner and Nick got to talking."

"You stupid fucks wanted in on the action," Tek said.

"It was Nick's idea, not ours," Ice said. "We thought we could mop up any stragglers that were running from the scene."

"Oh! That makes everything all better then! You want me to give that message to Mr. Jones? It was Nick's fault that *you* disobeyed his direct order?" Tek was fuming. "'Cause I'd love to be the one who gets to judge you two fuck-ups for this."

Bricks placed a calming hand on Tek's shoulder. "What happened next?" he asked Ray-Ray.

"After Nick convinced us it was the right thing to do, we ran towards the gun shots. It wasn't long before we ran into these two white boys, kind of professional looking." Ray-Ray shook his head. "I still can't believe it. Nick asked a few questions, trying to figure out who they were, before going into straight jack mode once he saw them carrying duffel bags. Johnny tried to talk them into handing over the bags peacefully when someone fired a shot. Next thing we knew, Johnny was on the ground bleeding from his eye and Nick had a bullet in the stomach."

"Before we could respond, they had their guns pointed at us," Ice said. "They were so quick. It happened so fast."

"I knew that Nick kid was no good," Tek muttered.

"And they just let you two walk?" Bricks said.

"We had no option," Ray-Ray said. "We had to do what they told us. We dropped our guns when they told us to, then booked it out of there." His fear of punishment was evident in his voice.

"Any chance they ran with Stacks?"

"Naw, they didn't talk like any muscle Stacks would use. They ain't from these streets."

"Jones is going to be pissed. Johnny was special to him." Bricks could only shake his head at Tek. "What did they look like?"

"I'm not sure," Ice said. "A couple of late twenties whities in dress shirts and slacks."

"Every time you talk, you make me want to hit you more," Tek growled. His anger was boiling over.

Ray-Ray said, "One had blond hair, the other black. They looked like businessmen."

"Businessmen who shot like hit men," Bricks murmured.

Tek rubbed his face in frustration. The good news they'd just received would be overshadowed by this new turn of events. "Shit!" he spat. He composed himself before speaking again. "OK, this is how it's going to play out. I'm going to walk upstairs and tell Mr. Jones how Nick and Johnny got jumped by a pair of professionals. You heard the shots and came running to help. By the time you got there, they were both down and the pros had their guns on you."

"But . . ." Ice started.

"Or," Tek said, "we can tell Jones how you two jackasses, under explicit orders to be off the street, tried to stick up some guys, then left Nick and Johnny to die. I'm sure Mr. Jones will understand."

"No, Tek, your story is good," Ray-Ray said quickly.

"That's what I thought. Now, bounce the fuck out of here before I change my mind. We'll talk later about what we're going to do with the two of you." Tek turned his back on the two failed bodyguards.

Ray-Ray and Ice slouched away with their heads hung low, neither one speaking to the other.

"Thank God for that phone call. At least we can soften the blow of Johnny a little," Tek said as he watched the two disgraced Niners leave.

"We? *I* got the call from *my* informant. You can deliver the bad news after I tell him about Raef's success."

"We still need to find more information on Johnny," Tek said.

"Why don't you make some phone calls before we head back upstairs? You know, give you some time to find out where they took Johnny."

"Fine, but you're helping me. We can split up the hospitals and start calling."

THE PAWN SHOP was painted by red and blue flashing lights as Walcott and Dats arrived in their Charger. Walcott was trying to make sense of the day, but this last stop was well outside Niner or Young Gunz territory. Nothing from today's events should have spilled this far northwest, into Little Russia.

They pulled alongside the front of the building, where a detective in a long tan trenchcoat waved them over. Detective Johnson was a former member of Walcott's South Boston anti-gang unit, a smart, fiery guy of Irish descent. A good detective, Johnson had one of the highest clearance rates in the department. He combined street smarts with good community relations. His downside was in his innate love for the drink, as if he was deliberately perpetuating the Irish stereotype.

Uniformed police had placed a cordon around the building. Yellow tape flapped in the breeze as Walcott stepped out of the Charger. He noted immediately that Johnson's nose was beet-red. He approached Johnson, analyzing the detective's every move.

"I was off duty when I got the call," Johnson said. "I'm not sure if it's connected, but I figured with all the shit that went down in your district today, you'd want to check it out yourself." Johnson's spoke clearly and directly, as if Walcott was still his supervisor.

"What do we have here?" Walcott asked.

Johnson led them to the front door of the pawn shop. Walcott scanned the perimeter but couldn't see any signs of forced entry.

"If you will follow me," Johnson said at the entrance, where he paused for a moment, as if for dramatic effect. "Tonight, the criminal infrastructure of Little Russia has been rocked." He swung open the door with a grand gesture and ushered the two detectives inside.

Walcott entered, followed by Dats. There was a corpse on the floor, next to a chair wedged behind the door. A doorman on watch, no doubt, a low-level thug not privy to much insider knowledge. What concerned Walcott was the apparent lack of wounds and the lack of blood splatters. Walcott put on a pair of latex gloves before fully examining the body.

"No discernible cause of death on that one," Johnson said. "The only thing I could think of was strangulation, but there are no abrasions around the neck. But there is definite hemorrhaging around the eyes."

Walcott lifted the dead man's head, tilting it to the left and right. He gently laid it back on the floor and took stock of the rest of the pawn shop's front room.

In front of the entrance was an untouched cash register. It sat on top of a dusty glass display case filled with mundane jewelry. To the right, there was a collection of mountain bikes and newer holographic projection devices. On the opposite side was a tall display case, taller than Walcott, filled with newer electronics: ocular contact players, holo-projectors, tablets, anything a crook could easily sell on. A thin layer of dust coated everything.

"Not much foot traffic," Dats absently commented, looking at the dust and the dirty tiled floor. She moved over to the collection of electronics and rifled through them.

"We believe this one was the last to die," Johnson said, pointing at the body. "The point of entry was the rear entrance. The chair beside the corpse was wedged behind the door when we arrived." He flipped up a hinged section of the counter and led the pair to the room out back.

Walcott walked into the cluttered, chaotic mess of the supply room. Shelves upon shelves lined the walls from floor to ceiling, turning the room into a maze of junk. Walcott inspected the exit that led to the back alleyway. There were no scratch marks on the door or lock.

"No forced entry," Walcott said. The concept of an inside job had already formed in his mind, with the killer having a key to gain entry.

"I'm thinking someone let the perp in, or he had a key," Johnson said, echoing Walcott's thoughts. "There are no marks on the keyhole, so I don't think he picked the lock."

"My first instinct says this was an inside job," Dats said. She'd produced a pen-sized flashlight and was scanning the dusty floor near the back door. "Only one set of footprints from the door. He must have had a key."

"It would explain a lot." Johnson stood in a doorway to the left, the door barely hanging by one hinge. "Now, for the real show. I hope you didn't eat recently."

Blood had leaked from the adjoining room and was pooled in a small patch on the supply room's floor. Johnson stepped around it and into the room. He stumbled as he accidentally stepped on the hand of the first body. He composed himself, and pulled out a handkerchief, using it to cover his nose.

Walcott was taken aback by the brutality of the scene as he entered. Pieces of torn flesh and unidentifiable chunks of meat were scattered across the floor. One thug had a broken neck; others had fatal gunshot wounds. Walcott took a quick count: nine fatalities in various post-mortem contortions. Unlike the doorman out front, the causes of death here were plainly obvious.

Dats was staring intently at one muscle-bound Russian with his throat ripped out. Patrolmen had already gathered photographic evidence, capturing the scene in its untouched state for the prosecution's eventual courthouse use. Dats located a lump of human flesh that might have been this victim's throat.

"Through here the weirdness factor increases," Johnson said, moving through this room's horrors. He led them into a tiny windowless room containing a round table and three chairs. In each chair was a well-dressed, older mob boss. All were slumped forward, heads on the table.

"From what we can conclude so far," Johnson said, "it seems the three czars all had heart attacks. Possibly induced by a poison, but we won't know for sure until we can get a toxicology report to confirm it."

"Doesn't look like they were having drinks," Walcott said. "How did the poison get into their systems? Find any injection spots?" He examined the men slumped over the table.

"No. And no excess moisture on the lips. Maybe a gas of some sort. What freaks me out is the fact that none of them left their seats." Johnson looked down at the bodies. "You'd expect one at least to fall out of his chair during his last moments, clutching his chest or something."

"Sounds like a coup," Dats said from the blood-soaked room behind them, where she was bent over a dead bodyguard whose eyes were missing.

"That would answer some questions," Johnson said. "But we heard no chatter about it. We're up on a few of their phone lines."

For the first time, Walcott noticed that Johnson's speech was very slightly slurred.

"Who could have pulled off this job on not just one, but all three of the czars?" Walcott said. "And to what end?"

"I don't see any nine-millimeter shells on the ground," Dats said. She'd moved on to one of the less grotesque bodies back in the supply room, whose cause of death appeared to be a gunshot wound.

"We can match each shell casing to a round in each gun of the bodyguards," Johnson said. "Either they shot one another, or somehow the intruder wrestled the guns away from the Russians."

"One man versus nine trained bodyguards?" Walcott murmured to himself.

"Doesn't sound like it's connected to our cases today," Dats said. "It seems the Niners and the Young Gunz weren't the only opportunists."

"Come on, Dats," Walcott said. "You just want to run home to your fiancé before he starts bitching that you're working too late again."

"And you don't *ever* want to go home lately," Dats fired back.

"I have to finish the job," Walcott said. He nodded to Johnson. "Thanks for the call. I'll touch base with you tomorrow morning. Call me sooner if you catch any scent of Niners or Young Gunz involvement."

A FEW MOMENTS later, Walcott and Dats were back in the Charger, Walcott sitting behind the wheel. Dats clicked on her phone, checking for missed calls.

"Crazy day," she said absently as she flipped through the phone's home screen.

"Just think," Walcott said with a wink, "the night is still young." He scrunched up his face. "Twenty-four hours until the big day."

"Not this again." Dats rolled her eyes. "After all the shit that went down today, you want to bring that up?"

"Hey, I meant it in a good way. You'll get out of here for a while. A break might do you some good."

"The captain is going to revoke my leave."

"Only beat cops and senior detectives like me get forced overtime. Did you get a promotion that I didn't hear about?"

"Didn't you say the night was still young?"

"It almost sounds like you *want* the captain to revoke your vacation time. Getting cold feet?"

"I love him," Dats said defiantly.

"Well that settles that." Walcott turned the key in the ignition. "Did you ever cheat on him?"

"What?" Dats's eyes widened.

"Eight years is a long time tied down."

Dats considered lying but only for a moment. "I did, once . . ." Her voice trailed off at the admission, and she stared out the window.

Walcott said nothing, so Dats went on, "We hadn't been together long. Turned out to be a disaster."

"He found out about it?"

"I told him, almost right away. Guilt wouldn't let me sleep."

"Wow," Walcott said and whistled through his teeth. "Little Ana Dats isn't quite as perfect as we all thought."

She scowled at him, but he smiled his most disarming smile, and she just shook her head.

"You are royally fucked," he said. "You know that, right? People don't forget these things. *Guys* don't forget these things. You gave him a free pass to win any argument you guys have for the rest of your life."

He laughed expansively and pulled quickly away, heading back towards headquarters.

I N THE SILENCE of the dead night, the white van rolled to a gentle stop behind a beat up black Altima. The side of the van was plain, apart from two dirty stripes where a company logo had recently been sprayed over. The city's dimmed street lights cast everything in deep shadows. A squatter shuffled drunkenly across the street, disappearing into one of the many abandoned structures.

Two spray cans rolled along the enclosed rear cab, clanging against the rear door of the van. There were two captain's chairs in the front, and Richard crouched between them. The events of the evening were traveling too fast for him to fully process. He had used his power twice in less than twenty-four hours. On other occasions, he'd rested at least a week in between each use. Now, he'd agreed to help with Matt and Jake's ludicrous scheme. He had a nagging suspicion about his ability to effectively heal again in such a short span of time.

What if the power doesn't come when I call it?

Richard kept his worries to himself. He knew how determined these two could be. He'd rather try and fail than not try at all.

After leaving Richard's apartment, the group had taken a municipal bus that had restarted its route after the riots died down. A short ride and a shorter walk later, they'd picked up a work van and supplies from Jake and Matt's office. Then they'd driven to a small mom and pop hardware store to acquire the spray paint. Matt had paid in cash.

"Are you guys positive you want to go through with this?" Richard tried one last-ditch effort to talk his friends out of this mistake.

Jake swiveled his head around to glare at Richard with cold, emotionless eyes that said all that was needed. Richard could see the pain behind the thinly-veiled wall of anger bricked up in Jake's stare. He thought back to the source of that pain—Andrea. Jake's wife's death had left him alone to raise his two-year-old son. She'd been a kind and sweet woman who hadn't deserved what happened to her. Nor would she have approved of Jake's current course of action.

"Okay, forget I said anything." Richard threw his hands up in concession.

"Do you need us to go over the plan one more time?" Matt asked from the driver's seat.

"What's there to go over? You guys hop out, I drive two blocks down and wait to hear shots fired. I call the police from the payphone and take off once you guys get back to the van. Simple enough on my end. I'm not sure about being so far away from the action. What if you get hurt and can't reach me?"

"We're not letting you go with us, and that is final," Jake said. "We're prepared to deal with the risks. You stay out of harm's way. You're our support. Besides, if you were hit, who would heal you?" Satisfied when Richard didn't answer, Jake turned back to Matt. "You ready?"

Matt nodded and opened the van's squeaky door. The two men jumped from the van as Richard worked his way to the front and inched himself behind the steering wheel. Once Matt and Jake were clear, Richard adjusted the rearview mirror and drove down the street, watching the pair in the mirrors for as long as they remained in view.

JAKE'S BLOOD WAS boiling as he walked side by side with Matt down the empty street. He pulled a balaclava out of his back pocket and tugged it over his head, then slipped on a pair of leather gloves. Matt followed suit. Jake wasn't sure if this was the same gang that had been involved with Andrea's death, but he would count it as vengeance either way.

Matt pulled the stolen nine-millimeter handgun out of his pants, and checked the chamber and the magazine. Jake pulled out his own confiscated Niner weapon and ran through a similar inspection.

"It's so loose, held up by only the belt. I don't know how these gangsters move around without a holster." Matt shoved the gun down the back of his waistband and tightened his belt.

Matt wasn't taking the operation seriously enough for Jake's liking. He feared that Matt was underestimating their opponents, which could be a potentially costly mistake. Matt and Jake had performed countless ops together during their time in the Marines and then in the USMC Special Operations force, but that was some time ago, with military drone surveillance piping information into their helmets and HUDs. Civilian life could dull the warrior's instincts, but Jake had never had such strong emotions coursing through his veins during those operations as he did now. The proximity to his personal life created a glee-like vengeance deep inside him.

Jake could easily see that Matt shared none of these feelings. Matt had walked away from Jake when he'd started interrogating the Niner in the alley. To Jake, this showed that Matt didn't condone his actions, but he tried not to give it another thought. Matt was here and he was loyal. Matt would not abandon his friend and partner.

Jake's mind wandered to his son Andrew. He had a brief, terrifying flash of the boy growing up alone if tonight went wrong. He quickly dismissed the vision. Now wasn't the time to get distracted, else the vision might become a self-fulfilling prophecy. It was time to give in to the rage that he held inside as it swelled, day after day. It was time to focus that rage.

"You seem distant." Matt was looking at Jake. "You thinking about her?"

A flood of memories assailed Jake, nearly drowning him. He didn't want to admit the truth, but he knew he couldn't sneak a lie past the one person who knew him best. "It's been so long," he said quietly. "Some days, Andrew forgets what her face looked like. He begs me to see pictures of her, to remind him. We spend whole days just looking at old scrapbooks Andrea made. Then he asks me why she had to die."

Jake couldn't meet Matt's eye. Instead, he focused on the street and the darkness. Even in the ski mask, he found it difficult to hide the pain. "I've never been able to give him an answer you know, but tonight, I'm going to give these assholes one." Jake's eyes lingered on a City Watch surveillance box that stood unlit, most likely disabled by the guards inside the Niner house.

Jake put himself back in that moment, when Andrea was taken from him. That moment when the world broke away from him and things lost their meaning. He was ready for tonight's task.

They neared the end of the quiet side-street, turning left onto the main road. Their target was an abandoned two-family house, four lots down on the right-hand side of the street.

"Maybe I should do this alone. Sophia is still so young. I don't think I could live with myself if she grew up without a father."

"Not a chance in hell," Matt said. "We play it smart and they're down before they know what hit them. Let's go over the particulars one more time."

Jake smiled a little to himself. The threat had put the detail-oriented Matt back on task. "They have seven men guarding the money and drugs. Runners drop off the count and re-up their supply here. Then, they deliver it to the lower-level street dealers who trade in their cash for the re-up." The dying Niner in the alley had been explicit in his answers during the interrogation.

"Minus the two we took down in the alleyway, that should leave only five guys keeping watch over a large stack of drugs and cash," Matt said.

"Unless they replaced them. Although that seems highly unlikely. The kid said they were stretched thin from the turf war. In a few hours, a lieutenant will pick up the daily count from the surrounding neighborhoods, and bring it to wherever they have their headquarters. We need to break in, subdue any threat, grab the cash, and get out again before he and his entourage arrive."

"That's the house there," Matt said, pointing at a two-storey building that had seen better days. It was a two-family home, split down the middle rather than by floor level. The front porch was in disrepair. It creaked and swayed in the light breeze that caressed the city. Sheets of particle board were nailed over most of the windows, covering broken glass. An owl hooted as it took flight from a poorly-patched hole in the roof.

"The nearside of the building, on the second floor—there's a light on," Jake said.

"Didn't the kid say they mostly kept to the first floor, especially when they were short on numbers?"

"He did, and that light worries me. Let's enter through the window of that room." Jake pointed to the side of the house. "If there are any surprises, I want them out in the open rather than when our backs are turned."

The pair crossed the street two houses away from the stash house and crept through the shadows between the smashed and lightless streetlamps, hopping over a chain-link fence that encircled the yard. On the side of the stash house, a drainage pipe ran alongside a second-floor window.

"Did you catch that camera mounted next to the front door?" Matt asked.

"Poorly positioned. You could barely get the gate in view from that angle."

"True, but be mindful of others. We don't need to give these clowns any advance warning. Or worse, be identified later."

Jake took a few steps forward, placing his hand on the warm drainage pipe, testing its sturdiness. "I think it should hold us, one at a time. I'll go first." He deftly climbed up the pipe before Matt had a chance to respond.

The plywood covering this window had long-since rotted away, leaving the bottom half of the window exposed. The Niners probably used this as a secondary lookout spot when they operated at full capacity. As Jake clung to the pipe beside the window, he heard one half of a phone conversation from the room beyond.

"It's bullshit," a throaty voice said. "We're two men down and with all the shit that went down today, do you think they sent replacements? Of course not, that would make too much fucking sense. Stacks and his boys could be casing the joint right now."

Jake pulled himself level with the exposed part of the window and peered over the sill. The voice belonged to a heavyset Niner who wore the gang's red colors proudly in extra-large sizes. He was loudly talking into a cell phone pressed to his left ear, with his back to the window.

"Nick and Johnny never showed. Rumor is, they got took out. No one has heard from either of them and Tek got pissy when I asked him about it." The Niner paused, listening, then said, "All right, baby. I'll talk to you in the morning. I gotta get downstairs before the boss starts tripping."

He removed the phone from his ear and pushed the red *END* button on the display. Jake slipped through the window, landing softly on a ratty mattress in the corner of the room. He hopped forward and pressed the barrel of the stolen gun into the back of the Niner's head.

"Make a noise and your head gives the wall a new coat of paint."

The fat guy froze, and Jake used the brief moment to take stock of the room's contents. The bare, stained mattress lay on warped and broken floorboards. The only other thing in the room, apart from Jake and the trembling Niner, was a dresser missing most of its drawers. The wallpaper was peeling from the walls, revealing a lime green paint job that made Jake's stomach uneasy.

The Niner's hands slowly rose in surrender. Jake, using his gun as a prod, nudged the Niner farther into the room and silently shut the door before guiding the man to the mattress.

"Face down, now," Jake said, jamming the barrel into the back of the pudgy Niner's skull. "Do it quickly and quietly and you might live."

The Niner regarded the stained mattress, paused for a beat, then crawled onto it. Jake reached into his back pocket and produced multiple sets of plastic handcuffs. He bound the man's hands behind his back with a set, then applied a second set to the ankles. Jake didn't have anything to use as a gag, so he simply pistol-whipped his captive. It was no big deal; he'd done it more times than he could remember.

He turned back to the window and signaled an "all clear" gesture to Matt, who was waiting below, crouched in the shadows of the building.

Matt scaled the pipe and climbed into the room. He glanced briefly at the man on the mattress. Jake motioned for Matt to join him by the door, both understanding the necessity of hand signals from this point onward. Jake eased the door open a crack and peered around it.

They were at the end of a four-door hallway, two doors spaced equidistant from one another on each side. From his earlier inter-rogation, Jake knew the two doors closest to him were a closet and a bathroom that hadn't had running water since before the Niner occupation.

At the end of the hallway there was another Niner with his back to Jake. This guy wasn't tall, but he was freakishly wide across the shoulders and back. Metabolic enhancers were the only way to pro-duce a body as bulked-up as that. The man was a tank. Tough, lots of firepower, and a low center of gravity to keep him right-side up.

Jake moved silently down the hallway, gun in both hands, point-ing at the Niner's massive body. Matt grabbed Jake's shoulder, halt-ing him mid-step, and shook his head. He slipped past Jake with his gun tucked behind his back.

Matt crept stealthily towards the Tank. Once directly behind him, he paused for a moment then sprang onto Tank's back, wrapping his arms around the Niner's neck and clamping down hard. Matt leaned back and levered the Tank off the ground by his throat, effectively preventing air from getting in or out. The Tank made no sound at all.

Matt used his height advantage to increase the leverage on the choke hold as he pulled the Niner down the hallway into the bedroom. He was closing in on the doorway where Jake stood, when the Tank's flailing leg collided with a weathered end table, knocking over the glass gas lamp that provided the illumination in the hall.

Matt jerked his elbow underneath the Tank's chin, securing the hold even tighter. As the last of his oxygen left his system, the Tank's arms went limp. Matt hurriedly dragged the unconscious gangster into the room with the mattress.

Jake locked eyes with Matt. "Shit," he muttered.

DOWNSTAIRS, GED, THE boss of the house, was in the middle of packaging small heroin capsules together in bags destined for corner-level dealers. The next resupply was due within the hour. He sat on a mangy couch as he worked at a rickety little table, listening to the music that poured from a small portable speaker. He watched as Marcus, one of the misfits in his charge, counted and stacked wads of money next to him.

There was a large bay window at the other end of the room, covered by blackout curtains. Another of his charges, Tony, stood there, acting as a lookout. Tony was the youngest member of his crew, having just celebrated his fourteenth birthday. Pimples dotted his cheeks and forehead.

Ged lay back on the couch, stretching and rolling his shoulders, when the sudden sound of shattering glass jerked him back upright.

"What the hell was that?" Marcus cried and leapt from the couch.

"Those assholes upstairs must be going at it again." Ged sighed deeply. He switched the speaker off, leaving the room in eerie silence. "If you catch a beating 'cause you keep fighting with your partner out on the corner . . . well, you'd figure they would smarten up."

"Hey Tony, why don't you go upstairs and check it out?" Marcus said. Ged was getting sick of his attempts to bully the kid.

"I'm the lookout. That means I look *out*, not *in*." Tony's voice varied wildly between deep bass and high-pitched squeaks. "If Po-Po comes stormin' in while I'm upstairs, it's my neck that gets lynched, not yours. I been judged twice this year and my shoulder still ain't right, all cause of one motherfucker stomping on me while I was on the ground."

"Fuck you. Don't be a bitch your whole life." Marcus turned to Ged. "Tell him, boss, he has to go. I outrank him."

Ged puffed out his cheeks and rolled his eyes. Mr. Jones really wanted to test his patience with this crew, nothing but a bunch of screw-ups who couldn't be trusted out on the corners during wartime.

"Tony's got a point," Ged said. "We need a lookout at all times. But don't worry, Marcus. The money will still be right here waiting for you to count when you get back."

"This is fucking bullshit," Marcus muttered as he headed towards the stairs behind the couch.

"What was that?" Ged called over his shoulder.

"Nothing," Marcus grunted as he stepped onto the first step of the staircase.

THE TWO SUBDUED Niners lay motionless on the filthy mattress. Matt was using a set of Jake's plastic cuffs to secure the wrists and ankles of the Niner he'd rendered unconscious. Jake was monitoring the hallway from behind the door, which he'd left open a crack.

"The music's stopped," Jake whispered, turning to Matt. "I can hear voices coming from downstairs, but I can't make out the words. No one has come up yet."

"You jinxed us again, you know," Matt said.

Along the hallway, Jake saw the top of a head appear as someone started climbing the stairs.

"I hate it when you're right," Jake groaned. He closed the last half-inch of the door and checked the stolen gun again; he didn't trust a weapon he hadn't cleaned and assembled himself.

"Yo idiots, where you at?" a voice bellowed from beyond the door. Jake stepped back as the doorknob slowly turned.

The door creaked open, and a young Niner stood in the doorway. He stared at the two guys on the mattress, then at the gun Jake was pointing at his head.

"Don't make a sound," Jake murmured.

The kid's eyes widened and beads of sweat formed on his forehead. His hand hovered close to the Berretta at his hip. Jake watched him frantically look for an escape route.

"Step forward, slowly," Jake said, the gun rock-steady in his hands.

The Niner took a step into the room. His hip turned, and Jake lost sight of the Berretta.

"We got a situation!" the Niner called out, and reached for his gun.

His voice was cut off by a quick double-tap from Jake's stolen firearm. The first shot tore through the kid's patella tendon, instantly dropping him. The second shot caught his gun hand. A metallic *ting* sounded as the bullet passed straight through the meat of his hand and ricocheted off the gun's dull handle. There was suddenly a good deal of blood in the hallway.

Matt dashed out of the bedroom. He looked at the Niner writhing in agony on the old warped floorboards, then shot a curious look at Jake.

"He was reaching for his gun," Jake explained.

"I guess it's safe to assume we no longer need silence then," Matt said. He started the timer on his watch. "Richard's making a phone call. We don't have long now."

"I know, I know."

The felled Niner groaned as Jake flipped him over and cuffed his hands behind his back. Matt unwound a roll of duct tape and wrapped it around his injured leg and hand, slowing the bleeding. He quickly slapped an extra strip of tape over the crying kid's mouth. Both Matt and Jake carried him back into the bedroom and dumped him onto the bed next to his captured comrades.

TWO GUNSHOTS CAME from above. Ged jumped to his feet and Tony began sweating immediately. The gun at his hip felt ten pounds heavier and his heartbeat fiercely accelerated in his chest. The thought of his heart bursting under the stress briefly raced across his mind.

"Boss, is it Stacks?" he cried. "Holy fuck. I'm not ready to die. I knew we should have got replacements for Johnny and Nick." His voice jumped the octaves.

"Shut your mouth. We'll check it out together. Make sure you have a round chambered and the safety's off that thing." Ged pointed at the shaking gun and Tony slid the charging handle back, loading a bullet from the magazine into the chamber.

They walked cautiously to the foot of the stairs. Silence greeted them from the floor above. Tony turned toward his boss, waiting for the next instruction.

"Go on up," Ged said, nodding to the top of the stairs. "I'm right behind you."

Tony closed his eyes and inhaled deeply. He ascended the stairs one creaky step at a time. His feet felt heavier with each one. As he neared the top, he dropped to his belly and crawled up the remaining steps.

Two men emerged from the last room down the hallway. They wore black masks and gloves. No part of their skin was exposed. Tony had his gun in his hand, but before he could aim, the two masked intruders unleashed a hellacious volley of gunfire. Plaster exploded all around him and the air filled with noise and dust. He jerked backwards down the stairs, cracking his head on a step, and retreated back to where Ged waited.

AT THE END of the hallway, Jake ejected the spent magazine from his gun. He loaded new rounds into the magazine with the deft precision born of long practice. Matt, not as heavy with his trigger finger, still had a few shots to spare. He kept his gun trained at the spot where the Niner's head had briefly appeared.

"That was just a kid," Matt said.

"Yeah. A kid with a loaded gun."

"We have your friends up here, alive," Matt called out towards the stairwell. "We won't kill you if you surrender. Your life doesn't have to end tonight."

"Go fuck yourselves." The voice originated from halfway up the stairs, and a single round was discharged which lodged in the ceiling. A flat chunk of plasterboard dropped to the floor.

Jake and Matt ducked into opposite side rooms on each side of the hall.

"I guess we can take that as a no," Matt said.

They crawled back into the hallway on their bellies.

"Too bad we didn't smuggle out any grenades before we left the service," Matt said. "One would come in real handy right about now."

An idea formed in Jake's mind, and he grinned. He winked at Matt.

"Play along," Jake whispered, then, more loudly, "Shit! I'm jammed!"

"Hurry," Matt said, now also grinning. "Clear the chamber. I'm still reloading."

There was a pause, and, for a moment, Jake wondered if the Niners weren't as dumb as he'd hoped. Then, without warning, two figures rose up from the stairwell and made a charge for the hallway.

The young kid fired off another round, which passed well over the prone Jake, and Matt squeezed off a couple of shots, one of which caught the kid in the throat. There was a puff of pink mist and the kid went down like so much meat.

The second guy was older and a lot bigger. He didn't have time to shoot at all. Jake fired off four shots, two groups of two. The first hit the older guy in the left side, the second went wide to the left, and the third and fourth hit him in the chest, dead center, with a noise like someone slapping a side of beef. He collapsed to his knees and swayed there for a moment, staring at Jake as blood frothed from his mouth. Then he toppled forwards onto his face and lay still.

"You think that's all of them?" Matt asked Jake. Neither had moved from their prone position.

"The fat kid on the phone said they didn't replace the two from the alleyway. We already took out five. If there were any others, they would have been right behind those two on the stairs."

"We need to move quick," Matt said and glanced at his watch. "It's nearly two minutes since the first shot was fired. We grab the cash and bail as fast as possible."

GOING BY THE response rates of the police department, the pair didn't have long left until more company arrived, so Matt hustled down the stairs into the open living room. Wads of cash and bags of drugs covered a coffee table in front of a worn-down sofa. Next to the sofa was a half-filled garbage bag. Jake's hard footfalls sounded on the stairs behind him. Matt dashed to the garbage bag and pulled it open. Inside were the gang's daily counts from the region, just as the tortured Niner had said they would be.

Matt grabbed the wads of cash that littered the coffee table and threw them into the larger plastic bag, which he hoisted over his shoulder as Jake made his way towards the back door. Matt followed as Jake pulled the door open and sprinted towards a fence that separated the house from the one behind it. Jake deftly hopped over the fence in a fluid motion.

Matt tossed his bag over to Jake, then grabbed the top of the fence with both hands and hauled himself over. He landed softy on the other side and sprinted after Jake who had made it out to the street with the garbage bag. They both ran down the road towards the meeting spot where Richard was supposed to wait with the van.

Matt rounded the corner ahead of Jake and spotted their work van idling where they had planned. He ran to the back of the van and popped open the hatch. Jake jumped inside with the garbage bag and Matt closed the hatch behind him. He ran around to the passenger door.

As soon as he climbed into the seat, he was assailed by the strong odor of alcohol. He looked back at Jake, who'd already begun separating the garbage bag's contents into three separate duffle bags.

"Richard?" Matt said.

"Yeah. Yeah. I got it," Richard slurred.

Matt peered at his friend and saw that Richard's eyes were glassy. There was a flask half-tucked into his pants pocket.

"You're drunk," Matt said.

"I just had a few sips. I'm fine to drive."

"No, you are not. Get in the back. What if we get stopped by the cops?"

Jake must have overheard; though Matt hadn't heard him exit the back of the van, Jake appeared at the window next to Richard. He opened the door.

"Come on, Richard," Jake said. "We can't take chances. Get out."

Matt watched Richard lower his head and get out of the van. A moment later he popped open the back hatch and crawled inside. He pulled the flask from his jeans and took a long swig.

"Do you have a problem?" Matt asked. He knew Richard was fond of the drink but finding a drunk Richard getting ready to drive the van put it into a new perspective.

"I need it. I healed Jake earlier," Richard said before taking another gulp.

"What does that even mean?" Matt said.

Jake pulled away, his attention focused on the road. He didn't seem to be aware of—or didn't care about—the situation.

"It's the only way to stop the visions," Richard murmured, just loud enough for Matt to hear before he downed the rest of his flask.

NSIDE THEIR SPLIT-LEVEL house on the outskirts of the city, Detective Dats tossed back and forth in her bed next to her fiancé, John. In her dream, mounds of paperwork were piled impossibly high on top of her desk. She tried to fill out the forms, but her hand was weighted down by a hunk of rock that was attached to her finger.

On the nightstand next to the bed, a cell phone began to vibrate, disrupting the dark and tranquil bedroom. Dats stirred from her slumber and shuffled over John's inert form, rousing him, too.

She picked up the cellphone and glanced at the display. "It's the station," she said softly.

She rubbed her eyes before answering the cellphone. "This better be good," she said irritably into the handset.

She'd expected to be greeted by one of Walcott's usual remarks, but as the voice on the line began talking, Dats's eyes popped wide open. She sat up straight.

"Yes, Captain?" Dats said.

"Dats, there was another incident tonight. A Niner stash house was raided by an unknown group. We have multiple injuries on site, including three gunshot victims and two fatalities."

"You said three were shot?"

John's complexion lost all color and he raised a hand to his face, covering his mouth and neatly-trimmed goatee.

"Were we able to flip anyone on Mr. Jones yet?" Dats asked.

"No one yet, but we have several Niners in custody," Levi answered. "The mayor wants all personnel in tomorrow. I hate to do it to you, but I need you in."

"Yes, sir. I'll be in first thing in the morning. Goodnight."

I'll be in first thing in the morning.

Giving voice to those words set off alarms throughout Dats's mind. John's face tensed as the words sunk deep, and his eyes narrowed as she placed the phone back on the nightstand. He shifted on the mattress, facing her.

"You do realize we have a lot of things to settle tomorrow. And we leave the day after." Dats winced as John's voice wavered to stay in control.

"Babe," she started, like she always did. "You have to understand, this past twenty-four hours, it's been a madhouse in the city. We have two rival gangs, full of hatred, engaging in a war and using a riot to mask the evidence." She tried to put her hand over his, but he snatched it away before she could get close.

"And if this 'war' continues, are we going to cancel our wedding and honeymoon?" He turned away but his tone was steadier than before. Dats counted it as a win, but she knew she was still in a critical situation that could turn in a blink.

She put her hand on John's shoulder, trying to think of an answer that wouldn't make things worse. "What do you want me to say? We have over a dozen murders on our desk and the city is going to Hell. What am I supposed to do, John? What am I supposed to do?"

"What I want to hear," John said, "is that you want to get married. That you didn't say yes just to avoid breaking up."

"Babe." She put her hand on his shoulder blade.

He jerked around, shaking off her hand.

"Just tell me the truth, Ana," he said quietly.

She took his chin in her hands and guided his face back towards her. She looked deeply into his eyes. "I love you more than anything in this world," she said. "If my captain tries to order me in another day after tomorrow, he'll have my gun and my stupid badge on his desk. We'll figure everything else out when we get back."

John's face softened. Dats could no longer see the doubts, but whether they were erased by her words or only in hiding, she didn't know.

"Ana, you don't need to do that." He inched closer to her. "I just needed to hear you say the words. I know how much the job means to you, and I know I kind of pushed for such a close date. If the worst happens, we'll lose the deposits."

She leaned forward and kissed him gently. She closed her eyes and lost herself, but he abruptly pulled back.

"But, it's your overtime checks that are paying for the next deposits," he said.

Dats smiled. She pouted while he laughed at his own joke, then pushed him back onto the mattress.

"So you think you're the boss around here?" she said and climbed on top of him, straddling his belly, pinning him beneath her. "We'll just have to see about that."

THE GETAWAY VAN rolled to a gentle stop in front of Richard's apartment. The back door opened and Richard clambered out into the quiet stillness of the post-midnight street. He stretched his legs as he walked along the cracked sidewalk to the passenger door.

Matt rolled the ancient vehicle's hand-cranked window down. He had finished separating the night's score into three duffel bags that now lay at his feet. He reached between his legs and grabbed Richard's bag. He levered it through the open window.

"Here's your cut," he said when Richard didn't immediately take the bag.

Richard shook his head, hands held up in refusal. "I can't accept that," he said and took a step away from the van.

"Take it, you earned it. You made the call and minded the van." Matt pushed the bag farther out the window. It sagged down the side of the door.

"I did it as a favor to the two of you. I wanted to be close at hand, in case anything went wrong. Money never played into it." Richard shoved the bag back through the window.

From the driver's side, his face gently lit by the dashboard's display, Jake said, "Just take the money. Use it to get out of this shithole of an apartment."

Richard glanced over his shoulder at the four-storey building. The exterior paint was peeling and even from here Matt could smell the stale mold from the hallways.

"I kind of like this place. Feels like home. I've been living here for two years now. That's the longest I've lived in one place since . . . well, since the car accident." Richard seemed surprised by the notion.

"Are you sure you won't take it?"

"I'm positive," Richard replied with a smile. "Split it between the two of you. Consider it a present for the kids."

"Alright, man. If you're positive," Matt said, disappointed. "Are you going to be all right here by yourself tonight?"

"I'll be fine. Just get home to your families. They must be worried sick."

Matt watched as his troubled friend turned and headed for the worn-down apartment building. For a passing moment, Matt swore he could actually see the immense weight that Richard seemed to be carrying. It was a load that Richard refused to share. Instead, he carried the burden by himself.

After the stresses of nights like tonight, it was no wonder Richard didn't call often. Matt thought of himself as a good person, as a good friend, but was he really? Tonight, he'd killed a young boy in cold blood. What kind of friend would involve others in a horrid affair like that, one that had already left at least four men dead? Would a good man rob and kill, even if the victims were "evil?"

"I'm hungry. Want to grab food someplace?" Jake asked as he shifted the car into drive and pulled onto the street.

THE LARGE WAREHOUSE was unoccupied, having been abandoned years ago. Raef lifted the large steel shutter of the loading dock and entered first, followed by James, who struggled to climb the two-foot lip; the cash-filled briefcase was heavy and threatened to unbalance him completely.

"I swear," James said, "this is more money than my father could have made in ten years." As he entered the darkness of the warehouse, the gnawing inside him couldn't be ignored any longer. "Can I ask you a question?" he said.

Raef stared at him. "What is it?" he asked through clenched teeth.

"How did you break into that place, and get to the leaders? I saw at least nine guys go in there."

"Don't worry about it, James. I have my ways. You just concern yourself with driving the van."

"You're one of those *Others*," James said. "You can't deny it."

"If that's the term you wish to use, then yes. I am."

"Well, your powers then. I already know you can like read minds or something. And you can take down a bunch of bodyguards. How do you do it?"

"You are very astute, James." Raef seemed to be in an oddly talkative mood. "To be honest, some of that first power you spoke of was enhanced by the *Sphere*, the tool I handed over to Midnight."

"I never saw you with anything in your hands," James said. He mentally replayed his moments with Raef, as traumatizing as they were.

"I carried it in my inner jacket pocket." Raef tapped his right chest. "The link was established mentally. It enhanced my own ability to scan people's mind. It also had other useful powers."

"But, how are you able to do it?"

"There are three types of people in this world," Raef said. "*Others*, *Carriers*, and you. We are all connected to the *Network*. You are sheep who will never understand your role in the greater scheme of things."

"Fine," James said. "But even if I'll never understand, I still have another question."

Raef's stare hardened. "What?" he said flatly.

"Why don't you like being called 'sir?'"

"That," Raef said, "is a personal question."

"I was just curious, is all." James was ready to let the question die, but a little part of him yearned to know more about the man who had saved him, only to enslave him.

"I suppose it couldn't hurt to tell you. After all, you will most likely disappoint me again and I will have to dispose of you." James didn't doubt Raef's sincerity.

"A long time ago," Raef said, "back in my homeland, I was often called 'sir.' I liked the sound of it. I reveled in the authority it gave me. But horror came and . . . I failed. I am not cut out to be a leader. I learned that lesson the hard way. I vowed that no one would ever again call me 'sir.' Now, horror seems to walk by my side wherever I go. I've even come to call it friend."

"What kind of horror?" James asked. He'd not seen this side of Raef before. He'd never truly considered the complexity of the man. He was too occupied by the "horror" that accompanied Raef.

"It is not the time to discuss such things," Raef said. "Just know, sometimes befriending horror is your only option for survival. Now, put that bag in the back office."

James walked the length of the building, unseen detritus crumbling under his feet in the dark. As he moved farther into the back, he passed multiple drums of gasoline. Raef had ordered him to bring the drums inside when they'd first arrived here. Even though all of the barrels were sealed, the smell of gas was almost overpowering and it instantly gave James a headache. Behind him, he could hear Raef dialing numbers into his cellphone.

"Why don't you make a pot of coffee while you are back there?" Raef called. James glanced back, and saw Raef standing in the dock entrance trying to improve his signal.

James pushed open the creaky door to the tiny back office and switched on the light. The makeshift office space contained a desk with an old 1970s computer-chair behind it. The phone on the desk had accumulated enough dust to render its keypad illegible. The electrics—lights, coffeemaker—were hooked up to a small gas-powered generator that James had to fill once a day.

Next to the doorway, the coffeemaker sat on a small end table. It was one of the few things you could touch in the building without getting grime on your fingers. James switched it on and placed an empty glass pot on the hotplate.

He slipped the briefcase under the desk, then walked out of the office, trying to stay out of Raef's eyeline.

"Mr. Jones, please. He is expecting my call," Raef said into the phone then waited, staring out at the calm, dark waters of the harbor.

"Coffee's on," James softly called from his hiding spot. He wasn't sure if Raef heard, for he made no acknowledgment. James took a few steps closer.

"Good evening, Mr. Jones," Raef said. "The deed is done."

James drew a picture of Scott Jones in his head as Raef spoke.

"I was fortunate," Raef went on. "An opportunity presented itself and I took full advantage. I could meet you tomorrow for the remainder of my fee."

Excitement filled James. If Raef had completed his work in the city, he would no longer have need of James, who'd finally be able to resume his journey to Maine. For the first time in days, he felt hope.

"It was no trouble at all," Raef said. "I actually still have some business in town to which I must attend anyway." James's hopes floated into the darkness with Raef's words.

"More work, you say?" Raef said, his smile widening. "My constituents are constantly hungry. More work is helpful to our cause. I'll fill in Mr. Anderson on the details and he can text you the fee. I'll see you in the morning."

A short buzz alerted James that the coffee had finished brewing. He went back to the office and poured the coffee into two mugs Raef had bought from a local gas station. For an instant, he wondered if he might be able to find some old rat poison to put in Raef's coffee, but even if he could, he doubted it would work—Raef probably used it as a sweetener when he ran out of sugar.

"Your coffee," James said listlessly as he returned to the loading dock.

"Good. Be ready for tomorrow. It seems Mr. Jones would like to hire us for another job." Raef sipped the coffee, swirling the contents around in his mouth before swallowing.

"I'll be spending the rest of the night in the office," he went on. "I need to meditate. You know, that means do not disturb me for any reason. And don't get notions of flight into that little brain of yours. You failed to escape last time. This time I may just skip looking for you and find Taylor."

"And if I thought things were bad for me, wait until I see what you'd do to my brother. Right?" James surprised even himself with his defiance.

Raef stood there for a moment, staring at James. Eventually, he seemed to decide to let the comment pass. He stalked away to the office and locked the door behind him, leaving James alone in the darkness of the empty warehouse.

Day 3

AFTER THE LONG night's ordeal and just under half a bottle of scotch, Richard rested peacefully in his bed, not quite asleep, but far from awake. His earlier cleaning frenzy had left his room spotless, save for the half-drunk bottle of scotch on the nightstand next to the bed. Immediately behind the nightstand was the room's window, with a fire escape bolted to the exterior.

Richard shifted in the bed. He could see himself outside on that fire escape, smoking, back in the days before he'd quit. Even though he knew he was half-dreaming, he could feel the breeze on his face, and the smoke in his lungs. He could see the figure of his own silhouette against the night sky. As his eyes fluttered, the figure dissolved into scintillating particles and dispersed into the dark before slowly rematerializing next to his bed, cloaked in shadow. He watched as it took a moment to take stock of the room. It snorted in disapproval.

"Wake up," the shadowy figure commanded. It floated over to the nightstand, carefully picking up the bottle of liquor. Holding the glass close to its eyes, the shadow inspected the label carefully.

"Wake up," it repeated a little louder. Richard continued to stare at it, but when he didn't move, a smoky, translucent hand smacked his forehead.

"What?" Richard muttered, shifting under the covers. "I'm asleep." Webs of sleep clung to his eyes, making them difficult to open fully. When he finally focused properly, he realized, with shocking suddenness, that he was awake. And the figure remained, staring down at him.

"Who . . . what are you?" Richard drew his knees up and braced his back against the headboard.

The shadow was absolutely motionless, making it hard to resolve its features from the natural shadows swirling around the room. It still held the bottle up. Richard tried to focus on the figure's face.

"You know," it said suddenly, its voice a chorus of whispers, "this stuff is bad for you. It's one of the reasons I've had such a hard time tracking you. It's bad enough with the *Vortex* distorting everything."

"What are you talking about? Who are you and what do you want?" Richard's head was spinning and pounding simultaneously. Could he still be dreaming or was this another one of his visions?

"I'll take that one question at a time. First, I am talking about your drinking. It makes your connection to the *Network* fuzzy."

"The *Network*?"

The shadow took a step forward, bathing itself in pale moonlight and resolving itself as a man. Richard didn't recognize him, but there was a sense of familiarity all the same. The man's black leather trenchcoat seemed to melt into the gloom of the room, making only parts of his body visible.

"Young one, it has been called many things throughout history. The *Network* is the name we have used during the modern age. It is our lifeblood. Without it, our powers would cease to be. All those people you have healed over the years would be a pile of corpses."

Richard crouched on the bed, getting into a better defensive position. "How do you know about that? I've never met you before." The hairs on Richard's body rose as a tingling sensation enveloped his body.

"That's not quite true," the intruder said, and placed the bottle of scotch back on the nightstand. "If we had met face to face, my problems would have been eradicated a long time ago. But, to say we have never met before today, well that would be a lie."

Richard couldn't be sure, but he thought the apparition cracked a smile.

"What are you talking about?" Richard said. He knew he was on the verge of learning something vital about his powers, but the source of the information scared him to his core. "You said *our* lifeblood, *our* powers. Can you heal people like I can?"

The man laughed, the chorus of whispers becoming deep and throaty. "Oh, the naivety of youth. You truly haven't figured it out yet. *You* can connect to the *Network* and use its power to heal people. *My* powers, while derived from the same source, are quite different from yours. And much more powerful.

"Now, when I say we have met, I mean to say . . ." He paused, looking for the perfect combination of words. ". . . we have interacted in the past."

Realization dawned in Richard's mind. He'd been wrong all along—his power wasn't cursed.

"You!" he cried. "You gave me all those visions, gave me all those nightmares. You ruined my life, caused me to alienate everyone I cared about. All because we both share some weird power?" Richard jumped from the bed and faced the shadowy figure.

The man laughed again. "I do not *give* you nightmares," he said. "I *am* your nightmare."

Something seemed to snap within Richard. He howled and charged at the figure. "You ruined my life!"

The figure fluttered briefly as Richard passed harmlessly through it. He collided headfirst with the far wall, denting the plasterboard.

"You still understand nothing," the man said, standing over Richard.

"Why me?" Richard groaned and rolled onto his back.

"You make my head hurt," the man said.

"What?" Richard said. It was *his* head that was throbbing. "I don't understand."

The figure bent over, his face just inches away from Richard.

"*You make my head hurt!*" he screamed.

He stood back up, taking time to smooth the creases out of his smoky leather jacket. He composed himself, taking a moment to gather his center. "I do not like to repeat myself," he said.

"How could I hurt your head? That doesn't make sense."

"I will be honest. I have yet to fully comprehend our connection. What I do know is that you are my opposite, the yin to my yang. When you use your powers, you sever my connection to the *Network*, leaving me vulnerable. It feels as if someone is caving in my skull. I am indeed lucky that my master has granted me permission to finally remove you. Unfortunately, outside powers are currently preventing me from doing it here and now."

The words sank deeply into Richard, chilling him to the bone. For once, he wished this *was* a vision. Such a fantasy didn't seem as bad as the truth, if truth this was.

"Why waste all this effort? Why not just kill me? You've had plenty of chances." Richard had a sudden vivid memory of filthy water filling his lungs from a mop bucket.

"It has been hard," the shadowy man said. "Though I hate to admit it. You moved around so often that it made it difficult to lock onto your location, and my own distance from you just compounded the problem. I have been very far away, you see, on important business. One cannot deny the master's call. My duties have kept me from unleashing my full power upon you.

"My only option at the time was to torment you. I hoped that the visions would do the job and you would take your own life, saving me the considerable trouble of doing so. And you came close, didn't you? Your resolve was dwindling, but you moved to this city, and regained your composure."

"Sorry to disappoint," Richard said bitterly.

"No matter. My previous assignment is complete. I am close to you, and you have now used your power inside your own home. *Sphere* or no, and *Vortex* be damned. It is only a matter of time before I will finish the job."

A frenzied panic raced through Richard's body. He jumped to his feet and bolted for the door. He grabbed the doorknob, ready to flee, but something struck the back of his head. Richard felt the immense impact a moment before the object expanded, swallowing his head and pulling him downward. His legs gave way and he flopped to the floor as the world went black.

MATT AND JAKE were seated in a booth near the back of the '50s-style all-night diner. The few other patrons seemed to be those types whose business was best conducted under the cloak of darkness. In front of Matt, a greasy burger leaked gray juice onto the plate and made the side order of fries soggy. Jake had opted for an early breakfast of two runny eggs, sausage, and home fries. Matt was exhausted, and, judging by the weary look in his eyes, so was Jake.

"That was a hefty score tonight," Matt said and took a reluctant bite of the burger. It tasted, surprisingly, pretty good.

"I guess crime does pay," Jake said.

"Listen, Jake," Matt said. "I've been mulling something over, ever since we dropped Richard off at his place."

"Oh yeah, what's that?" Jake put down his fork and gave Matt his full attention.

"Could you buy me out?" Matt said.

"Buy you out?" Jake said. "What're you talking about?"

"Our business," Matt said. "It doesn't require two people to operate it."

Jake stared at Matt for a long time. "You've been mulling this over?" he said at last.

Matt nodded, though he said nothing about the unease that had been growing within him since watching Jake's interrogation. And now he had the death of a kid on his hands tonight, too.

"I knew there was something wrong," Jake said. "I figured it was just because of today, you know, you shooting someone for the first time since we left the service. But I had no idea . . ."

"Melissa's been talking about moving down to Florida," Matt said. He realized he couldn't meet Jake's eyes. "The property prices are pretty cheap there. With the cash from tonight and a buyout, I could open my own auto-body shop. Those retirees down there don't take too kindly to bots working on their classic cars. I could finally put all my certifications to use." He mushed the fries on his plate absently with his fork.

"You serious?"

"I've had it with Taxachusetts. The weather sucks and you can't drive a decent car here, since the potholes have their own zip codes." Matt stopped talking as the image of his abandoned car flashed across his mind. "And now the gangs and riots, it's all too much for me to handle. This state is going to hell in a handbasket." He kept the other reasons to himself.

"I hear you, but I don't have the extra cash to buy you out."

"Why not? You were always the saver. If you used the cash from tonight, you could afford it." Matt surprised even himself with his reaction to Jake's answer. He stopped playing with his food and stared intently at his partner.

"Private schools for Andrew cost a lot," Jake said quietly.

"I'd hate to have to sell out to some random guy."

Jake was quiet for a while. He regarded the uneaten breakfast on the table, then said, "Justin."

"Justin?"

"Sure. My cousin is back from Ukraine. He always wanted a piece of the business. Remember when he was home on leave? He took over my duties while I went on vacation. He could buy in as a partner and we could run it together."

"Justin doesn't have that kind of disposable income."

"So we hit another stash house," Jake said immediately. "We still have their schedule and if we act quickly, it'll still be viewed as a Young Gunz operation. I can buy you out and work out a payment plan with Justin."

Matt had stuffed a fistful of fries into his mouth as Jake was talking. He stopped chewing and swallowed hard. "You know you're crazy, right?"

"Crazy smart, you mean." Jake grinned.

For just a second, Matt assumed it was a joke. When the grin didn't waver, he realized Jake was serious. "What about Richard?"

"I don't think we should involve him again."

"No?" Matt thought about all the ways the robbery could turn south, and all the ways Richard could be of help.

"I'm not comfortable putting him anywhere near harm's way," Jake said, leaning in close.

They resumed eating in silence, preferring to let the extra risks hang unspoken between them.

MATT CAREFULLY SLID his key into the keyhole. He tried his best to quietly turn the knob. The near-full moon hung high in the sky, casting faint illumination over him. Silently, he eased his front door open.

The interior was dimly lit by pale moonlight coming through the windows, allowing Matt to navigate the chaos of toys that littered the floor. In the kitchen, he opened the fridge and grabbed a Sam Adams from inside. He noticed his cold supper on a shelf, wrapped in plastic wrap.

He silently popped the cap off the beer and gulped it down in two long swallows as he walked along the hallway. The first door on the right belonged to his daughter, Shelly.

He eased the door quietly open and peeked in. The room was dimly lit by a night-light with a unicorn on it, a present from Sully for her second birthday. More toys were strewn about the floor. Shelly lay in her bed, wrapped up tightly in blankets and surrounded by a legion of stuffed animals. A wave of emotion welled up in Matt, making him blink with the ferocity of his feelings for her.

Then he flinched as the young Niner's agonized screams echoed in his head, and he had to take a moment to flush the memory from his mind. Yes, a quiet, rural setting was the right place to raise Shelly. This place was no good for her. The sprawl of the megacity inched closer to their town year by year. By the time she was in high school, the town would be reclassified as a district of Boston.

Matt and Melissa's room was at the end of the hall. Light came through the half-open door. Matt did his best to push all thoughts of today's violence to the back of his mind.

Inside, Melissa lay on the queen-sized mattress, the covers half-hiding her naked form. To Matt, the only thing more impressive than her looks was her even temperament. She took life's blows on the chin, but never let them knock her down. Matt was reminded of how lucky he was.

Tonight though, he wasn't sure of the type of reception he would receive. Melissa may be even-tempered, but it was an unwise man who riled her. It took a lot to upset her equilibrium, but when she snapped, well, you'd better stand well back. He smiled to himself, despite the risks of incurring her wrath. He wouldn't have her any other way.

He had done his best to keep her up to date with fake reasons for working late, via text message, never the most accurate communication method from which to judge responses. Her *Fine*s and *OK*s had left him no wiser.

"Late night?" Her voice made him start.

"The city's on the verge of madness right now," Matt said as he unclipped his gun and holster.

"Was it because of those shootings earlier?" She had a high level of empathy that Matt simply didn't possess.

"Yup. When it's bad for the public, it usually means Jake and I will be making extra cash. How was Shelly today?" He tried to change the subject as fast as he could.

"She was fussy tonight. She gets like that when you don't come home." Even without high-level empathy, he could hear the frustration in her voice. "How'd the rest of the night go?"

Matt placed his gun on top of the antique bureau, using the opportunity to give a completely fabricated account of the evening's events. He removed the magazine and ejected the round from the chamber, which bought him enough time to spin his tale, though he couldn't look at her. He kept his story simple, and skipped over the incident in the alleyway. He knew he'd sold the lie when Melissa expressed concern over his Ferrari, but that only added to his guilt.

"How'd your day go?" Matt asked, shifting the conversation.

"Not too bad. I took another contract to work on the local school district's database. It's a remote job. Shouldn't take more than a few hours."

"I've been thinking," he said, finally turning to face her. "This state is too cold for me. How about we pack our things and move down south. Shelly hasn't started school yet. I'd rather do it now instead of later."

"You mean move to Florida?" Melissa sat up in bed, the covers slipping down, pooling in her lap. An excited look came over her, like a child on Christmas morning.

"Jake and I discussed having his cousin take over the day-to-day operations of the business. Jake will handle the paperwork and payroll. With his buy-in, I can open a garage down there."

Matt beamed a smile as he tried to partition his mind, and hide the true source of the cash. Melissa could never know where the money had come from. He just had to carry on for a few more days. He'd done it before. It's how he'd always gotten through the most inhuman times.

AFTER HE DROPPED Matt off, Jake drove to the next town over, fifteen minutes away, where his mother lived. The streets were deserted at this time of night but the autodrive feature was still forced to activate the brakes at stop signs. The quiet of the dwindling middle-class suburbs was in stark contrast to the constant commotion of the city.

Jake pulled into the driveway of a two-storey raised ranch. The front light had been left on, awaiting his arrival. He tramped up the two stone steps to the matching stone landing and made to unlock the front door, but as he did so, it swung open before him.

His mother, Sarah, stood in the doorway. Despite having four grown children of her own, she retained much of her youthful spirit. Jake's small group of friends had crassly bestowed upon her the dubious *MILF* distinction, which Jake had found neither humorous nor appropriate.

Her husband, Jake's stepfather, was sitting on the couch in the upper half of the split-level house, watching a boisterous action movie. He wasn't too much older than Jake himself, which had caused some initial friction when he'd first started dating Jake's mother.

"Do you have any clue what time it is?" His mother's voice was shrill with worry and frustration.

"I know, I know," Jake said, looking at the ground.

"And all day and night, I had to watch riots on TV. I was worried sick."

"We were caught up in some stuff, that's all. That's why I'm so late." He wasn't going to go into any more detail.

"Is everything all right?" Her voice softened and she gently touched his shoulder, as if she could sense what had happened. "Where's Matt?"

"Relax, Mom. I dropped him home before coming here."

"You've changed your shirt. Also, I thought he drove today. Where's his car?"

"It broke down. He had to get it towed to a garage. We're fine, Mom, just late." Stress and lies worked heavily on Jake, wearing his patience thin.

"You could have called and let us know you were okay."

"I sent you a text," Jake said. "It was just a work thing." He rubbed his eyes. "Mom, it's late and I'm tired. We can talk in the morning. For now, I just want to go to bed."

"Dad?" Andrew had emerged from the hallway and stood at the top of the stairs behind Jake's mother. He dragged a broken-in security blanket, which Jake had given him after Andrea had passed away. When Jake went to prison, Andrew had carried the blanket around with him everywhere.

"The prince awakens," Jake said grinning, and walked up the stairs, swooping his young son into his arms. He embraced Andrew tightly before returning him to the ground. "I'm so glad to see you, buddy. I've missed you."

"I missed you too, Dad." Andrew yawned, his eyelids drooping.

Jake took Andrew's hand before descending the stairs. "Thanks Joe, thanks Mom." He stopped and kissed his mother on her cheek. "I'll talk to you tomorrow."

"Be safe driving home." His mother followed them to the front door, halting at the entrance.

Outside, the damp spring air was filled with the chirps of crickets. Jake and Andrew walked hand in hand past the sporty SUV and the late-model pickup truck, until they reached Jake's sleek, obsidian Honda Civic. He buckled Andrew securely into the passenger seat then climbed in behind the wheel.

"Daddy was like Batman tonight," Jake said softly to Andrew, but his son had already fallen asleep.

THE SUN GENTLY crept into the office through a small crack in the blinds over the windows. Tek lay peacefully on the couch after a long night on call. Bricks, showing up for the morning, entered the office and immediately disturbed the tranquility of the room.

"Damn," Bricks said. "Did you get any sleep last night?"

Tek rolled onto his side and forced open a stubborn eye. Bricks's massive bulk lumbered toward him like a horror from a nightmare.

"Just be glad Bones dialed my number and not yours," Tek said, half into the pillow on the couch.

"Trust me, I am. I deliver the good news and I get a full night's sleep."

Tek struggled into a seated position and fished in his pocket for a cigarette. "A smoke and a coffee are what I need right about now." He flipped open the pack and plucked out a cigarette and a lighter.

"You light that in here and Bones will be pissed."

"Right. He's already going to be in a bad mood." Tek lit his cigarette and inhaled deeply. "The window is open and we can light the candle," he said and puffed out a smoke ring. "Hey, did you hear about the storm coming tonight? Tropical storm winds this early in the year." He shook his head. "Crazy stuff."

Bricks walked back to the open office door and mumbled something to the Niner standing guard outside. Tek couldn't hear the exchange, but it was a different guard from last night, so the shift change must have occurred while Tek was sleeping.

Bricks closed the door and returned to Tek.

"No, I didn't hear nothing about any storm. My ass slept last night," Bricks bragged. "Coffee is coming, so out with it."

Tek blew out another drag. "Shots were fired inside the stash house," he said, "and an anonymous tip alerted the cops. A lieutenant saw two people running from the place and followed them. He lost them when they got into some kind of work van, waiting a couple blocks away. Before you ask, he didn't get the license plate number. The cops arrived before our boys could swoop in and clean up the place. Five-0 arrested Marcus, Garrett, and Dwayne. I don't know which, but one of them was taken to the hospital. Ged and Tony weren't so lucky. Their families went to the morgue early this morning to identify the bodies. No money was recovered and the stash got confiscated."

"You think it's the same two that took out Nick and Johnny?"

"Looks that way." Tek half shrugged. "Johnny and Nick knew the rotation of the stash for this week. Johnny had to, 'cause Bones put him on guard duty indefinitely until things with Stacks settled down. He wanted to keep Johnny out of the crossfire."

"Well, that didn't work out as planned." Bricks walked behind Jones's desk, where a scented candle sat. Johnny's mother, Monica, had given it to Jones, and it had been invaluable when they'd first moved into this place and the smell of mold had dominated the entire building.

Bricks popped the rubber-lined glass cork off the candle. He snapped his fingers and Tek tossed him the lighter. "So, is this some vigilante bullshit we need to deal with now?"

"Not us," Tek said as his cigarette burned away.

Bricks turned sharply. "Who else would Jones trust with this, besides us?"

"Bones wants to lay a trap," Tek said, and slowly sketched out the plan, enjoying the feeling of being in the loop when Bricks wasn't. It wasn't too often that Bricks wasn't in on the formulation of a plan, so Tek wanted this to last as long as possible. "Jones figures they know the stash house locations for each day this week from either Nick or Johnny. We bait the house and act as if everything is normal. When they hit us, we spring the trap."

"I follow you. So you're the one to spring the trap then?" Bricks went through a list of all possible soldiers who could pull this off, but quickly crossed out all the names on his list.

"Get this," Tek said, enjoying the reveal. "Raef Deos."

"The freak?" Bricks blurted out.

There was a loud knock at the door and both Niner lieutenants looked at each other.

"Come in," Tek called out. His hand instinctively went to the gun strapped to his hip.

The guard entered with two cups of coffee. Knowing better than to say anything, he placed them on Jones's desk. Bricks gave the young man a quick nod of thanks and slipped him a twenty-dollar bill.

"Deos? Really?" Bricks said after the guard had left. He handed one of the coffees to Tek.

Tek sipped the piping hot liquid thoughtfully. He thought about getting an iced coffee later, now that it was spring and the weather was heating up, though he still refused to drink iced coffee in the morning, no matter how hot the weather was. It lacked something, as far as Tek was concerned, something essential that helped him wake up in the mornings.

"He did such a good job with the Russians," Tek said, "why not try him out on a domestic model?"

"Yeah, I guess," Bricks said, and shuddered. "Still, I don't know what it is, but I get a weird vibe out of that guy."

Bricks had yet to take a drink of his coffee. The thought of betrayal flashed through Tek's mind. He saw Bricks meeting with Stacks in Roxbury yesterday and the pair plotting to take down the Niners from the inside. Tek imagined Bricks having poisoned coffee brought in, while having already taken care of Jones before arriving at the office.

Jesus, he thought. *If you don't get yourself under control, paranoia will consume you whole.*

"Bones wants them alive," Tek said, trying to shed the treacherous feelings. "He needs them to talk before we gut them. Raef promised to make them talk." He eyed his coffee before taking another sip. He'd already taken two sips; abstaining at this point would be pointless.

"That adds some unnecessary risks." Bricks finally took a sip of his coffee and Tek let out a loud sigh. Granted, Bricks could have still poisoned Tek's coffee, but he didn't believe Bricks would trust anyone to hand him the correct cup.

"We gotta get all the details," Tek said. "Apply some pressure and make them blab information. We need to know if there are any more out there and find out why they attacked us. It's a risk, but a calculated one."

"All right. I see your point." Bricks walked towards the open window. "Any word on Stacks?" He didn't face Tek as he asked the question, but stared out at the morning.

Tek, in his turn, found it difficult to look at Bricks, so he stared at his shoes and wondered why he hadn't taken them off when he went to sleep. "No one has seen him," he said, readjusting the laces on his Converse shoes. "Last tip we got was that Roxbury place."

Bricks, staring off into the ever-expanding city landscape, spoke softly. "As long as he's out there, none of us are safe."

WALCOTT, WITH HIS cellphone clamped to his ear, disengaged the auto-drive feature of his undercover cruiser. He was parked in front of a convenience store owned by Lee Hyun. The sun had yet to climb high enough to cast out the shadows in the alleyway to Walcott's left, where two young boys had lost their lives less than twenty-four hours ago. The total death count from yesterday had yet to be reported, but estimates pointed to over one hundred fatalities and perhaps thousands injured.

Inside the store, a young, rather tall Korean man pulled a chain that flipped the small square neon sign from *Closed* to *Open*.

"Thanks, Barry," Walcott said into his cellphone. "Those Bruins tickets are yours if you can get the reports on my desk by lunchtime." He ended the phone call with the forensics officer and slid the phone into the holster strapped to his belt. A little give-and-take had always eased inter-departmental relations, and probably always would.

Stepping out of the vehicle, the detective scanned the street. There were a few locals out and about, some grieving, others already back into their normal routine of government-supported life. Yesterday they'd rioted from lack of work, but the outrage had been quelled by the violence. *With no solutions being passed by the government, what's going to stop it next time?* Walcott wondered.

It amazed him how quiet everything had become in such a short span of time, though debris still littered the streets, and broken windows dotted the landscape. Police tape still clung to a light pole near the mouth of a nearby alley. The morning was eerily calm, which made it hard to believe that a riot had gripped the city less than twenty-four hours ago.

Digital chimes rang as Walcott pushed open the store's glass door and entered. He crossed to the self-service vending machine, which filled the store with the inviting aroma of fresh coffee. He smiled politely at the employee behind the cash register, who was watching some e-sport competition on his tablet.

Walcott swiped his thumb across the machine's reader. A cup made of recycled plant fibers plopped into the cutout slot. The machine registered Walcott as the user through facial recognition software and his thumb print. It added the appropriate amount of sugar and cream without the need to press any additional buttons after the "size" option.

Walcott swirled the brew in the cup as he turned and stepped up to the counter. He placed his trifold wallet casually next to the register, letting it flop open to reveal his badge. It was an old but effective move. He plucked his omni-card out of the wallet to pay the clerk.

"You wouldn't have been working yesterday morning, would you?" Walcott asked innocently.

"I work every morning," the clerk said curtly and quickly scanned Walcott's purchase.

"So you were working while the shooting happened across the street?"

"I told the officer yesterday. I saw nothing."

"Come on now," Walcott said. "Even if you didn't see the actual shots fired, you must have heard them. Surely you saw if anyone went in or out of the alley afterwards." He pulled out a fifty-dollar bill and placed it on the counter. "Any information on this case would be greatly appreciated."

The man looked down at the note, then up at Walcott again. Without saying a word, he returned his attention to his tablet. Walcott dropped two more fifty-dollar bills on top of the first.

The clerk was only human after all, and the prospect of cash seemed to make the risk of trouble worth it. "I did see two men carrying metal briefcases," he said eventually. "They left the alley shortly after the shots were fired."

A few minutes later, Walcott walked out of the store, with his coffee in one hand and a satisfied smile on his face. He'd finally gotten his first break in the case. He placed the coffee on the hood of his car and slipped his phone from its holster.

"Hi, this is Detective Walcott, badge number seven-four-nine. I need a number for Yellow Cab Taxi Service, and the names of any commercial banks within a short driving distance of my current location."

SCOTT EDGED SLIGHTLY closer to the mourning woman seated beside him on the soft, overstuffed couch. It had been the hardest thing Scott had ever done—coming to this apartment to tell the woman he loved that her son had been transported to the Critical Care Unit of Brigham and Women's Hospital.

And, even worse, to tell her it was Scott's failings that led him to his fate.

Scott put his arm around Monica's trembling shoulders, but she shrugged it off. He turned his head away, unable to meet her sorrow-filled eyes.

"I'm sorry, Monica," he said. "I tried to keep him out of the line of fire. But I couldn't protect him." He focused his gaze on a picture hung on the wall across the room, a print of an idyllic Monet picnic.

"Johnny's all that I have," Monica said, her breath hitching between words.

"I know," Scott said. "I love Johnny like he is my own son. But you do have me, too."

Monica's hand flashed up in a blur and smacked Scott's cheek. Anger flooded into him for just a microsecond before he wrestled his emotions under control.

"He's my flesh and blood," Monica said, her jaw set defiantly.

"He's my son! Who did it, Scott? Who? Stacks and his boys? Tell me! You have to make them pay."

"Monica, try not to get yourself all worked up again. This wasn't Stacks."

"What do you mean?" Her eyes bored into Scott. "If it wasn't Stacks, who hurt my son?"

Scott didn't know how to word his thoughts. He broke his gaze with Monica. "Johnny and the others picked a fight with the wrong people."

Scott felt her fingers on his cheek as she guided his face back into her line of sight. "He was with Nick again, wasn't he?" Scott didn't have to give an answer. "That devil, I'm going to wring the life from his neck." Her hand tightened into a fist.

Scott shook his head. "I don't think it'd do much good to strangle a corpse."

Monica's eyes widened. "What?"

"He was killed by the same people, shot in the gut." Scott's phone vibrated in his pocket, the fourth time in the last half hour. "I have to go," he said. "There's still a lot to sort out today. When is your sister coming to take you to the hospital?"

Monica nodded slowly, her energy drained. "Angela will be here soon."

Scott stood up and grabbed the leather briefcase he'd personally packed before coming. He placed it carefully on the couch, next to Monica. She looked at him with hatred in her eyes.

"It's for Johnny's medical expenses. More will be coming soon. I'm going to make sure you're taken care of."

"Do you think I give a shit about money right now, Scott? All your money can't undo what was done. Throwing money around won't fix all your problems. When are you going to realize that?"

She stood and grabbed the coffee-table in front of the couch, flipping it over. Coasters and a centerpiece went flying across the floor.

Scott was glad he'd moved a few steps back. If he hadn't, he surely would have been on the receiving end of another slap. His cheek still stung from the first one.

He bent over and righted the table. He took his time to replace the centerpiece and the coasters. Then he turned to leave. With his hand on the doorknob, he faced Monica, who had slumped back down on the couch in a defeated pile.

"This is the only thing I can do right now," he said. "I have to go, but I will be back later to check up on you. And I will find the guys who did this."

DETECTIVE DATS WALKED through the bullpen of the overcrowded police station. It seemed she wasn't the only one who'd been called in to work on an off-day. She had to maneuver carefully through the bodies delivering paperwork or transporting detainees to the various facilities, lest she spill either of the two coffees she was carrying in her hands.

"So, the captain really *did* drag you in today?" Walcott called out from across the room. Dats spotted him near their shared cubicle. He had begun a slow clap as she approached the desks. The other officers who'd been conversing with Walcott vacated the area and nodded at Dats as they walked by her.

"Did John have a fit last night?"

"He'll be okay. Let's just hope the captain doesn't want me in tomorrow." She handed Walcott his coffee before blowing on her own steaming cup and taking a sip.

"Wait a second. You come in this morning with coffee and— dare I say it—a glow about you? Maybe it wasn't such a bad night for you at all."

"Very funny. You're here early, and in a good mood," Dats said.

"The reason I'm here so early," Walcott said, "is because I received a call last night about a raid on a Niner safe house. Seeing as

I am the lead detective of the gang unit, I thought I might show up to the crime scene."

"Ever the civil servant."

"I'll let that jab slide, but since I was in so early, I also picked up a lead on that alleyway shooting."

"The uniforms were whispering it was going to be a guaranteed cold case," Dats said. "How the hell do you have a lead already?"

Walcott had picked up the receiver from his desk phone and punched in a few numbers. "Hold on," he said to Dats and held up a finger. "Hey Cap, can you come out to the pit? There's something I want to run by you."

"You were saying?" Dats said.

"Let's wait for Captain Levi. I don't like to repeat myself."

A few moments passed, and Levi eventually appeared and strode across to Walcott's desk. He'd been a fit man once. He'd patrolled the streets when he first joined the force. That was before numerous promotions had landed him a squad car, then a detective badge, and ultimately a desk. Life behind a desk was starting to show around his midsection, but his famous mustache, which had spawned many jokes around the office, was still as bushy as ever.

"This better be good, Walcott," he said in his gruff, permanently perturbed-sounding tone. "I have a conference call in half an hour with the commissioner and the mayor. I have a feeling they want my ass for breakfast."

Smiling, Walcott relaxed in his chair. "I have an appetizer that may just save your day."

Levi glared at Walcott, who said nothing else. "Then spit it out," he snapped.

"Let me start at the beginning. The first shooting occurred fairly early in the day, at the vacant Clark's corner store. I noticed a Ferrari abandoned in the middle of the intersection. Several spent rounds were retrieved from the car's body. Not a common car, so I filed it away in the old mental file cabinet." He tapped his temple. "My next clue came a few blocks away, in that alleyway shooting. I returned there earlier this morning."

Dats's eyebrows rose in surprise. She wondered if Walcott ever went home anymore. "We've canvassed that area," she said. "No witnesses, no evidence."

Walcott had a twinkle in his eye and a broad smile on his face. "Police work and comedy have many things in common," he said, pointedly looking at the captain. "But one of them is timing. I went back to the Korean store directly opposite the alley around six this morning. And what do you know?" He paused for a full second, playing for dramatic effect. "The owner, a nice young fellow, well, he recalled seeing two well-dressed white males carrying metal briefcases. They fled the scene after he heard several rounds discharged."

"Descriptions?" Levi said.

"Both were in their late-twenties or early-thirties. One had blond hair; the other had darker hair, possibly dark brown or black. Both were under six feet tall. The dark-haired one was gripping his shoulder and had a blood-soaked shirt. Most likely a gunshot wound from the alleyway."

"It wasn't just another dustup from the gang war?" Dats said. She was trying to process the new information as fast as she could.

"I don't believe so. I checked the hospital records for the surrounding area and no one matching that description sought treatment for a bullet wound to the shoulder. I had a hunch from the description and those briefcases. I caught a lucky break with the ballistics report."

"They told me two weeks," Dats said. "How did you get our order moved up the list?"

Walcott opened his mouth to answer, but Levi said, "I don't want to hear how you guys bend the rules."

"Fair enough," Walcott said. "But the guns who killed our two Niners were forty-five caliber. As we all know, neither the Niners nor the Young Gunz have used anything but nine-millimeters since their rise to power." Walcott leaned back triumphantly.

Captain Levi sighed and shook his head. "So, we put out an APB for two white males with briefcases, that it?"

"No sir, but if you let me finish."

"By all means," Levi said, and made an *after you* gesture with his hand. "But hurry up. I want something more to tell the commissioner than my lead gang unit detective doesn't think it was directly related to gang activity."

"This is where the car and the briefcases come back into play," Walcott said. "A couple years ago, I responded to a shooting at a convenience store in the general neighborhood of our alleyway shooting. A private security guard foiled an attempted robbery, and in the process shot one of the perps. He worked for a company called JM Security. That's where I recognized the car from. The owners of the company had arrived in that very car to check up on their man. Both owners were young, white—and one had blond hair, the other jet black. Sound familiar? And they secured that store's deposit in a metal briefcase while they were there."

"How do you remember all this?" Dats asked incredulously.

"It's all in my report from the incident." Walcott tapped a manila envelope on his desk before pointing a finger at Dats. "Make sure your write everything down in your reports. It may not be helpful to the particular case you're working on, but you'd be surprised at how many cases overlap. Plus, I still have their business card. They offered me a job." Walcott glanced at the captain. "I wonder if they actually pay out overtime."

"Not now, Walcott." Levi glared at the lead detective. "Where does the stash house come into it?"

"I was just getting to that, Cap. After talking with the Korean shopkeep, I called our impound lot. Guess whose name is on the title of the abandoned Ferrari?" Both Captain Levi and Dats simply stared at Walcott, so he said, "Matt Nader, one half of JM Security."

"Now that is some damn fine police work." Dats was legitimately impressed, even though Walcott's reputation for thorough case work was well known.

"Thank you, I thought so too. I pulled Mr. Nader's, and his partner Mr. Talbot's, gun registrations. Both have forty-five calibers registered in their names."

"And this information ties into the stash house shooting how?" Levi said.

"The two Niners shot in the alley," Walcott said. "They were mid-level enforcers. But one of them has a special connection to our man Jones. He's the son of Jones's girlfriend. No weapons were found at the stash house, but we did find spent nine-millimeter casings."

Dats leapt from her chair. "You think Nader and Talbot hit the stash house as well, using the Niners' own weapons against them?" She thought for a second, then said, "My only question involves the motive. What did they have against the Niners?"

"Talbot had a run-in with some Niners a while back. He did some jail time for it. I'm still waiting to pull the arrest record on that case. My theory is that the alleyway was a robbery gone wrong by the Niners, and these two sought vigilante justice. The two bodies we pulled out of the stash house were shot with a nine-millimeter handgun. Our initial thought was the Young Gunz, but the method of infiltration into the house was highly skilled. They left survivors, and the drugs. The Young Gunz would have rushed the house *en masse*, murdered everyone inside and taken everything. The survivors and the number of shots fired does not support that scenario. The simplest explanation is Talbot and Nader, both of whom have advanced military training. Most of those records I didn't have clearance to view."

Levi nodded as Walcott concluded his series of hypothetical events. "Sounds like you're onto something there, detective. Tying in the stash house could prove difficult though. Shore up some more evidence on that front and issue APBs for Nader and Talbot. I want them in custody before the Niners find out what's going on, and try to dispense their own form of justice."

Both detectives nodded. "Yes, sir," they said in unison.

RICHARD AWOKE FROM the most realistic dream he'd ever had. The details were foggy but he could remember the mocking tone of a man in black. His head pounded and protested at any quick movements. His cheek below his left eye was burning and he wondered how bad the bruise was going to be. He would need to think of a good excuse for how he got it.

A still-image from the dream crystalized in his brain. He saw Julie bound by her hands as the man in black stalked around her. He carried a large blade. The smells of a salty warehouse had seemed so real, as if it wasn't a dream he was remembering, but an actual memory. The man in black's laughter had boomed in his head, filling Richard with dread. Then the man had smiled sickeningly before plunging the blade into Julie's chest, all the way to the hilt.

Richard broke out in sweat. It was only a dream, right? He suddenly wasn't so sure of himself anymore. The longer he thought about it, the less he was convinced. After all, you forget your dreams the longer you're awake, don't you? Yet Richard kept recalling more and more of the nightmare as he lay there on the floor.

His arms flailed wildly as he scrambled to his feet. He smacked into the end table, knocking over the lamp and a bottle of liquor, sending both crashing to the floor. A flashbulb memory of an insubstantial hand holding the bottle shook him. Disregarding the crash and broken glass, he bolted from his bedroom into the living room, where he leapt over the coffee table to the front door. He fumbled with the double lock and wiped his sweaty hands on his pants just so he could turn the doorknob.

He stood in the doorway, facing Julie's closed door across the hall. His heart pounded in his chest as if it were trying to escape through his throat. He took a deep breath and crossed the hallway. He pounded on Julie's door until his fist hurt.

"Julie!" he shouted, but there was no reply. Had something happened to her? Had his dream been some kind of premonition? "Please," he pleaded. "Answer your door." He slumped forward and rested his head against the wood.

A few of the floor's other residents poked their heads out of their doors. Recognizing Richard, a few promptly grew bored and went back inside. Those that remained simply stared at him, curious but apathetic.

Eventually, he heard a soft click from behind the door, and he stood up straight. The door opened and Julie stood there, red-eyed and blinking, her hair in corkscrews. Richard's breath snagged in his chest even though she looked like she'd just crawled out from under a bush.

"Richard?" she said groggily.

Exhaustion flooded through him, replacing the panic that had filtered through every pore in his body. He felt his shoulders sag as the adrenaline levels in his body receded. There she stood, unscathed. He found he was unable to speak.

What the hell is wrong with you?

"Richard," Julie repeated, now fully awake. "Is everything all right?"

Richard could feel himself blushing and he stared down at the floor. In the grain of the boards, he could almost see a crowd of wooden faces laughing at him.

"Yeah, everything is fine," he said, finally looking back up at her. "I had a bad dream that just felt very real." His answer made him blush even more.

"And you came here?" Her eyes widened with surprise or joy, Richard couldn't tell which.

"Yes, well," Richard said, "you were kind of there." He looked away. "In the dream, I mean."

"Oh, *really* Mr. Sullivan?" Julie's still-sleepy smile warmed him. "I usually charge people for dreaming about me." She tilted her head to one side and chewed her lower lip. "Then again, judging by the way you were pounding on my door, I take it that it wasn't a pleasant dream."

"You can say that again."

"I guess I could waive the standard fee, this one time, then," she said.

"Aren't you generous?"

"Only for the cute ones."

Richard smiled, but he reminded himself of his current situation. He couldn't get carried away. There were dangers in being associated with someone like himself. Even though he now knew where the danger was coming from, it didn't change the fact that it was present and close. So he said nothing and an awkward silence grew between them.

Julie cracked first. "You sure you're okay?"

"Yeah, I'll be fine." He could never tell her the whole truth.

"Do you want to talk about your dream?"

"It was just a bad dream, that's all." His mind had completed its repairs to the wall around his secrets, but his answer disappointed even himself.

"Richard, I care about you," Julie said. "I think I've made that obvious. I saw you and your friends leaving late last night. What happened? Let me help you."

"It's a long story," Richard said.

"If you never tell me, it's only going to get a lot longer. Richard, I'm not letting you leave without explaining yourself." She squared her shoulders in the doorway, like a prizefighter.

Richard couldn't help smiling, but he could also see the fragility of the walls that surrounded his secret. Julie's compassion was tearing them down as quickly as he could build them back up. He knew he couldn't go on lying to her for much longer. He finally had to admit how much he cared for her.

And that put her in danger.

"After work tonight, we can talk," Richard said. "I promise."

"I have time on the books. I can call out today. It won't be a big deal."

"No, no. Go to work. I'll be here and we can talk when you get home."

"Okay then," she said. "It's a date." She smiled a smile that was still two-parts sleep.

Richard returned her smile and she leaned in to hug him. He was momentarily lost in her warmth and she looked into his eyes and smiled again.

"Promise me you won't back out now," she said.

"What?"

"No bullshit, Richard. No last-minute phone calls. I'll come over earlier and we can talk before Greg comes up to watch the movie. Promise me." She held him frozen with her stare.

Richard hesitated. He didn't want to hurt her. He should just run, like he always did, before it was too late. How could he even begin to explain all of last night?

"I promise," he said eventually.

THE SUN CAST down oppressive rays of heat from the zenith of its daily arc. Jake stood ten paces away from his son, who held a yellow plastic bat. Jake picked up one of the two remaining wiffle balls near his feet and tossed it underhand. The strong wind made the ball dance in the air. Andrew swung the bat and narrowly missed the ball. It rolled gently behind him to join a collection of similar balls.

"That was close," Jake said. "Remember to keep your eye on the ball." He picked up the last ball and floated it through the air towards Andrew. The wind died down and the ball traveled in a straight line. The little boy swung, putting all of his meagre weight behind the bat. The ball connected solidly and sailed over Jake's head.

"Perfect!" Jake exclaimed, as only a proud father can. "See what happened when you kept your elbow tucked in like we talked about?"

Andrew dropped his bat on top of the makeshift home plate Jake had scuffed from the dirt, and began to do an impromptu victory dance. Jake was laughing at the spectacle when his phone vibrated in his pocket. The display told him it was Matt.

"Collect those balls so we can practice some more," Jake called, and answered the phone. "Matt, what's up?"

MATT WAS WALKING aimlessly around the department store while waiting for Jake to pick up his phone. Close by, Melissa, who was pushing Shelly in a stroller, browsed the clothes on the racks.

As Melissa picked up a pricey sweater, Matt couldn't help but wonder how much of a hole this shopping trip would make in the stolen stash. And whether his conscience could afford it.

Eventually, Jake picked up and said, "Matt, what's up?"

"Jake," Matt said quietly into the phone, not bothering with the usual greetings and small talk. "Listen up. I figure we hit them one last time, tonight. Then get out before the dust settles."

Jake paused a beat, then said, "Sounds good. How are we going to find out which houses they're using today?"

"We have five houses on the list. Since the cops are all over the one from yesterday, there's only one solution: a stakeout. With all the added 'Staties' on the road today, the Niners will have to con-solidate. Maybe operate out of only one or two buildings, at most."

"Great," Jake said, his voice dripping with sarcasm. "Just what I wanted to do all day today—sit in the van while the heat bakes us from the inside out. You got plane tickets yet or you going to wait until the situation has some time behind it?"

Matt chuckled. "We leave two weeks from now. I already or-dered the tickets. I gave enough time to settle our business affairs with Justin. We can meet up after I'm done shopping with the girls." He spotted Melissa walking towards him, bags full of recent pur-chases dangling from the stroller. "Jake, I gotta go. We'll talk later." He hung up before Jake could answer.

Melissa wore a satisfied smile as she approached. "Who was that, hon?"

"Jake," Matt said. "We need to meet his cousin today." Then his lies began. "We need to show him the ropes." He hated to lie, especially to Melissa, but the less she knew, the better for all involved. "A boring day of driving around the city and showing him a few of the stores we have under contract, and going over some financial reports. We probably won't even head to the office today."

In truth, Justin had only agreed to the deal in principle, and wouldn't be available for a tour for a few days yet. Matt found himself involuntarily holding his breath, awaiting Melissa's reaction. "I probably won't be home for dinner," he added.

"And I suppose you won't be home in time to do the dishes either," she said, pouting playfully, her hand on her hip in mock annoyance.

"Sorry sweetie, but if you want that dream home in sunny Florida . . ."

"Yeah, yeah," she said. "I get it."

Matt slid behind the stroller and placed both hands on the handle, gently bumping his wife out of the way with his hip. "I take it my lovely ladies are all set here?"

J AMES SAT ON the floor in silence, surrounded by the darkness of the poorly-lit basement. He had overheard that the house was ordinarily a drug resupply spot, currently shut down due to the increased police presence. The Niners had repurposed the house as a decoy to lure in a target.

James's nerves bit at him. His muscles twitched, and he ground the metallic tip of his shoelace between the toe of his sneaker and the unfinished basement floor. The dull, monotonous scraping filled the dark space.

Raef sat cross-legged in the middle of the floor. There were two hardcore gang members in the room above James's head, and that did nothing to calm his nerves. He scraped his toe against the floor one final time, and Raef's eyes snapped open. The pale man stared, and the look was so cold that it literally made James gulp.

Raef began to rise, signifying imminent punishment, but at the same moment, a small sphere of blue light winked into existence between them. It vanished almost immediately, and a muscular black man stood in its place. James held his breath, and his mind froze— the man was partially translucent, and James could clearly see anger, and recognition, on Raef's face through the newcomer's body.

"Rufus," Raef said.

The newcomer smiled, and James slowly stood up, trying not to draw attention to himself. He slunk into a dark corner of the basement, trying to squeeze as much of himself into it as he possibly could, wishing he could just dissolve into the wall itself.

"Raef," Rufus said, like a disappointed father. "Raef, Raef. You have been a very active man, these last twenty-four hours. You may be good at concealing your *Echo*, but you must have realized we would track you down."

"Your *Seekers* took long enough to find me," Raef sneered. "You are still one step behind. As always."

"Think what you will, Raef, but your time is coming to an end."

James felt a glimmer of hope spark inside him. He'd spent his whole life ignorant of the supernatural, but such forces seemed now to surround him. His life—and the world—had been broadened by these revelations, and by the beings who wielded these powers. And, it would seem, not all were allied with Raef and his master.

"Perhaps you're right," Raef said, rising from his cross-legged position. "I doubt that today is that day though. How far away are you, I wonder, as you project yourself now? I'd bet I still have plenty of time to finish my business and leave the city limits before you and your lackeys arrive. So, the real question is, what exactly are you doing here?"

"It's funny you mention 'business,'" Rufus said. "I'm not talking about your work with this group of degenerates, whom you persist in aiding, but about the one that got away. Richard Sullivan."

James saw a look of recognition in Raef's eyes, even if it lasted only for a millisecond before Raef regained his composure.

"Who is this Richard," Raef said, all innocence. "*Sullivan* did you say?"

"Don't play games. We have found a way to navigate the *Vortex*. You can thank Delphi for that. She is very talented."

Raef scowled. "He will come to me. Your seers must have told you that. You cannot protect him." Raef began pacing across the floor. James pressed back into the corner, an almost-instinctual response. "He will be a rotting corpse by the time you arrive."

Rufus wagged a translucent finger at Raef. "That has yet to be determined, but let's not get carried away. I came to pass on some information to you."

"I'm all ears, noble warrior of *justice*," Raef said.

Rufus frowned. "Oh, how I hope the day soon comes when I crush your skull with my bare hands." He paused for a moment, then said, "Do you remember operating out of this state, some twenty-five years ago?"

Raef shrugged. "I may have. My work does have me traveling a lot."

"There was a woman."

"Isn't there always," Raef said dismissively.

Rufus ignored him. "She'd just left a bar. She was looking for her car, while her husband finished his beer inside."

"Could you get to the point?" Raef said, folding his arms. "I do have a busy schedule." He began tapping his foot loudly.

"She never reached her car. You made sure of that. You had your way with her and left her there in the parking lot, cold and bleeding."

Raef waved a hand. "Add it to the list of charges the Agency has over my head. And anyway, since when does the Agency bother with such trivial matters? Did Agamemnon create a new sub-division?"

"It would be easier to make my point if you did not interrupt," Rufus said. "The woman you brutally raped, while not an *Other* herself, carried a lot of potential power. Her husband was an ordinary human, not an *Other*, nor even a carrier. And, as you know, he could not pass on the gift we share."

"Rufus, please, I already understand basic genetics. Agamemnon made us all sit through the lectures."

"The woman was born Grace Staibler. Her husband is called David Sullivan. Grace gave birth to their third son, who carried the Sullivan name, but not the seed."

Raef's eyes suddenly blazed and James could see energy slowly gathering around him. Whatever the new intruder had hinted at had set Raef off worse than calling him "sir." Much worse.

"The boy's name is Richard Sullivan, though perhaps we should call him Richard Deos. That's what you've been calling yourself lately, isn't it? We know you are hunting your son, and, more importantly, we know why."

Raef's eyes rolled back and his arms shot straight out. "You'll never understand what I had to face after being hunted!" he roared. "The sacrifices I made. Agamemnon made me seek power to survive, but I didn't know about the seed it put inside me. Now the desire to spread cannot be denied by you or anyone at the Agency. Be gone!"

Rufus's translucent body wavered under an onslaught of energetic waves. "You can cast my image out, but you cannot escape the consequences of your actions." Rufus's image became solid, fully blocking James's line of sight to Raef. It shimmered for a moment then silently exploded in a blinding blue flash.

Silence lingered in the air and James took a step away from the safety of his corner.

"Is what he said true?" James asked.

"Does it matter?" Raef said. "My orders remain the same. The boy holds a dangerous connection to me and must be removed to limit any interference with the next steps."

"But if he's of your own flesh and blood . . ." Suddenly, James's life with his father didn't seem so bad. Even though the old man drank too much, and on occasion roughed him up a bit, James could never imagine his father threatening his life. Having seen Rufus stand up to Raef, James was compelled to push his luck.

"*Sir,*" he said, chin raised.

Raef seemed to grow larger and wisps of blue smoke rose from his body. The muscles in his arms engorged to preposterous proportions. James could hear soft footsteps lightly echoing on the wooden stairs to his right. Out of the corner of his eye, he saw a pair of expensive sneakers descending. He took his eyes off Raef for only a second, but that was all it took. A fist smashed him in the face, sending him flying back against the wall.

He struck the bricks and sunk to the floor, all vision gone in his right eye. He raised his hands to block the next punch, even though he couldn't see, but Raef's next blow simply sliced through his defense and crunched into the bridge of his nose, shattering the bone. The taste of copper filled James's mouth as the vision in his good eye blurred.

He could hear the Niner on the stairs dialing on a cell phone. James's whole head seemed to swell, as if his face might burst through his skin. He struggled to stay awake. A third punch slammed him in the solar plexus, forcing the air from his lungs. He could hear the desperate attempts of his body to suck in air.

Darkness crept in from the outskirts of his vision. The pain melted away, replaced by an odd sense of acceptance. The narrow tunnel of James's vision was filled by Raef as he reared back for another blow. He closed his eyes before the fist collided with him once again.

BRICKS SHUT OFF his phone minutes before Mr. Jones walked into the office. He felt oddly naked without the phone attached to his ear after the volume of calls he'd received over the last two days.

"Afternoon, Boss," he said, slipping the warm handset into his pocket.

Jones nodded at Bricks and crossed to his chair. He sat down and closed his eyes. He exhaled loudly before opening them again. He leaned forward in his chair, elbows resting on the desk in front of him.

With his fingers steepled under his chin, Jones tracked Tek as he entered the office. Tek had gone downstairs to speak to one of his street-level scouts, corner boys whose top priority was to locate the whereabouts of Stacks and his high-ranking crew members.

"I just had a shitty morning," Jones said, dropping his hands to his desk, his palms slapping against the wood. "Give me some good news." Bricks heard a hint of desperation in Jones's voice.

"Wish I could," Tek said as he sat next to Bricks on the couch, giving him a curt nod of greeting. "No signs of Stacks yet. He's definitely underground and planning something. We had a hit in Mission Hill but by the time we got a crew there, we found nothing. On the plus side, territory-wise, the Young Gunz are practically wiped out.

Those who weren't scared off yesterday were rounded up by the police." Tek gave Jones a knowing wink, generating the first smile from Jones that Bricks had seen in days. "Their corners are deserted and our corner boys have been calling for re-ups almost as soon as we drop the package off. We may need to buy some extra supplies from the facility, considering the stash house was hit."

Jones nodded to himself. "Tell everyone to keep their eyes open. The situation seems too good to be true. The last thing we need is to get complacent and invite Stacks to strike while our guard is down."

Jones turned to Bricks, and the weight was suddenly on his shoulders. "It has been a lot of bad news recently, Bricks. Please tell me you can change that."

Bricks thought of the call he'd just received. Not knowing how Jones would take the news, he said, "We spotted the van from last night creeping around a few of our stash houses. They haven't made a move yet. We've moved the stash houses to the outer regions and set up the bait house. We figure they'll wait until dark like yesterday." Bricks hesitated, not sure how to continue.

Jones studied Bricks's face. "What are you leaving out?"

"It's Raef. Well more exactly, Raef's little puppy. The kid he was dragging around yesterday."

"Who?" Jones's face was perplexed.

Bricks couldn't think of the young man's name. "That jumpy kid with him yesterday, pale, sickly-looking." The image of the tweaky kid was clear in his mind, but the name eluded him.

"James," Tek said. "The kid's name is James."

"Yeah, that's him," Bricks said.

"So?"

"Raef killed him. Beat the life out of him, real brutal. I don't know if you want to do something about that."

Jones leaned back in his chair as he contemplated this new piece of information. Bricks knew that Jones approached every situation like a chess player, trying to plan ahead as many moves as he could without losing sight of the current position. A simple folly on the micro-level could unravel a perfect plan. Raef was a powerful force, one that Jones needed to wield for a little while longer. But they all knew that Raef had his own agenda, one that nobody could guess at. Jones leaned forward.

"Don't do anything just yet. Make sure Monk and Cutter stay on their toes. They're on their own while they babysit Raef. Shorten check-ins from an hour to half an hour. If anything else goes strange, send them some back up." Jones turned his chair to face the window. His eyes glazed over as he surveyed the cityscape. "Any other news?"

"Chop suey's the special today, down on the corner."

Jones hopped up from his chair. "Finally," he said. "*Real* good news."

MATT'S HOUSE SAT on a quiet street, in a symmetrical sub-urban layout designed for maximum efficiency, a few miles outside of the city limits. The driveways of the neighborhood were mostly empty, the occupants having left for work some time ago. A local police patrol car pulled into Matt's driveway, followed by Walcott's black cruiser. The cars blocked in the lone vehicle that occupied the driveway.

Two uniformed cops got out of the patrol car and waited for the detectives. Walcott waited as Dats adjusted her gun belt and checked the chamber of her gun, then they both climbed out of the cruiser together. Dats played the game by the rulebook through and through, Walcott reminded himself. They crossed to the awaiting patrolmen.

"You want to take the lead on this one, detectives?" the uniformed sergeant asked.

"Thanks for the offer, but this is your jurisdiction, so the call is yours." Walcott knew there was no way the sergeant would step on his case—his offer was simply a gesture of respect to the local officers.

"I have no qualms about you taking over," the sergeant said.

"Much appreciated," Dats said, and the sergeant nodded.

Walcott headed to the front door, which had a small patio attached. A child's toys were strewn all about. He maneuvered around them as Dats followed a step behind. He opened the screen door, and knocked three times on the sturdy wooden door behind it.

"Municipal P.D. Open up, please," Dats said loudly.

Walcott heard a scurrying behind the door. He could also hear the faint wail of a small child. Dats motioned for the patrolman and sergeant to circle around the house in case anyone was attempting an escape through a back exit. Once again, Walcott was reminded of his partner's textbook approach.

As the locals headed around back, the front door opened. A young woman stood in the doorway with a child cradled on her hip. The woman couldn't be a day older than twenty-five, and Walcott's instincts told him she was a babysitter.

"Can I help you?" she said.

"I'm Detective Walcott of the South Boston Gang Unit. This is my partner Detective Dats. Is Mr. Nader home?" Walcott sensed her relax at the question.

"Oh thank God," she said. "If you're looking for Matt, then you aren't here to tell me something has happened to him." She shifted the child on her hip, who was watching Walcott with big blue eyes. "I'm Melissa, his wife. You've missed Matt. He left for work about an hour ago. Is there anything I can help you with?"

Walcott's mind raced over a few things she could help him with but decided it was best to leave them unsaid. He'd turned a corner and those days of indiscriminate promiscuity were long behind him. He was confident he wouldn't act on his urges again, but there was nothing he could do to stop the thoughts darting through his mind. He closed his eyes while he centered himself.

"No ma'am," he eventually said.

"Why do you want to talk to Matt?"

"His car was abandoned during a shooting yesterday. We were looking to ask him a few questions about that." He didn't mention that her husband was also wanted for questioning in a murder investigation. He did this not to spare the wife, but so as not to spook the suspect into hiding.

"He mentioned he had to leave his car, but didn't say too much else."

Walcott fished in the inner pocket of his jacket and drew out a business card. He handed it to the worried wife. Her fingers gently brushed his as she took the card from him, and it sent his heart racing. He couldn't help it. "Here's my card," he said, ignoring it as best he could. "If you talk to your husband could you please have him call me, or if you have any more information, don't hesitate to call me yourself."

"Thank you, detectives. I'll make sure Matt calls you."

"Thank you, ma'am," Walcott said. Melissa closed the door before Dats released her grip on the screen door's handle.

"Now that," Walcott said, "is one good-looking broad."

Dats shook her head in disbelief. "What would your wife say if she heard you say that?"

"I'm not doing anything. I was just admiring the female form. Ain't no harm in that."

"Keep it in your pants, big boy," Dats said before nodding at the two approaching uniformed officers.

"Thermal drone didn't register any other movement inside the premises," the sergeant said while closing some program on his armband interface. "You want to pull a warrant for the property?"

"Not yet," Walcott said. "I think we're all set here, guys. Thanks for the backup. Let us know if Mr. Nader registers any hits with you guys."

"Will do, anytime."

The patrolman and sergeant headed back to their cruiser and Walcott's radio chirped.

"Walcott, you on?" the dispatcher asked.

"Yeah, go ahead."

"Units just checked in at seventy-nine Center Street. No answer at the door, no cars in the driveway."

"Received. We're returning empty-handed as well."

RICHARD LOUNGED ON the couch in his apartment, staring at the white, textured ceiling while the afternoon news buzzed in his ears. He feared drifting off to sleep after last night's scare. The event played over in his mind. That shadowed figure standing in his bedroom held firm in his memory, unlike the nightmare that came after.

He did his best to resist the need that was growing in his brain. Julie and Greg would be stopping by later and neither approved of his drinking habits. He touched his forehead again, still surprised by the lack of a mark. Even though he had no wound, his head was still pulsing with pain. A drink could easily dull that pain.

On the TV, the news switched from the weather report back to the news desk. "Looks like a scary storm on the horizon there, Chip. Thanks for the update, we'll check in with you later.

"Now, back to our main story. It seems that the tragic events of yesterday continued into the evening. Police were dispatched to an Oak Street residence, believed to be an abandoned house where they found two known members of the Niners street gang, Jason Serre, aged twenty-seven, and Anthony Sylvester, aged nineteen. Both men had been shot dead."

Dead.

Richard sprung from the couch and focused on the clean cut,

cookie-cutter anchor. "Three other gang members, whose names have not been disclosed, were bound with plastic cuffs, but did not suffer fatal injuries. Police also found several kilos of marijuana, and six kilos of cocaine in the basement. Earlier, the police commissioner held a press conference."

The picture cut to a furious police commissioner. "Let me be the first to say," he said, "in spite of what some are whispering, that this is a crime. The people who did this need to be brought to justice. Street vigilantism will not be tolerated in our city." He slammed his fist on the podium before him. The State Seal on the front shifted off-center.

"Let me reiterate," he went on, "two people were murdered last night. It matters not their background or past deeds. We live in the United States of America and everyone deserves the chance of a fair trial. The individuals who did this stripped those young men of that right." Spittle flew from his mouth, easily caught by the ultra-high definition cameras.

The commissioner ranted on, but Richard was no longer listening. He began pacing the length of his couch, turning at the arm rests. "What did you guys do?" he said.

"Friends of yours?" a husky voice suddenly said behind him.

Richard ducked as he turned around, braced for anything. The brute of a man in the room appeared to be only slightly older than Richard, but he had smooth, dark skin. Something in his eyes suggested he was much older—or perhaps wiser—than his appearance indicated. The man was pointing at the TV.

"I'm not afraid anymore. I know what you are," Richard said to the apparition.

"Oh really?" The man's muscles were practically bursting through the seams of his finely-crafted shirt. "You know what I am?

Then pray, tell me: what am I?"

"You're just an image or a vision, sent here to torment me."

The man's face softened into a half-smile, which chilled Richard, despite its apparent sincerity. "I'm impressed. You're close but not spot on. My name is Rufus, and my presence is indeed a projection. The reason I am in your living room is because of Raef." Richard tensed up at the name.

Rufus slowly raised his arms, palms facing Richard. "Yes, *because* of Raef, but not on his behalf. I'm here to extract you."

Richard snorted at the notion of a savior. "Extract me? I guess you're running late."

"I apologize," Rufus said, his smile gone. "During your Awakening, Raef responded to your *Echo* faster than we could. He is bound to you, and a *Vortex* has opened up around you. We do not fully understand the nature of the *Vortex* or what caused its birth, but it has been a barrier stopping us from reaching you."

Richard heard the words and understood the individual meanings, but none of it made any sense. "Was that in English?"

"Let me elaborate. There is a *Network* of power in this world, a source of unimaginable energy. By using the mind's subconscious, there are people who can manipulate this power into different physical manifestations. These people, we call *Others*. You and I are *Others*. When you use your powers to heal people, you draw power from this global reserve. We call this the *Network*."

"I have heard some of this," Richard said, and thought of Raef's words from the previous night.

"Interesting," Rufus said, almost to himself. "When an *Other* uses their power, they draw it from the *Network* which leaves an impression of their aura. This *Echo*, as we have come to call it, can then be used to trace the person who drained the energy. The *Vortex* that surrounds you scrambles your *Echo*."

"Raef said my *Echo* was fuzzy," Richard said, though he was still uncertain of what this really meant.

Rufus scratched his head—or his projection did, at least. "He must have meant it in a tracking sense. In addition to the *Vortex*, he has a kind of wardship over you that makes your *Echo* near-invisible to everyone but himself. Until he is killed—or until we are able to recover the device he has used to cast the ward on you—you will remain invisible to us. My people used Raef's own scrambled *Echo* to locate you here in your apartment.

"The 'fuzziness' was probably due to an inebriated state. Drinking or being high—hell, even a concussion—could have an effect on your *Echo*."

Richard tried to absorb the massive amount of information being thrown his way. "I get it. I think. Most of it, anyway."

"Good, that was the easy part. This next pill might be a bit more difficult to swallow."

"There's always a hard part, isn't there?"

Rufus wore a sympathetic smile. "For you, it appears so."

"Let's have it then."

"Your two friends from the TV are going to die tonight."

The words struck Richard's core. All the self-pity that had built up inside him was flushed out in an instant. He took two aggressive steps towards the intruder in his living room. "How?" he demanded.

"They are planning on robbing another Niner drop-point tonight.

But the Niners have laid a trap. And Raef will spring it."

Richard stared at the apparition. "How do you know about the first robbery?" he said. "And how do you know they are planning another one? They never mentioned anything to me."

Rufus shrugged. "Perhaps they didn't. But these gangsters are no joke. They contracted Raef to deal with your friends."

Richard snatched his cell phone from the coffee table in front of the couch. "Bullshit. There's no way I'm going to let them die."

He found Jake's number in his contacts-list first, and dialed it. After many rings, Jake's voicemail picked up.

"Fuck!" Richard slammed the phone back down on the coffee table, splitting it into three pieces. The back cover flew towards the TV while the battery popped out in the opposite direction.

"Calm down," Rufus said. "We need to get you to a safe place before Raef is done with your friends and comes looking for you."

"Calm down? *Calm down?*" Richard glared at Rufus. "Do you really believe I could abandon my friends?"

"I know it's difficult, but you must realize something. In the past sixty years, you are the only person who has been born with the gift of healing. You are a vital asset to the Agency. One that we cannot afford to lose."

"Agency? What Agency?"

"I belong to a group that is tasked with keeping renegade *Others* like your father in check." As the words left his mouth, Rufus immediately clamped it shut.

"My father? What does he have to do with any of this?"

"Your father? Did I say that?"

"'Renegade *Others* like my father,' you said." Richard suddenly didn't like the way this conversation was turning.

Rufus paused then sighed loudly. "I hate these sensitive missions," he said wearily. "It's much easier when they just say, 'There's the bad guy, go stop him.'"

"Forget all that, Rufus," Richard said. "What did you mean about my father?"

"You deserve to know the truth," Rufus said, and fixed Richard with a level gaze. "David Sullivan is not your father. Raef Deos is."

Richard opened his mouth to reply, to tell Rufus to stop playing silly games, but no sound emerged. Instead, he slumped onto the couch. There'd always been some hidden suspicion, buried deep in his mind, and there'd been the taunts and insinuations during his childhood. Richard had determined a long time ago that David Sullivan would always be his father, whatever happened. But to have the blood of a monster like Raef Deos in his veins . . .

It was too much for Richard to absorb. He couldn't process it.

"He raped your mother outside of a bar," Rufus said quietly.

"Enough, I don't need to hear any more." Richard didn't need the details. The fact itself was horror enough.

"I'm sorry. I didn't want you to think your mother betrayed Mr. Sullivan."

Richard dragged his hands down his face from forehead to chin, stretching the skin taut. "All those taunts and the ridicule, they were all true," Richard said to himself. Each insult was vividly clear as he relived them.

"It doesn't change who you are, or your importance to us at the Agency."

Richard shook his head. "Of course it changes who I am. But it doesn't change my importance."

Rufus smiled. "Good, I'm glad you understand. I recommend you leave the city and head south immediately. I'm heading north on a train as we speak. My associate and I could meet you someplace near Rhode Island."

"You don't understand," Richard said. "My importance is to my friends, not your Agency. I've been running for too long now. I've done enough running. Raef—my 'father,' if that's what he is—he must be stopped."

"Not a wise decision. Our seers have predicted multiple outcomes for what will transpire tonight. If you face off against your father, most outcomes end poorly for your friends. None end well for you."

"I have to save my friends!" Richard shouted. "Can't you understand that?"

"If you try, you die," Rufus said flatly. "In every possible outcome, the only constant is, if you square off against Raef, you die."

"And what happens to Raef?"

"Some of our seers say that karma finally catches up with him, while one says he walks away scot-free. There tends to be some degree of contradiction in their premonitions, something about the flow of time. Listen, you can save more lives by leaving this place. Don't turn yourself into a martyr. Besides, how can you save your friends when you don't even know where they are?"

Richard had a sudden thought, and he stood, taking a step towards Rufus's insubstantial image. "I don't need to know where they are to know where they're going," he said. "The only thing I need to do is to locate Raef and wait." He smiled at Rufus. "If he can track me using the *Network*, I can track him the same way."

Rufus shook his head. "It takes years of practice to hone one's tracking sense, not to mention that Raef is an expert in masking his *Echo*. You can't possibly hope to locate Raef without the proper training."

"Watch me."

RICHARD CLOSED HIS eyes and searched deep within himself. His eyelids fluttered as he felt his weight melt away. Images of his surroundings seeped into his vision, even though his eyes remained closed.

He was ascending a pale blue tube, the edges of which wept like a waterfall. Beyond the tube, the sky was splotchy black, lacking a sun. Dark, torn clouds rolled massively around, like the eye of a hurricane. Eventually, he recognized the busy city beyond the tube, the buildings swaying impossibly back and forth in the wind.

As he looked around, he suddenly realized that he had no perception of a body, that his mind was all there was to him. The shock broke his focus and he started to plummet back the way he'd come. He forced the horror of his incorporeal self to the back of his mind and concentrated. His fall slowed and halted. He rose once again.

The screaming winds and swaying buildings made it hard for Richard to see anything clearly. He concentrated on his vision, focusing on one building near him. After a moment, the wind died down and the swaying of the world outside eased.

High above the skyline of the city, Richard could see for miles around. Buildings were almost transparent, like thermal scans or x-ray images, and Richard could peer through multiple structures simultaneously. Little white sparks of light dotted the landscape everywhere he looked. Mixed in with the sparks of light were blue and red spheres of varying brilliance, though these were scarcer than the swarms of white lights.

If I can find that icy chill . . .

His thoughts were as loud in his mind as a raised voice.

A particular red speck of light in a high-rise building caught Richard's attention. He focused on it, and was immediately there. The shadowy outline of a man sat on a couch in a room near the top of the building. The red light originated inside the man's skull and radiated outwards. Richard had never seen this man, or this room, but he knew without a doubt that this man was not Raef Deos. He snapped back to his vantage point high above the city.

He scanned the horizon, mentally blocking out the white lights. He grasped the idea that those lights belonged to ordinary humans— it was as if the *Network* was teaching Richard about itself. He found he could completely filter out the white lights, and the hollow city grew darker without those specks, leaving only a few red and blue lights to illuminate it.

A red flare, like a rising sun cresting the horizon, drew Richard's attention. He flung himself across the city, towards the flash. A familiar chill penetrated his mind, and he mentally shuddered. The world wavered with him.

It was the largest red glow that Richard had seen so far, and though he'd flung himself so far and fast that he'd lost track of where he was, the light was emanating from a man in a basement room. He sat cross-legged on the floor, in some kind of meditative trance, and as Richard appeared before him, the man's eyes snapped open. His mouth did not move, but a voice spoke in Richard's mind. A voice Richard recognized.

"Rufus, you must be improving your interactions within the *Network*. I thought my ward would keep you away a while longer." Raef stopped speaking and stared at Richard. "You are not Rufus."

Raef stood up abruptly. Richard wasn't sure if Raef actually stood up in the real world, or if only his avatar stood up in this new world, independent from his physical body.

"Richard?" Raef sounded genuinely shocked. He walked around Richard, smiling. "Your skills impress me, boy. Now, the real challenge is to see if you can find me in the material world."

A flood of red energy erupted from Raef's body and rushed at Richard, engulfing him. Pain lanced through his mind and the new world around him faded to nothingness. When the searing pain finally dissipated, Richard opened his eyes and saw his apartment in natural colors and with solid walls. Rufus stood before him, arms crossed.

"I'm baffled," the muscular man said. "Not many people can access the *Fringe* without any proper training. Hell, even I'm still not that great at it." He shook his head and peered closely at Richard. "Judging by your return, I assume you found what you sought."

Richard struggled up from the couch and stepped past Rufus, giving him no more than a passing glance. He scooped up the bits of his cell phone, and placing the pieces back together, he went into the cramped bathroom. He dug inside the cabinet below the sink. He pulled the old revolver from its box and tucked it into his belt. As he left the bathroom he passed Rufus again, who stood motionless, watching.

"Wait!" Rufus called.

Richard stopped at the apartment's door and turned, making no effort to mask the irritation on his face. "What?"

"I can't stop you, can I?"

"I couldn't live with myself if I didn't at least try."

"Even if it cements your own death?"

"I thought we already went through this. I'm wasting time."

He turned his back to Rufus and pulled the door open. A weird notion washed over him: This would be the last time he would walk through his doorway.

Behind him, Rufus's image slowly faded. He turned his head to the left, away from the departing Richard, addressing someone who wasn't in the apartment.

"The kid is decisive," he said. "Got to give him that."

T HE EVENING SUN was setting as Matt and Jake slowly rolled down the desolate city block in their work van. The long, hot day of surveillance had left Matt feeling groggy and irritable. He blinked the strain out of his eyes, placing his binoculars on the center console.

"Any more activity?" Jake asked from the driver's seat.

"Not really." As the van approached the end of the road, Matt pointed towards a boarded-up house, from which a young man in baggy pants and a muscle-shirt emerged. He hopped into a black SUV that was parked at the curb. He carried a partially filled plastic garbage bag.

"We got another runner," Matt said. "Dropping off money and picking up the goods."

"That's the fourth drop-off we've seen here. This is the only spot on the list that has any activity." Jake popped a chewy fruit candy into his mouth.

Matt adjusted his chair, reclining back. The sun filled his eyes, forcing him to squint. He stretched his cramped legs, working out the slow accumulation of lactic acid in his thighs. "I can feel that warm Florida sand between my toes."

Jake smiled. "You'll be extra happy when you don't have to lug out a snow shovel this winter."

Matt extracted a folded piece of paper from his pocket. "Check this out," he said and passed the paper to Jake. "It's for sale, a nice garage with three full bays."

"Very nice," Jake said, scanning the printout and peering at the image of the garage at the top of the ad. "Did you place a bid yet?"

"Not yet. I've sent a real estate agent to check the place out and get me some more financial reports. She's supposed to call later and update me." Matt rubbed his hands together like an excited child.

"The deed has yet to be done," Jake said, "so let's try and keep our heads in the here and now, not in Florida. We still have to make it through tonight, with no safety net. Also, the chances of getting caught have risen exponentially." He gazed out the window contemplatively. "Are you sure it's a wise decision not to involve Richard?"

"You saw him yesterday. He was slinging back the booze even though he was supposed to be the driver. He looks like shit, an old man compared to us, and he hasn't seen half the horrors we have. He refused our offer of money and his visions are growing worse. It's for the best if he knows nothing about tonight. He doesn't need the added stress."

As if on cue, Jake's cell phone chirped. He looked at the front screen and his face dropped. "Speak of the devil," he said and pressed the *Ignore* key. "You're right, he did look run down." A sudden thought brought a smile to his face. "You know, we could stop by in a few days and accidentally leave him a present. Just a small amount to help him out. We'll say it's your cash. It's not like he'd go all the way to Florida to return it."

Matt laughed. "Knowing Richard, he just might."

RICHARD SHUT HIS apartment door behind him, leaving the fading image of Rufus alone in the living room. He flicked through his phone, ready to call Matt. He had to warn them. He was startled when he caught sight of Julie, still in her nursing scrubs. She was headed to her apartment across the hall. Richard quickly shut the door behind him and inhaled deeply, slowing his breathing, hoping his heart would respond in kind.

"Julie." Richard's mind was filled with his last words to her.

"Hey, Richard. I'm just getting off my short shift now. I'll head over in a bit."

"I'm so sorry, there's been an emergency," he said. He couldn't believe things had spiraled down even further from when he'd made his promise.

She crossed her arms and gave him a hard look. "What did I say, Richard? No bullshit."

"I know I promised, but it's too dangerous. I can't involve you, not now—"

Julie stepped up close and planted her soft lips upon Richard's. He was stunned. The brief kiss was over before he had time to react.

"I'm involved whether you like it or not. You promised."

"I've learned some things since I made that promise. If I'd

known before, I never would have made it."

"Richard, make all the excuses you want. I'm coming with you wherever you go, whatever you say. So, start by explaining 'some things.'"

"Where do I start?" Richard said. "I'm Saint Michael. What else? Well, I helped my two best friends rob some drug dealers. What's next? Oh yeah, some guy who is my father—who wants me dead by the way—is going to kill them tonight. Oh, and I almost forgot, he has crazy supernatural powers that I don't even know about probably. So now I'm going to go use some special power of my own to track down my 'father' before he can hurt them. Did I mention that this guy—my 'father'—wants to kill me?"

If he was lucky, she'd think he was insane, and maybe that'd be enough to scare her off.

She stared at him in silence for a long time. Eventually, she said, "I knew it."

She chewed her lip and turned in a circle on the spot, as if her body didn't know how to react to this information. She shook her head, chewed her lip some more. Finally, she gazed up at him, and her eyes were wide and shiny.

"The Saint Michael part," she said. "I always had a hunch. The rumors started shortly after you started work. I've read all sorts of articles online about people like you. Well, not healers like you, but other superhumans. People always think these things are junk, but I knew they had to be true. I'm so sorry about everything else. What are we going to do now?"

Richard was baffled. He couldn't understand why she was so willing to help him. They were pretty close and they'd talked about a lot of stuff, but this was life or death. His instinct was to run, but he knew he couldn't bail.

"Julie, I'm going to confront this guy and stop him. I can't ask you to do this."

"Well, I'm telling you I *am* doing this. You've been here for me when I needed you, but I couldn't be there for Claire when she needed me. You talked me through that rough spot in my life. You helped to heal me, Richard, without using your powers. I am going to be there for you when you need me."

"A million things could go wrong. You could lose your job if the police get involved. Or you could get hurt. Badly hurt." He saw a brief image from his dream. "Or worse."

"How much longer do you think I'll last as a nurse? Ten years if I'm lucky. With nowhere close to anything I can retire on. They are phasing us out. Soon only the richest hospitals will have nurses and with the first batch of gene therapy, babies will be graduating college soon." Julie snorted and shook her head. "I know what I'm doing, and I want to do this."

"Okay, but when we get close to Raef you stay far away from him. He's the most dangerous thing I know of, and he will use your safety against me."

"I promise," Julie said.

WHAT'S THE DEAL with this apartment building?" Dats asked. It wasn't the worst she'd seen. It reminded her of a place she used to rent while going through college. Not upscale by any means but she had fond memories of her old place.

"I told you already," Walcott said. "The taxi service said they dropped off two white males fitting the description I got from the Korean store owner. One of them had a shoulder wound."

"And the significance of this floor?"

"Two people in this building work for a city hospital. Both live on this floor. One is only a custodian, but the other is a nurse, Miss Julie Ezra."

Dats nodded as she followed Walcott's line of reasoning. "I get it. Since there were no hospital records for our suspect, that means he sought aid from a friend who had some medical experience."

"Exactly." Walcott pointed at a blonde girl dressed in scrubs. She was talking with a disheveled-looking man. She was younger than Dats, couldn't be more than a few years out of med school. "That looks like our nurse right there."

Walcott's phone rang in his pocket. "It's the station," he said, pulling it free and squinting at the screen. "They probably want an update. Start without me."

He retrieved Julie's bio, which the hospital had emailed to the police precinct per his request. He handed the photo to Dats. She approached the pair as Walcott wandered away down the hallway, speaking into his phone. She wondered what the connection between the nurse and the two suspects could be. The pair looked nervous.

"Excuse me, miss. I'm Detective Dats and that is my partner Detective Walcott." She pointed at her boss. "Could we ask you a few questions?"

The nurse paused and looked at the scruffy guy beside her, but eventually she said, "Yes. Sure. What's this about?"

"This may take some time," Dats said to the man. "Who are you?"

"I live in the building."

"Why don't you give us some privacy?"

The man started to protest but Julie stopped him. "It's all right. I'll be fine. I know you're in a rush and if I can I'll catch up somehow."

Dats watched the man walk down the hallway and past her partner, who was hanging up his phone. The guy took the stairwell that she and Walcott had just ascended. Walcott moved to join the conversation.

"Just getting started," Dats said to Walcott. He nodded and Dats regarded the suspect. "Like I said, I'm Detective Dats and this is Detective Walcott. We have some questions about last night. What were you doing around midnight?"

"I was home. I'd worked second shift, so I would've been either cooking or cleaning before bed."

Walcott grabbed two photos from his pocket. These were from

the ATF database. They were the license-to-carry photos for the two main suspects in the alleyway shooting, Matt Nader and Jake Talbot. Walcott presented the photos to the nurse.

"Have you seen these two people before?" Dats was glad that Walcott had let her take the lead here. Her more senior partner tended to get a little too chummy with younger female suspects like this one, and she couldn't stomach much more of *that*.

"Yes," Julie responded. "I've seen them."

Dats was thrown, just a little. According to Walcott's reasoning, this woman should have denied ever seeing these men, if only to protect herself. Dats saw the same uncertainty mirrored in Walcott's face.

"They came to you last night, looking for medical help," Dats stated. She left out the details. She should be happier than she was. This was the link to Nader and Talbot, but something wasn't sitting right with her.

"No," Julie said, blinking in confusion. "They looked fine to me."

"Don't lie to us. Why else would they have been here?" Dats asked. The nagging suspicion that something was amiss tugged at her harder.

Julie sighed. "Okay, fine. They got into a scuffle with some gang members. They got cut and came to me to get patched up."

Warning lights flashed in Dats's mind. She saw all the tells of a lie. This nurse was going to tell them anything they wanted to hear.

"They didn't come to see you," Dats said. Walcott's shoes scuffed against the wooden floor as he shifted his body towards her. She put up a hand in his direction without bothering to look at him.

"Who did they come to see?"

"Honestly, they came to see me. They were both hurt bad and I fixed them up and then they left."

"No they didn't," Dats said. "I know you're trying to protect someone, but you're only hurting them. Who did they come to see here? Is there a doctor you have a side job with? If you care about this person you will tell us before he gets himself hurt."

Julie looked down at the floor, then back up at Dats. Her eyes were wide and sad. "Okay," she said. "They came to see Richard." She chewed at her lip and frowned. "But he's a good man. He only helps people. He would never hurt anyone."

"Richard Sullivan?" Walcott said. "The custodian?"

"That's right," Julie said. "I'd just finished cleaning the kitchen and I didn't want my garbage stinking up the place. Richard passed me while I was throwing the trash in the dumpster out back and those two were with him."

"This apartment, right across the hall?" Walcott asked, pointing at it with his chin.

The nurse nodded and Dats said, "Did either of the men have a shoulder wound?"

"It was dark out, but I don't think so. They looked fine."

Walcott crossed the hall and knocked on the custodian's door, three loud, short raps.

"You just missed him, detective," she said, still biting her lip.

Dats was truly confused. All the evidence put those men at the murder scenes, yet this nurse couldn't confirm a gunshot wound. Dats was convinced these two were the men they were looking for, but a seed of doubt had been planted. Could they be following a wrong lead? They knew for a fact that one of the gunmen in the alleyway shooting had been wounded. Blood from the site confirmed it. She was trying to sort through all the conflicting information when Walcott suddenly sprinted down the hall.

"*Goddamn!* The guy was just standing here!" he shouted.

"At this point, I am placing you under arrest," Dats said as she pulled out her handcuffs. "We have more questions for you down at the station."

"I don't care what you do, just make sure you help Richard. I think you're right, he is in danger. He said he was going to fight some powerful guy, an *Other*."

Her words made Dats pause in applying the cuffs. She frowned at the nurse. *Is she off her rocker?* she thought to herself.

"Come on, Dats. He's already got a head start on us," Walcott called out from somewhere down the stairs.

RICHARD WAS EXHAUSTED as he rounded the corner of the next city block. Alternating between running and searching through the *Network* had left Richard both physically and mentally drained. The sun was setting as he scanned the street, and, unsure of which direction to head in next, he closed his eyes and hurled his consciousness high into the skyline of the newly-discovered *Fringe*.

Richard was able to locate the space that Raef still occupied. He did not dare get as close to the red light as he had before. Whatever power Raef had used on him earlier still left his brain raw, and focusing out the *Vortex* drained him even more. Richard could hear Raef's voice beckoning to him across the distance between them. Richard recoiled, snapping back to his body.

He peered around, once his senses had fully returned to him. A car had been following him for the last two blocks, and when Richard glanced behind, it rounded the corner he'd just left. Fear gripped him. Raef must have sent somebody to find and eliminate him before he could save his friends. He was shocked that Raef had acted so fast.

He turned and sprinted on, past a closed convenience store with shutters locked firmly in place, and then down an alley next to it. Glancing back, he saw the black car stop at the mouth of the alley.

"Shit!" He gasped. He was still looking over his shoulder when he ran into a chain-link fence that divided the alley. He bounced off it, fell to the ground, and immediately jumped back up to scale it.

From inside Walcott's cruiser, Dats watched as their latest lead slammed comically into the fence, like a stooge in an old silent movie. She couldn't quite contain her laugh. "Well, we've got him now," she said.

She hopped out of Walcott's car and headed down the alley. She drew her service pistol as Sullivan attempted to scale the fence.

"Police!" she yelled. "Down off the fence! Hands where I can see them! Now!"

The suspect complied immediately, which surprised her. He hopped off the fence and turned to her, a puzzled look on his face. "Police?" he said. "I think you have the wrong person, officer."

"It's *detective*, and I doubt it. You are Richard Sullivan." It was a statement, not a question.

"Well, maybe you do have the right person," he said. "Why am I under arrest?"

"Currently, you're not. You're wanted for questioning. Turn back around and put your hands on the fence."

He did as instructed and Dats cautiously approached and patted him down quickly and efficiently. She discovered the revolver in his belt immediately and removed it, stuffing it in her own waistband.

"I have a permit for that," Sullivan said.

Dats put a hand on his shoulder and turned him around. "Where you headed?" she said, watching him carefully, trying to gauge his reactions and motives.

"Nowhere in particular."

"Do you know Jake Talbot and Matt Nader?"

"Sorry, ah, detective, that doesn't ring any bells."

This guy's an amateur, she thought, for she could read his face like a large-print book. There were better liars in kindergarten.

"You know, I can ask these questions down at the station if you prefer," she said. "We have a witness who will attest to seeing all three of you leave your apartment last night." She tapped her foot impatiently. "The choice is yours. I'll ask again: Do you know Jake Talbot or Matt Nader?"

"I do," Sullivan said and looked at the ground.

"You wouldn't happen to be heading over to see them, would you?"

"Possibly."

"Tell you what, you can tell me where they are so me and my partner can have a little chat with them. How does that sound?" For the first time today, Dats felt as if they might actually catch a break in this case.

"I can't do that."

"Are we being difficult again?"

"It's not that, it's just . . ." Sullivan's voice trailed away as he evidently attempted to compose his thoughts. "I'm not exactly sure where they are."

"What do you mean?"

"I don't precisely know where they are yet, but I can find them."

"You waiting on a phone call or something?"

"Yeah, 'or something,'" he said.

Dats's weirdo-detector was ringing alarms all over the place. If this guy was unstable, she'd have to be careful and remain in tight control of the situation. "What do you mean?" she said, but she didn't like where the conversation was heading.

Sullivan's head snapped up sharply, and Dats took an involuntary step backward. He stared into her eyes, but she was suddenly sure he was seeing more than her meat and bone. She felt stripped bare. She still had her gun trained on the man but the situation was no longer in her control.

"If I told you what that meant," Sullivan said slowly, all emotion drained from his voice, "you'd take me to a mental hospital. And that wouldn't be good for my friends."

"Take it easy," Dats said calmly. What the nurse had said came back to her:

Other.

This needed a different approach now, so she lowered her gun and put it back in its holster. She could read Sullivan, and what she saw posed no threat to her. "Tell me what you're talking about."

He looked at her steadily, and Dats saw that he was terrified. "Screw it," he said eventually. "Here goes nothing."

WALCOTT SAT IN the cruiser, watching the exchange between his partner and the suspect. He was glad to see Dats growing into a fully-independent detective, capable of handling the increased responsibilities and pressures. At length, she took the suspect by the arm and led him back towards the cruiser.

Walcott grabbed the radio mic. "Dispatch, we have a person of interest in custody. Dats is returning with the perp to the car now. I'll check in again later." He slipped the microphone back into its holder as Dats opened the rear door and helped the hospital custodian into the back seat. She slammed the door shut and opened the passenger door, silently falling into the seat, eyes forward.

"Julie!" Sullivan said from the back.

Walcott examined the guy through the pane of bulletproof glass that divided the interior of the vehicle. He didn't look like much of anything, certainly not a killer, but Walcott had been proven wrong about appearances in the past. *The sight of the nurse in the back sure gave him a shock*, he thought.

"Hey guys, detectives. She has nothing to do with this," Richard said in a rush. "You can let her go. She doesn't need to go with us."

"Richard, just sit back. I'm coming with you," Julie said.

"So?" Walcott said to Dats, ignoring the pleas from the back.

Dats snapped out of her trance and blew out a long sigh. "This guy is either high as a kite, or . . . I don't know. He says he's going to lead us to Nader and Talbot. Just drive."

She shook her head and placed Sullivan's confiscated revolver in the glovebox of the cruiser before locking it. She turned to face the suspect.

"Tell my partner what you told me," she said.

M ATT WATCHED FROM a darkened alley as Jake climbed through the second-floor window of the stash house. Night had crept upon the city, concealing their infiltration, but suspicion tugged at Matt. While it had been fairly busy during daylight hours, no one had come or gone from the vacant house in over an hour.

Matt couldn't hear Jake's soft footfalls inside the building. Jake could be stealthier than a gentle breeze when the situation demanded it. Matt could feel tension building within him as he waited for the all-clear signal. It seemed to take an age for Jake's arm to appear at the window, waving.

Just like at the previous stash house, Matt scaled a drainage pipe to the window and hauled himself through.

"*Déjà vu*," Jake muttered.

Matt scanned the rundown bedroom that had been colonized by insects and rodents. Rat droppings littered the floor and a ratty mattress leaned against the wall.

"I don't see anyone tied up," Matt said.

Jake scowled. "It's not that. I just get a sense that we've been here before."

Matt had no such feelings. The room was about the same size as their breach point the night before, but this was in a worse state of disrepair. Water stains dotted the walls, and the ceiling was full of holes.

Matt motioned towards the doorway. "Check the hall." He pulled out his stolen nine-millimeter and flipped off the safety.

Jake crossed to the door, peered around it briefly, then went out. He strolled back into the room a moment later.

"Nothing," Jake said, frowning. "I can't even hear a whisper."

"Something isn't right here," Matt said. "With the amount of business they were running through this place, there's no way they packed everything up and left without us eyeballing them."

Jake nodded, then suddenly froze. He stared at the open door. "You heard that, right?"

"I didn't hear anything."

"There it is again." Jake turned around, facing the hallway.

"I can't hear shit. The last thing we need right now is for you to start losing your mind."

"How can you not hear that? It's coming from downstairs." Jake walked into the hallway and disappeared to the right.

Matt slowly followed, his gun at the ready. Jake was down the hallway, standing at the head of the stairs. As Matt walked forward to join his partner, Jake jumped, startled.

"Andrew?" he said.

Matt was completely baffled now. What would Jake's son be doing in a place like this? That made no sense at all. "What about Andrew?" he said as he drew up beside his friend. Illogical thoughts of the Niners kidnapping Jake's son briefly flashed across his mind, but he dismissed them as quickly as they appeared.

Suddenly Jake bolted down the stairs. He took the steps three at a time. Before Matt could properly take everything in, Jake was out of sight, leaving Matt alone on the landing.

This night was getting weirder—and more dangerous—by the second. They shouldn't have raided this stash house. They'd pressed their luck too far. These Niners weren't stupid, just neglectful of the law.

"Shit," he hissed, and, with no other option open, he descended the stairs, one creaky step at a time.

At the bottom, Matt peeked into the dilapidated living room. It held a couch with stuffing boiling from the cushions, and a small coffee table that was too new to have been left behind by the previous legal tenants. Both faced a television that might have last been used to watch the Berlin Wall come down. He crept past the couch, alert for an ambush.

"Jake?" he whispered. He passed through the living room into an adjoining hallway, which was pitch-black with neither lights nor windows. A person could be lying in wait for him and he wouldn't have a clue before it was too late. Gun braced, he walked the length of the corridor.

The kitchen ahead was dimly lit by pale moonlight and seemed to be empty. A dull thump from below the faded floorboards made him start, and he instinctively pointed the gun down towards it. He froze, listening, but the sound didn't come again.

In the darkness, he saw a door to his right. He eased it open, revealing a flight of stairs that led down to a low, unfinished basement, lit by a dim bulb.

"Fucking hell," he breathed and stepped onto the staircase.

He cautiously descended halfway, then crouched to get a more complete view of the area below. On the floor, off in the far corner, a body lay, ringed in blood. He raised his gun in both hands and descended the rest of the stairs with his back pressed against the wall.

As he reached the bottom, he saw that the clothing was not Jake's, nor was the body big enough to be his partner. The boy on the ground looked out of place, with his skintight jeans and *Misfits* T-shirt. Matt felt a pang of sadness for the lifeless teenager at his feet, an outsider in the wrong place at the wrong time.

It was then that Matt caught sight of Jake. He was on the floor across the room, slumped against the far wall with his legs splayed out. Matt could have sworn he wasn't there a moment ago. From where he stood, he couldn't see any obvious injuries that might have rendered Jake unconscious. Matt rushed across the basement.

"Jake!" he called, slapping his partners face and shaking him.

A sweet scent filled Matt's nostrils as a rag winked into existence in front of his face. It clamped over his mouth and nose, the smell becoming nauseating as he inhaled more of the substance. His vision blurred and the scuffs of his struggling feet grew distant.

As he fought to retain consciousness, he drove his elbow into the midsection of the assailant behind him. He heard a small grunt, but his knees gave out at the same time his vision faded. He tried to put the pieces together as his fall continued for far longer than it should have, but his thoughts refused to adhere to each other.

RICHARD'S EYES STUNG with sweat as he opened them and caught his breath. Finding his body in transit had proven more difficult than he'd expected. He'd tried to snap back to his body much like he had when he'd hunted on foot, but he'd found himself back where he'd left his body, not where it currently was. Stranded in the *Fringe* world, a chorus of lights had encompassed him. He'd had no idea in which direction Walcott's car had been travelling while he was away. He'd launched himself high and searched for the cruiser, until he finally detected it working its way through the crowded city streets.

Richard forcibly exhaled when he returned to his body. He caught sight of Julie staring intently at him. He offered a weak smile and a nod before turning his attention to the front seat. "Take a right at the next stoplight. The house will be halfway down on the left."

Dats nodded. "Took you a while to respond. I thought we'd lost you there for a second. It feels like we've been driving in circles."

"More like a spiral," Walcott said. "At least we'll get to the bottom of this soon."

Richard was woozy from his exertions, and as the car decelerated into the turn, his stomach rolled uneasily. He focused on the mats under his feet, trying to control his breathing. He felt Julie's hand on his back.

As Walcott slowed, he switched off the headlights and slipped the car into an inconspicuous parking spot, well away from the alleged stash house. Three figures stood outside the vacant building, talking animatedly. None took any notice of the vehicle as it parked.

"There they are," Richard said, pointing at the three figures.

"Yeah, okay," Dats said, pressing Richard's extended arm back. "Settle down." She turned to Walcott and said, "What's the game plan?"

Walcott was watching the activity in front of the house. Two of the Niners had placed a large, tarp-wrapped object into the trunk of a car that was idling at the curb. The third directed them back into the house, while he remained outside with the vehicle.

"Who's the tall one?" Walcott said.

"Never seen him before," Dats answered. "Doesn't dress like your run-of-the-mill gang banger." She grabbed her cellphone and used its camera to zoom in on the tall guy, capturing his image.

"That's Raef Deos," Richard said as he looked at Dats's cellphone screen. "He's been working with the Niners."

"That's *him?*" Julie whispered in Richard's ear and he nodded.

The two Niners returned with a second tarp. A limp arm hung out of the tarp, and Richard's heart lurched. He instantly knew it was one of his friends, either Matt or Jake, but he couldn't be sure if they were alive or dead. The Niners placed the body in the trunk as well, then slammed it shut. Raef jumped into the passenger side of the car, followed closely by the two Niners. The car slowly pulled away from the curb.

Walcott waited for a moment, then pulled out and followed.

"I'll radio in this location and get some units to lock it down,"

Dats said. She turned to Walcott. "Where do you think they're going?"

Walcott used his mirror to study the entrance of the stash house. "We'll have to follow them and find out," he said. "I didn't see any blood trails, so I'm assuming we have an abduction here. Unless they poisoned those guys." He glanced at Dats. "Right now, we've only got a portion of the workings. Let's see what else we can find."

"You don't have any clue what you have here. That man is bigger than the whole gang," Richard said.

"Just be glad we took the cuffs off you two. You're still wanted for questioning," Walcott said.

They followed the vehicle as best they could. When Raef's car started gaining distance, Richard launched himself into the *Network* and followed with the aid of his *hollow vision*. As long as Walcott's cruiser stayed close to the target, Richard had no trouble locating his body.

Using his newfound power, Richard could see two white lights in the trunk, and a pulsing red glow with two more white lights in the cab of the vehicle. At least Richard knew that his friends were still alive, even if they were in Raef's clutches. He decided not to get too close to the vehicle, worried that Raef would be able to sense him.

The car turned into the old harbor district, and Walcott followed. Night had fully gripped the city now, and the vacant warehouses that lined the harbor were shrouded in darkness. Raef's car stopped in front of a large, five-bay warehouse, with a small pier attached to the rear. Raef jumped out and opened the steel shutters of the middle bay.

The two Niners opened the car's trunk and pulled out the first of the two bodies. Richard could see them struggling with the dead weight. They hauled the tarp up to Raef, who stood on top of the loading dock. He took the weight without apparent effort and carried it into the warehouse and out of sight.

"Want me to radio this in?" Dats's voice drew Richard's attention back into the undercover cruiser.

"Not until we know more about what's going on in there," Walcott said. "I don't want this place lit up like a Christmas tree, or patrolmen trampling all over potential evidence."

"We already know what's going on," Richard said. "How about two kidnapped people who've just been dragged into the building?"

"Don't worry," Walcott said. "We'll head in ourselves to make sure nothing happens to them. You two stay in the car until we come back."

"Bullshit," Richard said. "I didn't come this far to sit out the final innings. You guys wouldn't even know about this place if it wasn't for me. Besides, you've got no idea what Raef is capable of."

"Relax, we can handle this," Walcott snapped.

Richard saw Dats give her partner a disapproving look, and he knew he had a chance if Dats took his side.

"Seriously, you guys have to believe me. You don't know what he's capable of. He has powers. I know it sounds ridiculous, but you just watched me track that car."

"Could be you're just lying to us and knew the location the whole time," Walcott said.

"If I'm lying, then what? I'm no threat to you two. You confiscated my gun. I'm a healer; it's what I do. And I can stop Raef. At the very least let me come with you in case the worst happens."

Richard watched a wordless exchange pass between the detectives. His hopes grew as Dats's features softened, just for a moment.

"What does the book say about this situation?" Walcott said to Dats. "We could end up eating a lot of shit for this."

"Name one time that's stopped you before," Dats countered. "This situation is already well beyond the norm." She turned back to Richard. "How can you stop Raef?"

"If I use my power, at least enough of my power, I cut Raef off from the *Network*, our power source. That's why he wants me dead. Please, you have to let me go with you."

"All right," Walcott said, throwing his hands up in defeat. "The weirdo can come with us, but unarmed. And the nurse stays in the back." He looked directly into Richard's eyes. "Your gun stays here. Keep your trap shut, and don't make a sound."

"I didn't come this far to get cut out now," Julie protested.

"The weirdo gets to go only because the three of you are convinced of some sci-fi bullshit. So, unless you have some special power, too . . ."

"Julie, he's right," Richard said. "Raef would try to use you against me."

He was prepared to do whatever was necessary to aid his friends. He hated to leave Julie, but he'd barely gotten Walcott to agree to let him go. A part of him hoped he could prove Rufus's "seers" wrong on all counts. He hoped he had a couple of tricks that they hadn't thought of; after all, they had never met Richard Sullivan.

"Just be safe, Richard," Julie said as he exited the vehicle.

RAEF PACED CIRCLES around the two unconscious men. His loaned lackeys had just finished tying the pair to a couple of steel chairs they'd found in the back of the warehouse. Raef took a step back and pierced the veil of the world's fabric, momentarily looking at the pair through the *Fringe* to confirm what he had suspected earlier. One of them had a blue pulse emanating from his shoulder; the other had a similar—though faded—pulse of blue swirls mixing across his stomach and knee. Each pulse reeked of Richard's aura. Raef had already rifled through their pockets and identified them from their driver's licenses—Matt Nader and Jake Talbot—though the names meant nothing to him.

The effects of the ether Raef had used on them earlier were beginning to fade, though full consciousness was still some way off. Raef couldn't afford to wait for them to come to their senses. He needed them of sound mind if he was going to be able to pump information out of them. He slapped the face of Talbot, the black-haired one.

Raef was shocked when the blond—Nader—spoke first. "Where are we?"

Talbot opened his eyes. His first sight was of Raef, inches from his face. "What the hell?" he cried and jerked his head back.

"How long have you known Richard Sullivan?" Raef said. He had no time to mince his words.

"Fuck off." Nader possessed a foul mouth, even with a groggy brain.

"You two are the link," Raef muttered. "I see that now." He looked the pair over again, finally pointing at Nader. "You must have known him a while."

Moving back to Talbot, Raef poked him in his once-wounded shoulder. "You're the one he healed yesterday at his apartment. I should thank you."

"What is this asshole blabbering about?" Nader said.

"Maybe he's off his meds."

Raef smacked the disrespectful mouth in front of him, adding a tiny sizzle from the *Network*, which would leave a long-lasting burning sensation that would spread throughout the skull. "Tell me where he lives."

"Who?" Nader said.

Raef's smack would leave Talbot speechless for a few more minutes. "I don't have time for your games. You know who I'm talking about: the one who healed you, Richard Sullivan."

"The man who healed me?" Nader said. "Why that'd be the one and only Jesus Christ, praised be His name. He resides in heaven at the right hand of the Father."

Raef had reached his boiling point. "Very well," he said. "Remember, I asked nicely the first time."

He slipped between the two chairs, with both captives' heads in close range. He could almost taste their fear as a sweet nectar on his tongue. There was a risk in doing this. Without the aid of the *Sphere*, he would have to suck in more power from the *Network*. The more power he demanded, the faster the Agency would be able to track him. He was already cutting it too close for comfort.

Comfort. Raef hadn't felt that since he'd handed the *Sphere* to that simpleton Midnight. He had thought about keeping the *Sphere*, but he'd known the master would never allow it. Without the *Sphere*, he had no way to mask his *Echo*. He had no way to track Sullivan if he went on the move. That damned *Vortex* still hung in the *Fringe* over his head. It ate up Richard's *Echo* too fast for Raef to track.

The Sphere *though, that could track anyone with the most minute trace of an* Echo.

Raef blew out a long breath. As soon as he opened the conduit into the subconscious of these two, Rufus and the whole Agency would be able to pinpoint his location.

Raef hadn't caught a scent of Sullivan since he'd appeared in the basement earlier. He was probably still at his apartment, cowering in a corner after the jolt of energy Raef had sent at him. In truth, he was disappointed with the boy. He would have to eliminate Richard at his apartment before Rufus's arrival spoiled everything, although that would entail finding out his physical address from one of these two. Passing through the *Vortex* without the *Sphere* disoriented Raef, and he hadn't been exactly sure where Richard's apartment was when he'd visited last night.

Raef clamped a hand down on each of his victims' necks, below the base of the skull. He formed a conduit and sent forth a surge of energy.

AKE AWOKE IN a familiar alley with a sense of *déjà vu*. He couldn't believe it had been a dream all along, though he couldn't recall when he'd nodded off. The last thing he remembered was hoofing it towards the bank. Trying to remember recent history gave him an intense headache, a sure sign of a concussion. Matt should have been close by, unless he'd gone for help.

Jake slowly stood up and took in his surroundings. He immediately noticed the brick wall that split the alley in two. His instincts told him he'd originally come from that direction, but he couldn't have come over the wall. Perhaps it was the concussion. A stench of face-cringing potency filled his nostrils, emanating from an industrial-size dumpster baking in the midday sun. He covered his nose and turned away.

Behind him, four gangsters stared down the alley at him. Jake realized he still had a metal briefcase in his hand. Two of the group were the boys that he and Matt had gunned down in his dream, but his brain couldn't dwell on the notion long enough for Jake to make sense of it. At the end of the alley, all four drew pistols and aimed at him. Jake bolted for cover behind the dumpster, reaching for his gun. There was just one problem: his holster was empty.

A hail of gunfire erupted. Shots and ricochets roared and zinged around him. He was trapped with no avenue of escape. The briefcase tugged on his arm. The locking mechanism consisted of a keypad with a small LCD screen, unlike the simple combination lock of his usual briefcase. Jake frowned—this briefcase wasn't his.

A soothing voice reverberated in his mind, reminding him of his recent security upgrade. The voice told him that inside the locked case, in addition to the firm's deposit, there was a loaded handgun with extra ammo. The lock's password was Richard's address. Jake shook his head, trying to clear it. Too many odd things were piling up, if he could only sort out the details. A sudden thought came to him.

His captor from the dream hadn't asked about the robbery or murders, only about Richard. Jake realized he was dealing with a being on the same supernatural level as Richard, possibly stronger. His mind spun. This might not be real, but if he was killed here, wherever here was, would he die in the real world?

A bullet ricocheted off the front of the dumpster, snapping him out of his brief reverie. The hail of gunfire died down and Jake peeked around the edge of the dumpster. The teenager he'd previously tortured was slowly walking down the alleyway, his eyes filled with hate.

Behind the teen, his companions held a small child that Jake recognized immediately as Andrew. Jake jumped up, ready to charge, but a single round ricocheted off the wall behind him, and a chunk of brickwork sliced across his cheek. Whatever reality he was in, pain felt the same.

He jerked back behind the dumpster. The implications were clear now: save your friend or your son.

This isn't real, he reminded himself. *Isn't real.*

DARKNESS, CEASELESS AND complete, surrounded Matt.

The air was damp and the reek of something rotten filled the air. He couldn't remember how he'd arrived here or for what purpose. As he stood there, his eyes slowly adapted to the darkness, which wasn't complete after all. The faintest trace of his surroundings became visible, and he saw that he was in a corridor with a dirt floor and stone walls close at either side. Since there was little else he could do, Matt began to creep cautiously along the corridor, trailing his left hand on the cool stone wall.

Despite his careful shuffling, Matt stumbled over a depression in the hard-packed dirt. He fell to his hands and knees and discovered that grass was growing sparsely in the dirt, nature's first attempts to reclaim this place. He lifted his head, and was enveloped in a filmy cobweb.

He spat and clawed the web from his face. He hated spiders, always had. For as long as he could remember, his stomach had clenched at the very sight of one, even if it was on a screen. The simple presence of a web was enough to set him off balance.

Ignoring the imaginary sensation of a million spiders crawling over his skin, Matt rose to his feet and resumed his cautious progress. He kicked something metal that scraped along the dirt floor. He paused and dropped to his knees, searching for the item. He eventually found a small metallic object, with a top that flipped open;

it easily fitted the palm of his hand. He couldn't believe that he'd found a lighter in this dark labyrinth. After a few attempts, he managed to spark the lighter to life.

A tall man was standing in front of him. As the lighter's flame illuminated his face, Matt realized that this was the same man who'd abducted him.

The man did not speak a word, but pointed towards the wall. There was an old map etched into it, surrounded by hieroglyphs that Matt couldn't decipher, but he understood that the map depicted the layout of the lost temple in which he now stood.

"Matt? Where are you?" Melissa's voice reverberated down the corridors, seeming to come from all directions at once, carried on a cold breeze.

"She is in the middle of the temple," the tall man said.

Matt took one last look at the ancient map before pushing past. "Get the hell out of my way."

He didn't have time to think things through, but he reasoned that this guy possessed powers on the same level as Richard. Matt's only conclusion was that he'd been "transported" to this place along with his wife, and presumably his daughter as well. Rage welled up in him.

"There are more markers, keep your eyes open," a voice called out from the shadows.

Matt hustled through the corridors, now searching for the labyrinth's center rather than its exit. He took only right-hand turns whenever the option presented itself. He found two more markers along the way, each with a red dot indicating his location in the temple. As he came upon them, each marker informed him that he was getting closer to the center.

A sudden blast of cold air struck him, extinguishing the lighter's flame. He thumbed the ignition wheel, but the spark failed to catch. The lighter was out of fuel.

"I have more lighter fluid, if you will let me help you." The voice was directly behind him.

Matt spun around but could only make out the shadowy outline of the tall man. "What do you want in return?" Matt asked.

"You already know what I want. His address."

"I won't do that." A thought had dawned on Matt. If this man was working for the Niners, why was he so interested in Richard?

Somewhere in the darkness, Melissa's cracked voice called, *"Please Matt, hurry. I'm scared."*

The shadowy man held up a small bottle of lighter fluid in the darkness. "I'm a man of my word, Mr. Nader. You help me, and I'll help you."

THE TWO COPS got out of the cruiser, and Detective Dats unlocked Richard's door from the outside. He climbed out, and the three of them crouched low as they hurried across the small parking lot to the front of the warehouse. Raef and his cronies had left the shutters of the loading bay open.

A quick glance inside revealed a large, nearly empty warehouse with a tiny office in back and steel barrels lining the left wall. Next to them were leftover industrial-size waste receptacles. Empty, rusted racks and rotted shipping pallets filled the right side of the warehouse.

Farther along the exterior wall was a conveyer belt that fed through a small opening, three feet above the ground. It was a tight fit, but all three of them could squeeze through the hole one at a time.

Walcott was the first to crawl through, belly pressed into the worn rubber of the conveyer belt. Dats was close behind, nearly on top of him. Richard followed last, clearing the hole in time to see Walcott gracefully roll off the belt and duck behind a fifty-gallon drum.

The stench of gasoline assailed Richard's nostrils as he slipped off the stationary belt and slid in beside the detectives. He was feeling woozy from the fumes already. He spotted Matt and Jake tied to a pair of chairs in the middle of the floor; each had a look of horror etched upon his face. Raef stood behind, a pale hand touching the base of each of his friends' necks. All three had their eyes closed.

"What the hell is he doing?" Dats whispered.

"Whatever it is, we have to stop him," Walcott said.

Dats stared at Walcott. "You know, it's going to take a lot to top today."

The pair simultaneously stepped out from behind the drum, an unspoken plan of action already formulated. They had their guns aimed at Raef before he noticed any movement.

"Boston PD! Hands in the air!" Walcott shouted.

Richard only caught sight of the two Niners as they rushed in from behind the stacks of barrels at the back of the warehouse. They started shooting even as they were moving, and the discharges echoed like explosions throughout the warehouse.

Walcott was quick to react. He swung around and dropped one of the two shooters. Raef made no move nor opened his eyes, even with bullets zipping around him. It seemed he was oblivious to his surroundings. The shooting grew more sporadic as the remaining Niner took cover.

Both detectives moved towards the center of the building, trying to pin the shooter down. There was a sudden burst of fire and from the corner of his eye, Richard saw Dats collapse in a heap. He crawled over to the fallen officer on his hands and knees, trying his best to keep behind cover.

As he approached, Richard could easily see the wound in Dats's neck; the bullet had torn a raw hole in the side of her throat, and blood poured from it, pooling on the floor under her head. She weakly applied pressure to the wound, and Richard saw the wild trembling of her hand as blood pressed between her fingers. Her mouth silently opened and closed. She coughed up blood between desperate gasps for air.

Richard grabbed her by the shoulders, cradling her head in his forearms. Another volley of shots rang out, and Richard dragged Dats behind a couple of waste bins.

Walcott fired off two more rounds as the last remaining gunman poked his head out from behind cover. The last round struck the Niner in the forehead, and the wall behind him was sprayed with gore and hair. Walcott turned and aimed at Raef, who remained motionless. Walcott looked over at Richard, and saw the wounded Dats for the first time.

"Oh Jesus, Dats. What the hell happened?" Walcott lowered his gun and rushed to his partner's side. Richard could see the tears brimming in Walcott's eyes as he pulled his jacket off, and tugged at his shirt sleeve. He ripped a length of fabric free and balled it up. He pushed Richard's hand out of the way and applied pressure to Dats's neck himself.

"You said you were a healer," Walcott said. "Look at her. She's dying. Do something. *Heal* her." He stared down at Dats, and she looked back up at him, her mouth opening and closing, her eyes blinking furiously. "Don't you fucking die on me, Dats," he said. "Don't you *dare*. That's an order."

Richard was already weakened from tracking Raef and from healing Jake yesterday. He had never before exerted himself through the *Network* this often. He couldn't be sure if he still had enough energy left to heal, or if he would even remain conscious throughout the procedure. But he had to try.

He began gathering power from the *Network*. A surge of energy rushed into him, and he was at once alert and renewed. He cupped his hands around the wound on Dats's neck. Exhaling slowly, he channeled the pent-up energy through his hands.

Blue light encompassed the area around Dats's injury, originating from Richard's palms. The surge of energy quickly fled, leaving Richard drained when he needed to exert the most control over the energy from the *Network*. The light winked out too quickly. Richard felt the discharge of energy, but it hadn't had the time to penetrate the wound deeply enough. The bleeding slowed and formed irregular clots, but Dats was still dying.

"What the hell was that? She's still bleeding, Sullivan," Walcott snarled. "Fix this shit or you won't make it out of here."

"Give me a moment, please," Richard said, exhausted. "I've used my power too much. Just let me catch my breath." His head was pounding, and his stomach ached with hunger. Even breathing was heavy labor.

He closed his eyes and took a couple of deep breaths. Dats gargled blood and gasped desperately for air. He cleared the sounds from his mind and thought about preventing her death.

Not this one. Not this time, he told himself and demanded power from the *Network*.

From beyond the waste bins, Raef let out a scream. Walcott turned to look at Raef, who had collapsed to his knees, hands clutching his head.

"Damn you, boy!" Raef roared, his open eyes filled with rage.

Richard felt a surge as the *Network* responded to his call with a flood of energy. The hairs on his body stood up as he struggled to contain it. He channeled the waves through his arms. The light leapt from his hands and into Dats's wound.

"You really can heal people," Walcott breathed, and the light dissipated.

Dats's eyes fluttered open. She slowly sat up, looking around. "What happened?"

Richard had propped himself up against a barrel. His legs were trembling and he could barely catch his breath, but he managed a weak smile at Dats. He wanted nothing more than a good meal and a week's worth of sleep.

"Does that count as Matt and Jake's 'Get Out of Jail Free' card?" Richard said, and hauled himself to his feet. "Now, if you'll excuse me, I have some business to settle."

Walcott helped Dats to her feet while Richard sprinted toward Raef, who'd managed to bring himself to his knees between the two chairs. Matt and Jake were stirring fitfully.

Richard didn't slow as he approached Raef. He drew back his foot and kicked Raef in the face as hard as he could. Even through his shoe, he felt Raef's nose break. Raef sailed backwards and Richard, unbalanced by the force of the kick, skidded onto his back.

"Goal!" Matt groggily cried.

Richard crawled over to Raef. He grabbed the back of Raef's hair and lifted his head from the ground. He drew his other arm back as far as it would go, then landed a punch square on Raef's fractured nose. Dropping Raef's unconscious head to the floor, he struggled to his feet. He untied his friends, though the hand he'd punched with felt as if it was swelling like a balloon.

"How did you find us?" Jake rubbed his wrists where the rope had chafed his skin raw.

Richard smiled slightly. "Don't worry about that. I've got a few tricks up my sleeve."

"Those cops with you?" Matt said and nodded in the direction of the two detectives.

"Yeah," Richard said, concentrating on undoing Matt's bonds.

"We're fucked, aren't we?"

"We all might get out of here, if we play our cards right. They owe me." Richard looked over at Raef. "Keep an eye on that one there."

Movement caught Richard's attention, and he looked over at the open loading bay. A dozen red-clad people crowded into the opening. All had guns in their hands. Richard assumed that these were more Niners. The last man to enter wore a crisp, expensive business suit with a red tie. He looked out of place in this company; he looked more like the CEO of a bank than a member of this ragtag troupe.

He stepped to the front of the group. "Well, what do we have here?" he said. He looked over at Raef, who appeared to be coming to. "I hadn't expected the great Raef Deos to be taken down so easily."

The Niners corralled Richard, Matt, and Jake with the two detectives. The man in the business suit, their obvious leader, stepped forward.

"Derek?" he said and stared at Walcott. "What are you doing here?"

Walcott still had his service pistol drawn, but it was pointed at the floor. "If it isn't Scott Jones himself," he said. "I see you still need your goons by your side, as always. Hello Tek, Bricks. It's a rare thing to see all three of you out together." He holstered his firearm. "You're sticking your nose pretty far out, making an appearance here."

Scott Jones smiled warmly at Walcott. "With our agreement in place, I've found it much easier to walk around without looking over my shoulder so much. I must say, it's a pleasurable experience."

Dats glared at Walcott. "Agreement?" she said sharply.

"It isn't what you think," Walcott said.

"I think it is," Jones interrupted. "Your partner and I made a little deal. He 'misdirects' information about my boys. In my turn, I keep the streets clear of bodies and the usual riffraff."

"You bastard," Dats spat.

Walcott looked away. "What do you want? It worked. Murder rates dropped, violent crime fell. The residents were never safer. It was perfect until Stacks split from the gang. That's when the peace got disrupted."

"Yeah. And all the while this guy's gang continued to expand and rot the city," Dats fired back.

Walcott shrugged. "I told them about a few wiretaps and surveillance ops. Do you know what happens whenever we take down a major player? I'll tell you. Nothing. Someone else moves in and sets up shop. If we remove Jones, the next person to assume control—Stacks, probably—well, you know how that would go."

"Yeah, yeah. I'm sure it was all for the good of the people." Dats looked away, shaking her head.

"I'll admit it," Walcott said. "I took money. I have bills and child support mounting up. The department refuses to pay the overtime they owe. I never claimed to be a hero."

Jones loudly cleared his throat. "Sounds like your girl doesn't want to play ball. Does she have any indiscretions that might help smooth the choice? You ever hear of her being a switch-hitter like you? I hear you knock it out of the park no matter who the pitcher is."

"You're an asshole, Jones," Walcott said. "And she never said that."

"She didn't have to. Come on Derek, let's get you out of here." Jones motioned to the skinny man at his right. "Tek, you know what you have to do."

The thin man pulled a fully automatic nine-millimeter submachine gun from his waistband. He held it comfortably, clearly familiar with its weight.

"No," Walcott said.

Jones appeared dumbfounded by the proclamation. "No?" He squinted at Walcott. "Do you really want to throw yourself in with this lot? Or, maybe have people find out about your little . . . secrets?" He glared at Walcott, but the detective didn't respond. "Have it your way, then. I will miss our little agreement. Luckily, I have agreements with other officers to fill the void that will be left by your death."

Jones turned his back on the group. Glancing behind the Niners, Richard caught sight of Raef rising to his feet. He glared at Richard and casually wiped the blood from his face with the back of his hand.

Tek aimed his gun at Richard. Suddenly, Richard's world shrunk to the size of the small, dark cylinder pointed at him. Rufus's comment about *Seers* and Richard's ultimate fate rang in his head. It was now, more than ever, that Richard wished he could have taught his skill to others. If nothing else, it might have enabled someone to heal his own bullet-riddled body.

Outside the warehouse, tires squealed to a halt, followed by multiple car doors slamming. Tek glanced across to the loading bay, and with the gun no longer pointing at him, Richard let out a breath he hadn't realized he was holding.

Gunshots boomed outside. A Niner at the open shutter crumpled in on himself. The Niners inside repositioned themselves to defend against the newly-arrived threat, leaving Richard and his friends unguarded.

A wave of newcomers, all dressed in green, surged into the loading bay. In the first seconds of the clash, it looked as if the Niners had this new group bottlenecked, but the kill zone didn't last long, as a second wave pushed through, sending the Niners scrambling for cover wherever they could find it.

Richard had trouble grasping what was going on. He thought back to the split that Walcott and Jones had spoken about. Was this new group controlled by "Stacks," whoever he might be? Richard was deep in thought when Matt pushed him forward.

"Hurry up, Sully. No time for daydreaming, we need to get out of here. Now."

The gunfire increased in intensity, but most of the shots seemed to be off-target, purely defensive. The Niners had attempted to form a semicircle around the entrance to the warehouse, preventing the newcomers from penetrating deeper.

Richard knew he needed to act quicker and think less. He gave chase to his friends, who had sprinted ahead. A stray bullet gouged the floor in front of him and he stopped abruptly, stumbling to a halt.

In the chaos, he'd lost track of Matt and Jake. He looked over his shoulder and caught sight of Raef, slipping out of a back office. A duffel bag was slung over one shoulder. He checked his watch before heading towards the back exit.

"You're not getting away that easy," Richard said through his teeth, and took off after Raef.

WALCOTT AND DATS dashed between a pair of old oil drums sitting on top of a pile of wooden pallets. Minimizing their exposure to hostile fire, they carefully worked their way to the conveyer belt near the loading bay. Walcott crawled onto it, dragging his chest along the rotted rubber.

Outside, he was grateful to find no one lingering around the perimeter of the warehouse. In the parking lot, vehicles were parked haphazardly, the doors of many still open. Walcott hopped off the conveyer belt and ran to his cruiser in a half-crouch. He heard Dats on the pavement behind him.

Julie was pounding on the backseat window of the cruiser. Walcott couldn't make out her muffled shouts, but when he popped the driver's door open, her voice was unleashed.

"What the hell is happening? I had to duck down in the seat when all these cars showed up and then I heard shots fired." She glanced around. "Where's Richard?"

"Just be quiet. I need to call this in first."

He grabbed the radio mic. Dats walked up behind him, still facing the warehouse, pistol at the ready. Walcott keyed the mic.

"Dispatch, come in dispatch. This is One Charlie Five, requesting immediate SWAT backup. We have multiple shots fired at the southwest corner of the old harbor. Suspects believed to be Niners and Young Gunz gang members. Repeat, we are requesting immediate SWAT reinforcements."

Walcott dropped the mic on the front seat of his cruiser.

"Where's Richard?" Julie asked again.

"We got separated inside, but he was with his friends."

"And you left him there? How could you do that?"

Walcott shut the door, not wanting to answer her questions. He turned and faced Dats, who still had an air of disappointment about her. "I'm sorry. I thought it was my only out." He couldn't find better words.

"What was with the baseball and 'secrets' talk, Walcott? You owe me that."

"I made some mistakes, Ana," Walcott said. He stared back at the warehouse and fidgeted with the torn sleeve of his shirt. There was blood on his hands. "Not just in my police work. I was stupid and listened to my dick instead of my head. I thought I could have everything. And for a time, I did. But I got careless and one night I got photographed with a guy I met at a bar. Somehow Jones got hold of the photos and he's hung it over my head since."

"A guy?" Dats said, eyes wide.

Walcott nodded. "I'm an equal-opportunities sleazebag," he said.

"Did your wife . . ?"

"Jeez, no. She didn't have a clue. Not about the guys. But she knew about the women. Some of them."

"Christ, Walcott."

"Yeah. I know. At least I had my job, until tonight."

Dats stared at the warehouse too for a moment, but her features softened, just a little. "I wasn't there when the deal was made with Jones. I can't say, if I were in your shoes, that I wouldn't have made the same call." She placed a comforting hand on his shoulder.

"We cool?" Walcott asked.

"Let's just see how tonight shakes out first."

BRICKS TOOK REFUGE behind a tightly-packed stack of rotted timber beams. He spotted Tek across the empty expanse of the warehouse floor. Behind Tek there was a member of the Young Gunz, taking aim at him. Bricks began to rise, voicing a warning.

As Bricks shouted, Tek dipped and turned on pure instinct. The Young Gunz member fired, but the bullet sailed high over Tek's head, embedding itself in a gas tank on the far side of the building. The newly-outfitted Young Gunz had been given incendiary ammunition by their new Russian benefactor, and as the bullet entered the tank, a ball of fire erupted into the warehouse. The searing blaze rolled along the vapor-rich air, engulfing the drums around it, which exploded in sequence, like toppling dominoes. Those gang members closest to the blast shrieked as they were charred and punctured by shrapnel. Tek quickly regained his footing and returned fire, putting two slugs into the chest of the shooter.

Bricks hunkered back down, untouched by the blast. He scanned the warehouse, desperately seeking his target. He mentally prepared himself for the task at hand.

"Come on, Stacks. Show yourself."

JONES CRAWLED TOWARDS the back entrance of the warehouse, leaving a trail of blood on the floor behind him. A bullet to the abdomen had punctured some vital organ, which was now ejecting blood at an alarming rate, and its exit had done something to his spine, rendering his legs useless. He hadn't seen his shooter, which meant that some nobody-thug was probably about to get a promotion. The whole situation had deteriorated too fast for Jones to wrap his head around. Stacks must have had a tail on Jones's car. It was the only way they could have found Raef's hideout, unless Stacks had made contact with Raef himself.

Head hanging, Jones reached forward, and found himself gripping a booted foot. He looked up, and when his vision finally cleared, he saw Raef standing over him with contempt in his eyes. Jones weakly grasped at Raef's ankle.

"Raef, help me," Jones croaked.

"No time," Raef said, and shook Jones's hand away. "You're dying anyway. It is a shame. I always enjoyed our time together."

Raef stepped over Jones and was almost at the back exit when a cascade of cardboard boxes crashed down on him. Jones spotted one of Walcott's young friends amid the boxes, reaching for Raef.

But Raef was quicker than Jones—or the boy—had expected. He turned at the last moment, using the boy's own momentum against him. Raef sent him crashing hard against the wall next to the exit. The boy lay dazed as Raef advanced upon him.

The alarm on Raef's watch chirped. He said something under his breath, but Jones couldn't make out his words. Raef turned away from the boy as he silenced the alarm, hurrying out the back door.

"Goddamn," the young man muttered and massaged the back of his head. He stared at Jones and his eyes widened. He looked at the back exit, then slowly looked back at Jones.

"I can't believe I'm doing this," he said to himself before meeting Jones's eye. "You're lucky that this benefits me as well as you."

He knelt down in front of Jones and rolled him onto his side. A wave of pain washed over Jones. "Try and relax. If you're able."

Jones couldn't muster enough energy to resist anyway, so he merely watched as the young man deliberately slowed his breathing. His hands emitted a soft blue glow, and Jones twitched in sudden panic. The boy placed one hand on the hole in Jones's chest and another over the wider exit wound. An intense itching sensation erupted right through Jones's thorax. The blue light winked out a second later and the young man removed his hands. Jones's pain dissipated with the light.

"I couldn't walk away and let you die now, could I?" the young man said, and collapsed against the rear door, his breathing ragged.

Jones sat up on the floor, feeling for the wound in the drying blood. He was woozy, almost as if he was stoned. "You saved me?" he said wonderingly.

"Yeah, I guess I did."

"I was about to have you and your friends killed," Jones said. He could see how much this miracle had taken out of the stranger.

"Don't remind me."

"Why did you do it?"

"In the practice of tolerance, one's enemy is the best teacher."

Jones was struggling to process these events, but the young man was struggling to rise, using the exit bar of the door for leverage.

"Wait," Jones called out, finding he too had to steady himself as he stood.

"What?" The stranger turned, but didn't remove his hand from the push bar.

"At least tell me your name."

"Richard Sullivan."

With the answer given, he shouldered through the door. Jones knew he would never see the young man again—he stood no chance in a face-off with the man Jones relied upon to eliminate his toughest enemies. It was a tragedy to see a person with the gift of life rush after death so quickly.

The sound of gunfire had died down since the blast that had briefly ignited half the warehouse. Jones turned back to the center of the building, scanning for threats. Satisfied that none existed, he began to follow his blood trail, looking for his lost pistol. He was unsuccessful in finding that, but he did locate something even more effective: his top lieutenant, Tek.

Tek had also seen Jones and was moving towards him, but a sudden blur of motion behind Tek stopped Jones dead in his tracks.

A squat, brawny man stepped into view from behind Tek. His head was shaved and he wore a black eyepatch.

"Tek!" Jones shouted, but it was too late.

"Hello, Tek," Stacks said and Tek turned around.

Stacks placed the barrel of his gun over Tek's heart. With a calm smile on his face, he pulled the trigger. Tek's torso rippled as the bullet shredded his innards in an instant.

The blast echoed in Jones's ears, confirming what his eyes refused to believe. He watched helplessly as Tek's body fell to the floor. Before the body could settle, Stacks fired another shot, which removed most of the back of Tek's skull. Satisfied, Stacks shifted his focus to Jones.

"No more hiding," Stacks said. "I've finally found you, Bones."

Jones had never imagined the end would come like this, his rise to power erased by a life-long friend, and his most loyal soldier struck down in front of him.

"You used to call Tek a friend," Jones said, and his voice sounded weak even to himself.

"Yeah, *used to*. Just like I *used to* have two eyes." Stacks stared down at Tek's remains. His emotions dominated his actions, and that was why he'd never regained control of the Niners after his incarceration. Rage consumed his logic whole. He fired another round into Tek's lifeless body.

He looked back up at Jones. "Any last words?"

Jones forced himself to look into Stacks's one good eye and he saw the madness there. "How did it come to this?" he asked.

Stacks snorted. "If you still don't get why I can't take orders from a soft prick like you, then you'll never understand. You lack the balls to lead. You had the largest claimed turf that Boston has ever seen handed to you, and you failed to snuff out me and my crew. Pathetic!"

Stacks moved around behind Jones and lined up his kill shot, execution style. "Say goodnight."

"Stacks!" a familiar voice yelled out, and both men turned to face it.

Jones wasn't sure where Bricks had come from, but he had never been as glad to see his last remaining lieutenant. Stacks smiled at Bricks, and that smile chilled Jones more than anything else—the last time Jones had seen that smile was right before Stacks had taken a shot at him, over a year ago. He wondered if he'd been wrong about more than just Raef.

"Bro, it's good to see you again," Stacks said. "Been a long time."

Bricks didn't reply. His gun was trained on Stacks, though it trembled. Jones couldn't tell if the tremor was from fear or anger.

"Shut the hell up!" Bricks shouted suddenly. "You do not get to call me 'bro' anymore."

Stacks raised his hands, the gun pointing at the ceiling. "Come on, man. You know I didn't mean for any of this to happen. Jones was greedy and weak. He would have destroyed all I built. He's the reason Leon is dead."

There was no warning from Bricks. Three trigger pulls, three rounds fired. Jones winced at each booming explosion. Stacks face briefly registered surprise, then he fell forward. A pool of blood quickly spread from beneath him.

"You will never speak Leon's name again," Bricks said tonelessly. Tears streamed down his cheeks. He nodded to Jones before kneeling down and whispering in Tek's ear, "I'm sorry I wasn't in time to save you." His hands hovered near the hollow cavity of Tek's head.

Jones took a step forward and a larger explosion rocked the building. He placed a hand on Bricks's shoulder. "It's not safe here," he said. They both knew that their friend's body would be cremated here, but they didn't have time to drag him out of the warehouse.

Jones swallowed the lump forming in his own throat. He coughed, trying to clear the obstruction, and looked down at his dead friend. "I don't know if I can do this without you, Tek. You've been a good friend and a loyal soldier."

Jones helped Bricks to his feet and the pair walked to the front of the warehouse. The bodies of Niners and Young Gunz littered the blazing inferno. Jones thought about the fire and his apathy towards which gang the bodies it would consume belonged to. He felt on the verge of an epiphany.

Somewhere above, a monstrous creaking reverberated throughout the warehouse. A steel support beam crashed down from the ceiling between Bricks and Jones, sending both men scrambling for safety.

"THE SHOOTING SEEMS to have stopped," Matt said as the dust that had been disturbed by the falling support beam slowly settled back to the ground.

"We need to find Richard and get out of here." Jake was crouched next to Matt. Neither had been armed during the firefight, a sensation neither had experienced before tonight.

"He was right behind us a moment ago."

Matt and Jake had sought cover behind a stack of wooden pallets in the least populated area of the warehouse. Matt spotted a fallen Niner nearby, whose pistol had dropped near his body as he burned. He took a quick survey of the surroundings before dashing into the open and grabbing the pistol.

He stuffed the gun into his waistband, and searched the body for spare clips. The sickly stench of roasted meat made him gag, and he breathed through his mouth, his head turned to the side. The corpse's roasted flesh was slimy beneath his hands and felt like it was sliding around on the bones, but eventually Matt found what he was looking for in a pocket of the pants, which had melted into the flesh of the body. There was one extra magazine, still hot.

He dashed back to Jake. He slid the clip out of the gun, checking the ammo. Only two remained, so he slid the two-round clip into his pocket, replacing it with the full magazine he'd found on the dead Niner.

"I don't see Richard anywhere," Matt said as he continued to scan the warehouse's interior.

"He must have made it outside somehow. Richard's a survivor, always has been."

"Hopefully we'll find him out there." He handed the warm gun and extra clip to Jake. "Take this. It's got a full clip and two extra rounds."

Matt took point as they headed for the open shutter at the front of the building. They had to cross most of the warehouse to get there, but saw no signs of continued fighting. Fires burned everywhere, the smoke coalescing near the ceiling and growing into a large, suffocating blanket.

They reached the loading bays, passing the two chairs with rope twined around them. Matt suppressed a shudder as he remembered the events of the night and the strange dream Raef had given him. Involuntarily, he swatted at a spider he thought he felt on his arm, though there was nothing there. He glanced back at Jake, and wondered what Raef had tried to do to him.

Matt turned back and stopped dead in his tracks. In front of them was the Niner's boss, limping, and supported by the guy Walcott had called "Bricks." The big man swung around, pistol at the ready.

"Don't take another step." Bricks's voice was barely steady, the toll of this night plain in his tone.

Jake already had his gun trained on the pair. Jones struggled upright. His shirt was soaked in blood. He pushed himself off Bricks.

"Lower the weapon, Bricks," Jones said.

"What?"

"It's okay, there's no beef here."

"I ain't lowering *my* weapon," Jake said.

"I would be dead right now, if not for your friend," Jones said.

"You saw Richard?" Matt asked with trepidation.

Jones pointed to the back of the warehouse, near an office. Matt could see a small illuminated exit sign back there. Flames roared in front of it, blocking the way. "He ran after Raef."

Matt watched as Jones fished in his pocket, knowing that Jake would be increasing the pressure on the trigger of his firearm. Matt raised a hand slightly behind his back, a subtle signal for Jake to relax a bit. Jones carefully removed his hand from his pocket. He held a set of keys that he tossed to Matt.

"Here," he said as Matt caught them. "There's a Lexus out back, near the docks. Find your friend and get your asses out of here."

Bricks stared at his boss. "What about the other half of Raef's payment in the trunk? Shouldn't we get that before they take off?"

"It's theirs."

"Payment?" Jake said, frowning.

"The second half of Raef's payment for two jobs he did for us. There's more money there than in the stash house you robbed. I hope Raef rots."

"Wait," Bricks said. "Are you saying Raef betrayed us, Jones?"

Jones shrugged. "Maybe. I can't be certain."

"Er, thanks," Matt said uncertainly.

"It's safe to assume we're even now?" Jones asked. "I don't want to open my door one day to find you two shoving a gun in my face."

Jake finally lowered his weapon. "Trust me, after tonight, you'll never see either of us again."

Jones offered his hand. Matt hesitated a second before extending his own hand and exchanging a brief handshake. Jake watched the pair as they headed off towards a side exit near the loading bay.

After a few moments, Matt and Jake walked in the same direction. A cloud of smoke billowed out of the opening and the dense fog blinded them as they hopped out through the open loading bay door.

BEYOND THE FIRE door, the darkness of the night made it difficult for Richard to see much of the harbor's water, but he could hear the waves lapping against the shore. A small, single boat dock was directly in front of him, and tied to it was a modest thirty-foot vessel.

Richard spotted Raef at the end of the dock, hunched over. Richard's plan had worked— using the *Network* to save Jones had rendered Raef immobile. His hands clutched his temples, trying to fight off the pain Richard had caused him.

"Raef!" Richard shouted. Adrenaline coursed through his body as he walked towards Raef.

Raef lifted his head at the sound of Richard's voice. Again, he checked his watch. "I don't have time to play catch right now, *son*," he called as he struggled to his feet.

Richard broke into a sprint. His feet pounded against the slick wooden planks, even as his muscles painfully protested. He lowered his shoulder, braced for an impact that never came. At the last instant, Raef smoothly pivoted away from the charge.

Raef turned Richard's momentum against him once again, lifting him off his feet. Richard grabbed a handful of Raef's leather jacket. Both men were pulled off-balance and they crashed hard against the weathered dock.

Richard rolled on top of Raef, pinning him down. He pummeled Raef with a series of wild haymakers, connecting as often with the wooden planks as with Raef's face. Richard's knuckles split and blood flew with every swing.

Raef caught the final haymaker with both hands and pulled Richard face-down into the planks while launching himself to his feet. Richard twisted away, but he'd already felt his nose break. He rolled in two complete circles before pushing himself upright. He tasted the blood from his smashed nose in the back of his throat.

Raef dashed towards Richard, who made a charge of his own. The two clashed, exchanging blows. Raef feinted a punch and Richard fell for it, lurching forward. Raef stepped back and dipped, then exploded upwards, focusing all the kinetic energy through his arm. His fist connected with Richard's exposed jaw in a mighty uppercut. The blow sent Richard sailing onto his back and Raef closed in.

WALCOTT FINISHED APPLYING the zip-tie cuffs to the last Young Gunz member who came coughing from the warehouse. Smoke billowed out of the loading bay doors, but Walcott couldn't see through the dense cloud that filled the interior of the building.

"That turned around quick enough for us," Dats remarked from over Walcott's shoulder. The fire had forced the survivors to disengage, seeking safety over revenge. The poisons from the smoke had left them gagging and blind as they exited the warehouse. The few who could still see had raised their hands above their heads when they spotted the red and blue flashing lights of Walcott's idling cruiser. Dats and Walcott had arrested them one at a time with relative ease.

"Who knew a set of lights on a cruiser and some smoke inhalation could lead to such easy collars?" Walcott said.

Dats nodded. "Should we head back inside and make a sweep? The bigwigs are still unaccounted for."

"I ain't going back inside there. It's not safe." Walcott motioned to the detainees lined up against their cruiser. "Besides, we're responsible for this lot, right? I'm fine with none of the others making it out."

"What about those two?" Dats said and pointed in the direction of the warehouse.

Two men were emerging from the smoke. They were both coughing convulsively. Walcott stood up straight as the two men approached.

"Good to see the two of you made it out alive," he said and smiled. "We were beginning to worry. Where's your friend Richard?" Walcott needed to make amends and thank the man who'd saved his partner's life.

"We were hoping you might have seen him," Matt said. He looked towards the corner of the building, behind which lay the docks.

"He didn't come this way."

"While we were inside, I only saw one rear exit," Dats added.

A moment of awkward silence passed between the group. Jake was the first to speak. "What happens to us now?"

"That is a good question," Dats said, and looked at Walcott with her eyebrows raised.

Walcott blew out a long stream of air. "In view of the extraordinary facts surrounding this case, coupled with Richard's . . . act for my partner here," he said, "I think we have some mitigating circumstances."

He walked up to Jake, pulling at his collar until the bare skin of his shoulder was exposed. Shaking his head, he did the same to the other shoulder.

"I don't see a shoulder wound," Walcott finally said. "The suspect we're searching for has dark hair and a shoulder wound. Guess it can't be either of you two."

"Seriously?" Matt asked.

"Go, before backup arrives. There's no way I could concoct a story that would explain how you ended up here. Then we'd all be screwed."

JAKE ROUNDED THE corner of the warehouse as sirens filled the air. He and Matt were sprinting the full length of the three-hundred-meter warehouse when an enormous explosion shook the ground, almost tipping Jake off his feet.

He looked up in time to see a huge chunk of brick and mortar tumble, dislodged from the top of the building. It plummeted down towards Matt, who stood frozen, mesmerized. A blur of motion passed in front of Matt, smashing into the chunk as it fell, and a cascade of pebbles and dust harmlessly showered Matt from the obliterated mass.

"Shit!" Matt blurted.

A man stood in front of them. His ebony skin glistened with sweat and his brawny muscles seemed to pulse with a life of their own. His face was stern. Jake stared at the newcomer in awe.

"Where is Richard Sullivan?" His voice was deep and carried a strange accent that Jake couldn't place.

"Who the hell are you?" Jake said. He didn't like the idea of *another* supernatural being hunting Richard.

"I don't have time to play games," the man said. "I am Rufus. I answered your question, now answer mine. Where is Richard Sullivan?"

Jake reached around his back, going for the nine-millimeter he'd recovered from the cooked Niner inside the warehouse. "Why do you want to know?" He snapped the gun around, barrel aimed at Rufus.

Rufus's hand moved faster than Jake's eyes could follow. In an instant, the gun was bent in half, barrel pointing towards the sky. Bewildered, Jake raised the firearm and peered closely at it.

"I told you, I do not have time to play around. Where is he?"

"We're not sure, we think he left out the back door." Matt's voice was anything but steady.

Rufus nodded curtly and jogged around the corner, springing from each step. It looked as if the man was barely exerting himself, but he moved with such speed that Jake and Matt were nearly at a full sprint trying to keep up.

Out back, Jake saw the wreckage of a dock; the explosion had blown out most of the warehouse's frame, which had landed on top of it. Fire poured out from the gaping hole in the warehouse wall.

On the shoreline, fifty yards away from the wreckage, Raef Deos rose from the waves, covered in seaweed, like a creature from a vintage horror movie. He bent over and expelled water from his lungs.

"*Raef!*" Rufus bellowed. "You will not escape me this time."

Raef squinted at Rufus and smiled. He pointed toward the wrecked dock. "I believe your top priority is lost somewhere under the water. Seems you have a choice to make." He turned away and took off down the shoreline.

Rufus placed a large paw on Jake's shoulder. "Raef is too dangerous to let him escape. Do your best to find Richard. I will be back shortly."

The huge man bounded after Raef. Jake looked at the black water and realized that they had no chance of finding Richard, but he also noticed Jones's Lexus parked in the nearly-empty lot.

Turning back to the sea, Jake thought, just for a second, that he could see something on the surface of the water. He waded into the sinking sand, working his way into the ocean. Waves washed over him and threatened to pull him under, until he was forced to stop. When he looked back up and tried to find the object on the water, it was gone.

SEAN B. CASEY

Day 4

RUFUS CAUGHT UP to Raef a mile down the beach. He tack-led Raef from behind, wrapping up his legs and dragging him to the sand.

"You're done, Raef," Rufus said. "You can't get away now." He got to his feet, standing over Raef.

"I didn't think you had it in you to let the boy die," Raef said, spitting out sand. "Time has hardened your heart, my friend."

"That has yet to be determined."

Raef rolled over, looking up at Rufus. "You could let me go. For old time's sake."

"You've been a bad boy since you left us. It's time to face jus-tice." Rufus could see the fear in Raef's eyes. Raef had always been in control; Rufus having the upper hand this time unnerved him. Rufus had seen the same look in countless targets over the years. "Justice, Raef, has finally come for you."

"Justice?" Raef shouted and shifted his weight. He sprang to his feet. "Does your Agency still drape itself in those false claims?"

The air around Raef crackled, and a black fog, streaked with bolts of red, flooded from his palms. The fog encompassed Rufus, bringing him to his knees. It squirmed into any orifice it could find, and Rufus collapsed backwards with a gasp as the fog vanished from sight.

"Really, Rufus? Did I overestimate your abilities all these years? Being cut off from the *Network* and with my reserves running so low, I thought I was in trouble." Raef approached the downed man. "Poor Rufus, Agamemnon's pet dog, sent to fetch whatever pleases his master. He is a tyrant who uses his 'laws' to justify his actions. Where was the justice for Alpha?" Raef grabbed Rufus by the collar, lifting him off the ground.

"You are blind," Raef hissed. "You can't see where Agamemnon is leading you. You think you are the saviors, but you will be the enablers of the coming doom."

Raef leaned in close and Rufus could feel Raef's hot breath on his cheek. Rufus stayed as still as he could, while Raef breathed in deeply, trying to suck in Rufus's essence. The pendant around Rufus's neck started to glow and became warm against his skin, just as Agamemnon had said it would.

The pendant emitted a lambent blue mist, which Raef inhaled. Immediately, his eyes bulged, and he choked, though he appeared to be unable to stop his inhalation. Once spent, the pendant ceased glowing and Raef collapsed, clutching his throat.

Rufus stalked towards Raef, who was thrashing on the ground, trying to force himself to vomit in an attempt to expel the ancient artifact's gift.

"A little present the boss gave me before I left."

Raef's mouth was moving but no words came forth.

"You know," Rufus went on, "I was worried you would flee the city before I arrived. Thankfully your fascination with Richard forced you to go against your better judgment."

"Yes," Raef said, struggling to get the words out of his throat, which was quickly filling up with blood. "And you let your personal grievance with me cloud *your* decision. You've let a *healer* die. The Agency won't be pleased with that. If it wasn't for that relic around your neck, you would have failed both of your assignments." He laughed, sending specks of blood into the air. "I never understood why you were Agamemnon's favorite."

"You plead your case for Alpha, but he was uncontrollable. Agamemnon gave you a fair chance." Rufus crouched and began searching through Raef's pockets.

"There is nothing fair about Agamemnon Duce, the irrational prick. He didn't have to obliterate Alpha's soul." Tears of blood began to roll down Raef's face, flowing from the corners of his eyes.

"He may have gone too far, even he will admit that. He lost his mind in the days after the Assistant Director's death. Every day, Agamemnon regrets the decision made in the aftermath of that tragedy. You could have seen it for yourself if you hadn't run. And you are one to talk—look at what you've become.

"I remember a man so torn by his past actions that he would do anything to make this world a better place. Then you aligned yourself with that entity, the one you call master, Thanatos. Rape and murder became commonplace for you. You feed off people as if they were cattle."

"It was the only way to escape Agamemnon's wrath. I had nowhere to turn. You say he regrets his actions? Well, that's only because I was here as a constant reminder that his power isn't absolute." Raef smiled, showing a row of blood-stained teeth.

"Where is the relic you recovered from the site? The *Sphere*?" Rufus roughly fished through Raef's pockets.

"Ah, so it wasn't the healer you were really after. I wasn't lying when I said you were blind. Agamemnon has his priorities out of line, or worse, he thinks he can make the prophecy go his way. Without lifting a finger himself, he will end the world." Raef coughed out dark phlegm, his words drowning in saliva and blood.

"Where did you hide the *Sphere*? I'm not playing your games anymore," Rufus said.

"Don't worry about the *Sphere*. I made sure it left the city a couple of days ago. Now please, I'm done arguing with you. The pain is too much. Do your old buddy Lukas a favor and kill me."

Rufus sighed heavily. He wished he could change so much of the past, but power like that eluded even someone as powerful as Agamemnon Duce, Director of the Agency. He pulled Raef up off the sand and placed a huge hand at each of Raef's temples.

"Take care of yourself, Rufus," Raef said.

Rufus began to squeeze his hands together. He felt Raef's skull crack and then crumple into his brain. As the last of Raef's lifeforce left the world, Rufus felt empty. There was no joy in this act. Rufus accepted the fact that even though Raef's case was now officially closed, the man's actions would be felt for a long time.

WAT VANS FLOODED into the warehouse's parking lot. A small army of uniformed police officers, decked out in full armor, quickly assembled. Dats watched as the backup canvassed the front of the building, taking stock of the devastation.

"How are we going to explain all of this?" she asked Walcott, who was helping the last of the cuffed gangsters get to a safer distance from the inferno.

"I'll figure something out," Walcott said. "Fudge up the reports. I can try to pin it on the Young Gunz and that Raef character. As far as Matt and Jake are concerned, I'll write a report that says we questioned them but no bullet wound was found on either. We had no choice but to let them go at that point. Then, we arrived at this scenario from a CI. Brass won't like it, might even cost me a promotion, but we'll manage."

"What about the Niners? Jones, Tek, and Bricks?"

Walcott motioned towards the blaze. "Our evidence against them is currently up in flames. No one will testify that they saw anyone of importance at the scene. That's if they even made it out alive. If they did, we'd be lucky to get past pre-trial."

"The wheels of justice continue to roll?"

"They never stop, Dats."

The two watched the flames dancing through holes in the warehouse for a while.

"So," Walcott said, drawing out the word. "Plane leaves in what? Less than 12 hours?'

Dats looked at Walcott and shook her head, smiling slightly. Over Walcott's shoulder, she caught sight of two silhouettes, one holding the other up as they walked behind the SWAT teams. She immediately sprinted towards them, without waiting for Walcott.

She could see the man with the limp wore a business suit like Scott Jones, and the one who supported him was built like a linebacker. That silhouette could belong only to Bricks. Dats's legs pumped faster. If she could catch these two at the scene, no lawyer on earth could get them off the hook. Flames lit their faces and confirmed Dats's suspicion as she neared them.

Bricks stopped walking and placed Jones gently on the ground. Dats stopped short and drew her pistol. Bricks and Jones exchanged quick words before Bricks turned and fired twice, without looking. The shots were wide and high, but still forced Dats to the pavement. She returned fire as Bricks bolted across the lot and into the darkness of the surrounding warehouses.

More shots ricocheted around her. Still prone against the pavement, she watched as Walcott strolled past and stood over Jones. Two SWAT officers helped her up.

"At least you have your other 'agreements,'" Walcott said as he looked down at Jones. "Maybe, you can work out a plea deal with the District Attorney." Walcott slapped cuffs on Jones's wrists.

"I'm sure the D.A. would love to hear all about you, Derek," Jones said, smiling back at the detective.

JAKE WAS SOAKED to the bone as he trudged out of the choppy ocean water. He'd failed to locate Richard and the increasing intensity of the waves had forced him to abandon the search. He spotted Matt in the parking lot and walked back along the shoreline, past the remnants of the dock.

The warehouse poured a plume of smoke into the harbor's skyline. Jake could hear police backup arriving around the front of the warehouse. Matt looked at Jake with despair in his eyes.

"Did you see him?"

Jake just shook his head.

"We can't leave without him," Matt said. "We don't leave people behind."

Jake looked at Jones's Lexus, still parked in the lot. He hated the idea of leaving Richard behind, but the odds of finding him had all but vanished, and the police would begin to circle around the building soon, now that the explosions had died off.

"Matt, we don't have long. Keep looking for Richard, but hand me those keys. I need to make sure everything is good with the car so we can jet at a moment's notice."

Matt glared at Jake before reluctantly handing over the keys. He turned back to the waterfront, scanning the dark water. He sighed as Jake moved towards the high-end vehicle.

The reality of Richard's death was starting to sink in. Jake balled his fists as he popped open the trunk of the Lexus. There was a metal briefcase lying inside. He popped the case and regarded the cash within. He closed the trunk again as anger began to boil deep inside him.

For the last two days, Jake had felt that he was doing the right thing. There was something calling him to take action against those who plagued society. Matt wanted to run away from those actions, which was why he'd told Jones he would stop hunting them.

This was a sentiment that Jake did not share.

He pressed the starter button on the Lexus's high-tech key. His mission had not been completed tonight. He would have to lay low for a while during the imminent police investigation, but once that settled down, Jake would hunt again. Only this time, he would expand his hunt beyond the Niners and the territory they controlled. There were many drug dealers and skin peddlers that needed a new form of justice.

"I can't see him anywhere." Matt's voice cut through Jake's thoughts.

"If we want to leave here as free men, we have to go now," Jake said. Soon, the responding officers would set up a large cordon around the area and the roads available to them would be filled with police.

"What about Richard?"

"We've got to have faith that Rufus is better equipped to find him than we are. It's the only option left." Jake didn't believe Rufus would save Richard. The man had chased after the psychotic Raef instead of saving their friend. Jake told the lie to try and comfort Matt.

"Yeah, Rufus could do it," Matt said. "He moved faster than lightning when he saved me from that falling brickwork. He can make it back in time."

Jake climbed behind the steering wheel. Matt took one long, last look over the ocean before getting into the passenger seat. Jake punched the address of J&M Securities into the onboard computer.

Neither Matt nor Jake spoke to one another as the vehicle accelerated away from the burning wreckage.

RUFUS USED HIS connection to the *Network* to pump his legs as fast as he could back towards the dock. The boat that had previously been tied to the pier thrashed about a few hundred feet from shore. Rufus could not find Richard, and Raef's comments came back into his mind.

You've let a healer die.

Rufus pulled out a cell phone and sent a quick text to an international number. Closing his eyes for a second, he took in a deep breath. He opened his mind's connection to the *Network* and established a link to his cell's *Seer*, Adelphia. He sent a homing beacon through the *Fringe*. It took only seconds for his brain to become occupied by another presence.

"I need your eyes to locate Richard Sullivan," Rufus needlessly said aloud.

Come now, darling. You know I can't see his Echo.

"Raef's dead. The ward should have dissipated," Rufus said abruptly.

He felt the foreign presence briefly leave his mind then return.

There is a chunk of the building submerged over there, my sweet. Your boy is trapped beneath it.

The cruisers had been parked out front for over a minute and Rufus knew his time was short. He ran to the water and dove under the surface. He easily moved the chunk of fallen wall from Richard's legs, and saw that a stout wooden leg had detached from the pier and was lying heavily across Richard's chest. Rufus picked it up with one hand and slid Richard onto his shoulder with the other. He thrashed his legs and swam to the surface.

He waded out of the water and placed Richard down on the shoreline. Richard's face was completely blue, and his chest failed to rise or fall. "I was too slow," Rufus said to himself.

Oh, my darling Rufus. Agamemnon is going to love reading your report.

"Thanks Delphi, but it's time for you to vacate my brain."

Rufus opened Richard's mouth and swept a finger around inside to clear any debris. He laid Richard back down, pinched the young man's nose shut, and blew into his open mouth as hard as he could. He waited for a couple of seconds then blew again. He put his fingers to Richard's neck and felt for a pulse.

Nothing.

He shuffled around and placed the heels of both hands on Richard's sternum. Rufus pressed down hard, arms straight, and compressed Richard's ribcage by a couple of inches. He winced as he heard a rib crack in there somewhere. He repeated the compressions, and more ribs crackled.

"Come on Richard," he hissed. "Raef is dead. It's time for you to start living."

Thirty quick compressions and two more breaths. Rufus felt again for Richard's pulse.

BOOTED FOOTSTEPS ECHOED down the side of the warehouse as patrolmen attempted to establish a perimeter around it.

Thick beams of light from their flashlights pierced the veil of midnight darkness.

But Rufus was already on the move. He pumped his *Network*-aided legs while carrying his charge. The police wouldn't spot him and Delphi was already on the way to the rendezvous spot. He cursed himself for thinking that he might have had a shot at getting the *Sphere* back. But at least he wouldn't be returning to the Agency empty handed.

Rufus checked Richard's wrist once again for a pulse while never breaking out of his sprint. Richard's pulse was still weak but he'd stopped coughing up water. Raef had done a good number on Richard before he'd gotten trapped underwater; his nose pointed off-center, and his eyes were swollen shut.

They needed to make it back to the Agency, but Richard was hardly in any shape to make that journey. Rufus knew that their best asset in this situation was in New York: Buddy Gecko was the financial farmer for the Agency. The man had a golden tongue and a knack for knowing exactly how the stock market would trend. He also had the connections in the city that could get Richard the medical attention and new identity he needed.

Once that was sorted, Rufus and Delphi would bring Richard across country by car. It would be easiest to take a plane directly to Majuro but after tonight, they couldn't risk Richard being caught by airport security, so they'd have to trust in the more lax security around the nation's coasts. Once they made it to southern California, they would take a boat from one of the Agency's private docks all the way to the Marshall Islands, home base for the Agency.

Rufus finally arrived at a parking lot a few miles away from the docks. Delphi had designated this area as the rendezvous spot. A few streetlamps illuminated the vacant lot adjacent to a foreclosed building that had once belonged to a shipping company. He laid Richard down on the concrete and lowered himself to listen to Richard's breathing.

Richard was unconscious and hyperventilating, short deep desperate breaths for oxygen, but at least he was alive. Rufus was glad Richard wasn't awake. He wasn't ready to answer any questions just yet. Delphi would be here any moment and she was much better equipped to handle that.

Richard's world was about to get a whole lot bigger. Rufus wondered at what his choice would be when Richard met with Agamemnon Duce. He would be offered a chance to join the Agency or assume a new life under constant surveillance. With no home life to go back to, Rufus couldn't see Richard turning down Agamemnon's offer.

A late model autodrive turned into the parking lot. Its headlights shone directly on the pair as it inched closer. Rufus had to shield his eyes from the blinding light before he could see Delphi in the front seat, her long, golden curls framing her child-like face. Looking at her now, Rufus still had to remind himself she was much older than the fourteen-year-old she looked like.

He gently picked Richard up and slung him over his shoulder. He headed towards the autodrive.

"Sleep now, Richard. When you wake up, the whole world is going to be different."

THE SUN HAD yet to rise above the urban skyline as Bricks cruised the streets of the city. It was *his* city now, he thought. With the police bearing down, Jones's last act had been to bestow the Niners on Bricks. Bricks was capable and he knew the operation better than anyone, but, in his opinion, Tek should have been the one to inherit the business. If only Bricks had made a more decisive shot a year ago. His regrets ate at him.

He drove to their headquarters. It was an uncomfortable and lonely ride, filled with silence. He needed to remove any evidence that could be linked back to him and the gang, but his phone had not stopped ringing since he'd lifted one of the vehicles the Young Gunz had driven to the warehouse.

Bricks tried to shake the thoughts from his head, but they proved stubborn and refused to be ignored. Bricks had killed Stacks. No matter what evil Stacks had done, he would always be the one who'd gotten Bricks into the clan. He told himself that he'd done what he had to do. Bricks tried to picture Stacks standing over Jones and Tek, but the image would not hold. Instead, a younger Stacks came to his mind, the one who'd shown Bricks the ropes of clan life. Stacks had taken him in after all the people Bricks believed cared about him had, in fact, abandoned him.

He punched the steering wheel of the SUV in frustration, producing a small honk from the horn. It wouldn't help Bricks if he continued to obsess like this. What was done, was done, and there was no going back now. Adjusting his mirror, Bricks's eyes caught sight of the black suitcase resting on the back seat. Inside were supplies and money that Jones had packed. It was enough to survive on for a few days, a modified bug-out bag for this specific situation.

Bricks would need to go into hiding for a short while. The warehouse fire had removed most of the clan's muscle. The Russians would be coming, especially now that Jones and Stacks were out of the picture. Bricks had acquired the clan at its lowest point and it was all on him to turn things back around.

MATT SAT BACK, breathing in the stale air of the downtown police interrogation room. It wasn't at all what he'd expected: four walls, a heavy steel door, but no two-way mirror with some big- shot behind monitoring his every movement. The table in front of him looked to be thirty years old, with flakes of faux wood veneer peeling off around the edges.

Jake occupied the cold metal seat next to him. Matt thought it odd that he and Jake were in this room together; he'd been trained to separate suspects under interrogation. He took it as a sign these cops were only really interested in signing off on paper work and closing the case.

It had been three days since the warehouse debacle and before today, Matt had believed they were in the clear. A phone call from a detective he'd never heard of changed all that. The cop explained that he needed Jake and Matt to answer some additional questions, to close the book on the case. Matt's flight to Florida was still over a week away, so he'd agreed.

Neither Jake nor Matt had heard from Richard since they'd left the warehouse. They'd barely spoken to each other in the last three days, aside from mandatory business talk. The authorities had found the body of an unidentified man a mile and a half down the shoreline, but his head had been crushed, as if with a heavy weight, and no murder weapon had been recovered. The body was linked to a case involving the local Russian Syndicate assassinations that was gaining a lot of media attention. Whoever it was, it wasn't Richard.

Dive teams had been sent into the water before sunrise of that morning, in search of Richard. The police held no hope of finding the young man alive. After the recovery of a boat registered under the name of Lukas Jager gave no new leads, the chances of recovering the body were extremely low. The search had been called off yesterday.

Matt and Jake had visited Richard's parents at their house an hour south of Boston. They'd offered their condolences to the grieving parents. Matt had found it especially hard to deflect questions about the crazy rumors floating around about their son, and his reasons for being at the warehouse. Richard had never told his parents about his powers, and neither Matt nor Jake were inclined to do so.

The heavy door to the interrogation room swung open and two detectives entered. Matt didn't recognize either. The first wore a tan suit with a red tie. Bald headed and heavy set, his face reminded Matt of an overripe fruit that had been attacked by insects, leaving small discolored patches all over its surface.

The other detective wore a fitted navy-blue suit with a matching checkered tie. He was taller than the first by half a foot, and Matt could easily see the time and effort he spent at the gym. They both wore the same grim expression. Matt began second guessing his previous notion that the police weren't taking this seriously.

The two detectives silently sat down across from Matt and Jake. The cops shared no more than a passing glance between each other. It didn't surprise Matt, for when he and Jake had conducted interrogations in Ukraine, they'd had a plan of attack devised before entering the room with their prisoner, too.

"Thank you, gentlemen, for coming in today," the scarred man said. "We have a few questions for you. To help us clear up our report." He smiled, a thin crack in his face. "Could you explain the situation that led you to abandon your car a few days ago?" The bright light from the ceiling fixture glared off the top of his bald head.

Matt explained the unfortunate circumstances of being in the wrong place at the wrong time. He spoke of the initial gunfire that had shattered his window and cut Jake in the process. He omitted the true events that had transpired in the alleyway. Instead, he explained that they'd walked through the alley, then skipped straight to the bank, which surveillance cameras could corroborate. Matt knew Jake's blood-soaked hands were not on that film and that the cab they'd taken to Richard's home was not equipped with a camera.

"What do you know about Raef Deos?" the gym rat asked.

"Not much," Jake said. "Only what Detective Walcott told us. He informed us that Raef was hunting our friend Richard, but he wasn't sure about the reasons behind it."

"Richard never talked about him?" The bald detective glanced quickly at the clock. It was a little after noon. For the first time today, Matt breathed a little easier. If this was a serious investigation, neither detective would be glancing at the clock this early.

"Richard didn't talk much about anything, let alone his personal life," Matt said. "To be honest, I couldn't even tell you if Richard was dating anyone."

"Sounds like you guys weren't that close."

"We were Richard's closest friends, but to call that guy reserved would be a big understatement."

"Can you please elaborate on your relationship to the Niner street gang?" the younger detective said, suddenly switching tack, a strategy Matt was well aware of.

"None whatsoever," he said.

After a moment of silence, Jake spoke, all emotion drained from his voice, his eyes drilling holes into the table in front of him. "A Niner murdered my wife a few years ago."

"And you wanted revenge," the hard-bodied detective said. It was the one string left hanging, linking Jake to the Niners and a pile of bodies.

"I killed the man who killed my wife. I did prison time for it, too. I've had my revenge and paid for it as well. You want to hang another charge on me because it fits your little scenario, that's fine. The court will prove my innocence." Jake's voice was a monotone, and it chilled Matt.

The bald detective had been making notes during the conversation. His pencil stopped scratching the paper as Jake spoke. He looked from Matt to Jake and moved his mouth as if to comment on the exchange, but something seemed to stop him. He resumed scribbling his notes.

"Surely you wanted to get even with the rest of the crew as well," the younger detective said.

"It was a stray bullet that took my wife's life. I killed the man who recklessly took that shot. I don't care who he played games with." Jake's lie was well told; Matt would have doubted it was a lie himself if he hadn't known Jake so well.

The bald detective looked up from his notes. "That pretty much answers all the questions we need for the report," he said. His voice was smooth and soothing. To Matt he sounded like that great narrator, Morgan Freeman. "Mr. Nader, you can pick up your vehicle release form at the front desk. We have waived any and all storage and towing fees, since the previous detective working the case claimed it as evidence."

"I want to thank you boys again for coming in on such short notice," the younger guy said, and Matt saw sarcasm in his eyes.

The comment irked Matt but before he could complain, the two detectives rose together and exited the interrogation room, leaving the door ajar. Without a word, Matt and Jake stood and walked to the reception desk.

J ULIE WAS NAPPING on her living room couch. The tidiness of her apartment had recently begun to slip in quality and care. A few dirty dishes sat in the sink, and a few little piles of clothes formed small dunes on the floor. The answering machine clicked on, waking Julie from her fitful slumber.

Her boss's voice came through the machine's speaker. "Julie, I hope everything is okay. I'm just calling to confirm that you're coming in for your shift tomorrow. We are here for you, and all of us miss Richard no matter what the news says."

Julie had tried her best to find any evidence of Richard after that night; she'd already exhausted most of her paid leave during her investigation. She'd scoured the beach behind the warehouse, but the police had created such chaos in the area she wasn't able to gather any new information. She'd spent the days afterwards talking to Jake and Matt, and looking for any signs of the mysterious stranger Rufus. Matt and Jake were convinced that he was an *Other*, but Matt was optimistic that Rufus had saved Richard.

She'd checked the surrounding buildings, or at least the ones that weren't abandoned. She was surprised when a few of the companies let her review their exterior surveillance tapes, under supervision, though her scrutiny had proven as fruitless as her search of the beach.

She'd lucked out when she talked to a night shift manager who'd been working the night of the warehouse fire. He didn't have much information, but he had seen a big man waiting in the parking lot across the street around the time of the incident. A car had picked him up after a while and vanished into the night.

That was the only lead that Julie had found, the only hint that Richard might not already be dead.

She looked away from the answering machine. On the dining table across the room, the draft leaflets she'd been creating were scattered haphazardly. Once she'd hit a dead end in her own search for Richard, she'd used even more paid leave to start a group to teach people about *Others* and how to help them. She'd spent the last few days organizing a meeting spot and drawing up the leaflets to spread across the city.

She wasn't going to let Richard down; she *wasn't*. She hadn't been there for Claire, and those detectives had kept her from helping Richard when he'd needed her the most. She wasn't going to let anyone else suffer. If the mainstream media wanted to keep denying the existence of *Others*, then Julie would be the one to spread the knowledge. She needed to teach people. If they understood more about *Others*, maybe they wouldn't be so afraid of accepting them.

She thought about the next day at work and the constant reminders that awaited her there. Though her own apartment building held its own share of reminders. She rolled over, burying her head in the couch's cushions. The frustration of the situation threatened to overwhelm her.

A loud and frantic knock at the door shocked her into alertness. The thought of ignoring the visitor crossed her mind for a second, but the banging came again. Reluctantly, she rolled off the couch, wishing her voicemail could answer the door too.

Wearily, she undid the locks and opened the door. Outside, Greg stood sobbing. His hair was a tangled mess and he wore shorts and a T-shirt. His face was puffy with grief and he held his phone up to Julie's eyes. Behind him, she could see the yellow police tape over Richard's door.

She'd heard Greg leave for school yesterday, but it wasn't until she looked at the screen and saw the date next to the headline there that she realized today was Saturday. The screen showed an online article by a local Boston blogger. A picture of the waterfront where Richard had gone missing accompanied the article. The headline read *Dive Teams Called Off*. Julie knew that it was inevitable, but a small part of her desperately hoped that Richard had somehow survived and was waiting to be rescued. The headline slid its knife through that last small glimmer.

She gently pushed the phone out of her sight. Greg stepped in close and she hugged him hard. He wept openly into her neck, and she rubbed his back through his T-shirt.

"I can't believe they gave up already," Greg said between sobs.

"It'll be all right," she said and stood back, holding Greg at arm's length. She looked him directly in the eyes. "It'll be all right. Richard wouldn't want you to be upset."

Greg sniffled, wiping his nose with the back of his hand. Julie knew Greg idolized Richard. Even with his faults, Richard was a selfless, hard-working man who valued his family and friends. Though he kept to himself, he was always willing to help those in need when the situation called for it.

She smiled at Greg, giving him a pat on the head before sending him downstairs. She closed the door and surveyed her apartment. She needed to get her act together. She'd been frantically running around the past few days and when she did stop, her emotions caught up to her. Her mother's tired, repeated words came back to her: *A clean house is the basis for a healthy life.*

She started with the kitchen sink. Over the roar of water splashing across dirty dishes, she heard the afternoon news program start on the TV. After a short intro jingle, the lead anchor quickly cut to a field reporter with new developments of an alleged murder at the Suffolk County House of Corrections.

"Thank you, Lucy," the reporter said. "As you can see behind me, activity at the Suffolk County House of Corrections has yet to slow since yesterday evening. Officials are baffled by an incident that occurred late last night inside these walls. Shortly before the evening roll call, a fire broke out in alleged drug kingpin Scott Jones's cell, where he was being held until his arraignment.

"Officials are keeping a tight lid on the details, but an insider close to the investigation has told us that they have a suspect in custody. Here at Channel Nine News, we were able to confirm that the suspect's name is Sergei Malatov, a Russian national who is in the process of being deported by ICE. Hopefully we can find out more details when the ICE Office of Public Affairs holds a briefing later today. Back to you, Lucy."

The desk anchor segued to a multi-day series the channel had been running on the Mysterious Wanderer. The media had given Richard the moniker after his nomadic lifestyle had been uncovered. They'd chosen not to use his nickname from the hospital.

If those damn detectives had only let me out of the car, I could have done something, Julie thought to herself.

Each news outlet was in a race to find the most interesting angle on Richard's tale. The past few days had been filled with reports from various parts of the United States, telling of the deeds of the Mysterious Wanderer. The lead story today was a local opinion piece by an investigative reporter, gauging public feeling about the enigma of Richard Sullivan.

Julie turned the water off; the dishes would still be soiled after the news program, and her curiosity compelled her to watch the report. She found herself back on the couch, focused intently on the first interviewee.

The sight of a familiar small girl brought a smile of remembrance to Julie's face. Sally Sanders had had a miraculous recovery, and Julie was one of the nurses who'd taken care of her during her stay in the hospital. An off-screen narration told the young girl's tale and underlined the bafflement of the doctors about the nature of her recovery.

"What do you think of Richard Sullivan?" the reporter asked Sally.

She smiled a broad, gap-toothed smile at Richard's name. "He was my angel," she said. "He cured me." She paused for a second, lost in a memory. "I wasn't supposed to tell anyone what he did. He said he couldn't do his work if I said anything, but he passed away." Her smile faded quickly, and her bottom lip began to tremble. "So, I don't think it matters anymore if I tell people."

The reporter thanked the little girl, giving her a hug before the scene was swiped away. Julie found her own eyes moist. The report cut away to an Indian man leaving a small two-storey house. Julie immediately recognized Mike Patel, Richard's supervisor. The neutral tone of the narrator clued the rest of the audience in a moment later.

"Hi, Mike Patel?" The reporter and cameraman had rushed from the sidewalk to meet the man at the bottom of his front porch.

"What do you want?" Mike looked visibly disturbed by this intrusion into his privacy.

"I'm John Longcoat with Channel Nine News. We'd like to hear your thoughts on Richard Sullivan."

Mike was shaking his head before the reporter had even finished his introduction. "Can't you let the boy rest in peace?"

"Our viewers want to know more about him and his life. As his boss you could provide some unique insights and possibly dispel some of the negative rumors about Richard. Do you believe that he had some sort of supernatural power?"

"Listen, Richard was a good man and a great worker. His passing has hurt me deeply. That is my only comment." He muscled past the cameraman and reporter to his car, where he sped off, and the camera lost him to a left-hand turn.

The last interview had been filmed later in the afternoon, judging by the high position of the sun. The shot was framed on an older man in his fifties who Julie could only think of as a stand in for "everyman." The narrator introduced him as a high-ranking former police officer and criminologist.

Julie lost interest as the man spoke of criminal profiles and the poor vetting of humans for remedial work. Off-camera, the same reporter held his mic close to the man's mouth.

"Do you have any thoughts or feelings you'd care to share with our audience?" The reporter's tone had changed dramatically from the meeting with Sally Sanders, growing deeper with a slight hint of anger.

The criminologist's face contorted briefly, revealing utter disgust. "He's a fraud," he said, and the whiskers of his mustache twitched when he spoke. "Just like those televangelists on TV. They all prey upon the weak. What I'd really like to know is how a custodian can get access to all these patients' rooms when no one else is around. If my child was at that hospital, I wouldn't be comfortable knowing that some whack-job could approach my child with no supervision. Not to mention his involvement with the street gangs. What kind of man even finds himself at that warehouse in the first place?

"This is why we need to consider mass implementation of the RFID program. All these questions surrounding this Richard Sullivan could have been examined if RFID chips were mandatory. Did you know that the return of abducted individuals who have RFID chips is over eighty per cent? If you are doing nothing wrong, you have nothing to hide. "

Julie pressed *Mute* on the remote control. She couldn't listen to people slander Richard's name when they had no personal experience with him. Even worse, this guy was using it as an angle for a political agenda.

Maybe she should be happy. At least the media was finally changing. They weren't burying Richard's story and they were, if anything, actually hinting at his supernormal powers. She shouldn't be surprised that people had latched onto the hot topic to earn a quick buck.

She had better things to spend her time on. She needed to make sure everything was ready for the first meeting of The *Other* Support Club before she started back at work tomorrow.

RAIN FELL IN sheets upon the thick grass of the deserted grave-yard. A solitary black SUV filled the single-lane drive. Bricks's Italian shoes left soft depressions in the grass wherever he stepped. Mud clung to the expensive leather. He moved toward a freshly packed mound of dirt.

Tek's gravestone had been ordered but was still being engraved. A small white cross stood as a placeholder, marking Tek's final resting place. Other empty grave sites had been marked off, though the occupants had yet to arrive.

Bricks knelt beside the grave marker. His knees sunk into the ground, ruining his expensive business suit. Since assuming leadership, Bricks had emulated Scott Jones, a man who dressed for success. Bricks was still getting accustomed to the new wardrobe.

"Tek," Bricks whispered the name as he would a prayer. "Man, I could really use your help right now. Jones is gone. He sacrificed his freedom so I could get away. I booked it out of there with SWAT guys on my back. I had to run three streets before I could jack a car and get away. You should have seen it!

"But man, the clan is a mess. Those Russians burned Jones alive inside his cell. Burned him alive! A few groups have splintered off from us. Rumors are circulating that the Russians are stepping up production. I'm barely holding on to the scraps."

Bricks clenched his fists. "Then there's Jones's distributors. First, they wouldn't meet with me. Then, when we finally arranged a meet, they informed me that the prices were going up. They claimed they need extra insurance until the new 'regime' proves itself." He let out a deep breath, calming his racing heart. "I can't even tell you how hard the police are hitting the street-level business. They got state troopers guarding the rails and administrative businesses, and the locals putting all the extra force out on patrol. Those riots made the city unlock an emergency fund, so now the police budget is bloated." Bricks shook his head, trying to rid himself of negativity. "On the plus side, I did manage to get a few of Stacks's former boys to come to our side."

One of Bricks's recently-promoted lieutenants approached cautiously, not wanting to disturb his new boss. He was a young man, barely into his early twenties. Though young, his actions during the past year had earned him enough trust to be awarded the promotion.

"Sir?"

"What is it, Wheezy?"

"The Russians, sir. You wanted to be informed if there was any activity at the pawn shop."

Bricks nodded at the young man. "I'll be along in a minute."

He turned back to face his friend's grave marker once more, waiting until his underling was out of earshot. "You'll have to wait until next time to find out what happens with the Russians. They've made headway back into the city. Starting to feel like the walls are closing in on all sides."

DATS WASHED HER hands in the tacky bathroom of the Old-ies diner. Her gold wedding band caught a ray of light from the recessed ceiling lights, casting a golden reflection on the din-gy wall. Dats was momentarily dazzled by the glow. Breaking the spell, she dried her hands under the machine, walking away from the stream of hot air before it turned off.

It was still early in the morning for most of the city. Despite that, the diner was already buzzing with business. Dats smoothed the creases from her suit as she made her way back to the table. She paused for a moment to get a better look at her ex-partner.

Derek Walcott was a broken fragment of his former self. After the warehouse inferno, Dats was granted special leave to go on her honeymoon, while Walcott was investigated by Internal Affairs. An Internal Affairs investigation was the one thing no cop ever wanted.

The investigation was drawn out and inconclusive, and resulted in no formal disciplinary measures against Walcott. He had, how-ever, been transferred to the Hackney Carriage Unit. The transfer was a death sentence for Walcott's career. He would spend his days writing up trivial violations and following up on lost items in horse-drawn carriages. He would never make another headline-catching bust, or see an upgrade to his rank or pay.

Dats slid onto the stool that was bolted in front of the bar. There were a few sips remaining in her coffee mug. Her breakfast plate had been ravaged, hidden now beneath a crumpled napkin. The waitress looked over and Dats tapped her mug for a refill.

"So, the wedding went well?" Even Walcott's voice was different. He had forfeited the cockiness that had defined his character when he'd lost the lead detective job.

"It was good. We kept it small, not that a lot of our friends could have attended a Caribbean wedding. But it went smoothly."

"Did you visit any nude beaches?" A hint of Walcott's former self still lingered behind those dead eyes.

Dats chuckled. "I did, but before you ask, no, I did not take any pictures."

Walcott smiled weakly as his inner demons went back to dismantling his soul. He looked away from Dats to his plate of leftovers. His shoulders sagged as the demons finished their work.

"I should be heading back. My shift starts soon." Walcott sat up, still not looking at Dats. He reached into his back pocket, instinctively going for his wallet.

"I got this one." Dats put her hand over Walcott's and pulled a small wad of cash from her pocketbook. She could feel Walcott's eyes upon her. She'd recently been paid all her due overtime pay. The Hackney Carriage unit hardly had cause to keep people past their posted shift hours.

"Still have cash from the wedding gifts," she felt obliged to say.

"Sure," Walcott said. "Thanks." He shifted on his stool, then stood. "Well, I should be going. Can't be late, boss already doesn't like me."

Dats shifted uneasily on her own stool, and fidgeted with the new gold band on her finger. "I'm sorry but I have to ask this," she said. "Did you have any involvement with what happened to Jones?"

"I won't lie and say his death didn't help me," Walcott admitted. "But no, Dats. I was ready for the law to hit me with everything they had when we arrested Jones. I guess I just got lucky."

Dats watched as Walcott draped his state-mandated jacket over his shoulders. She wanted to say something positive, something to buck Walcott up, but nothing came. He walked slowly to the glass door of the diner and out into the busy city street. Dats wasn't sure if she would ever see her former partner again.

The waitress arrived with a full pot of coffee. She noticed the money lying on top of the bill. "Did you want some more coffee?" The waitress was in her early twenties with a sweet voice.

"I've got time for another one," Dats said. Walcott had not made a single cringe-worthy remark to their waitress during the whole meal. Dats knew the man walking around in Walcott's skin was not the same man who'd trained her for the last year.

THE FLORIDIAN SUN had crested the horizon a little over an hour ago. A few fluffy clouds dotted the morning sky and the natives would complain about foul weather. After living in New England for most of his life, Matt could find no reason to complain.

He stood in front of a building that had seen hundreds of hours of labor over the past month. He was surrounded by family, friends, and important local figures. Today was the Grand Opening of Matt's mechanic shop, which had a gas station and convenience store attached. The plan involved Matt being the mechanic and Melissa handling the numbers for both shops.

Matt, Melissa, and Shelley were standing together under a large sign covered by a blue tarp. A thin rope ran along the edge of the tarp, coiling down to the ground next to them. Shelly anxiously toyed with the rope.

Behind Matt and his family were the locals, some of whom were elected officials or politically close to them. Matt had applied for a revitalization grant that he had discovered through the internet. Those attending the opening had either proposed the bill or had been early adopters, getting it passed through the legislative branch. The local media had decided to cover the grand opening since Matt's was the first business to open using money from the grant.

The politicians had wanted Matt to deliver the keynote speech, but he was never one for public speaking, so they'd compromised with Matt saying a few thankyous and introducing the mayor, who would deliver the speech. Matt performed this duty then hastily exited the small stage.

After the mayor's speech concluded, Matt gave a subtle hand signal to his daughter that they'd practiced all week. Shelly tugged hard at the rope, but she wasn't strong enough to manage the job with a single pull. She tried again, and after the third failed attempt, Matt moved in to give some assistance. Shelly glared at him, and before he reached her, to everybody's amazement, she yanked the tarp free.

It pulled away to reveal the auto station's sign. A twenty-foot post supported the large frame bearing the legend *Sully's Last Stop* in a fancy font. It was Matt's final homage to their missing friend. If Richard ever passed through, Matt hoped the sign would be a beacon.

After the ceremony, the high noon sun roasted the parking lot of *Sully's Last Stop*. Matt took a private moment for himself after the news crews had finished filming their segment for the afternoon show. He admired his newly unveiled sign as sweat poured off him.

"What's the matter? A little hot out?" Melissa said as she came up behind him.

"I think I might have caught something from one of those politicians."

"You did good today, even if you consider it selling out. We got a lot of free advertising out of it."

Matt chose not to argue the point. Instead, he looked back to the sign and gave voice to the thoughts that had plagued him throughout the day.

"They never found his body," he said.

"The Atlantic is a big ocean."

"He could still be out there, somewhere."

"Maybe. But you know Richard. If he *is* out there, he can handle himself. I know you haven't told me everything about that night, and I'm fine with that. But one thing I do know is Richard can handle himself."

Matt stared at the sign for a while, then turned and directly faced Melissa. "He could still be alive." He felt the need to say the words aloud. He spoke them like a mantra, as if Richard could be brought back from death as long as everyone believed it enough.

"And if Sully ever wanders through these parts, the sign will draw him to us."

"Or if he happens to be in the area now, and watching the news," Melissa said, smiling, "doesn't it make all those handshakes with the slime worth it?"

Matt nodded, now smiling too.

"For Richard," he said, "yeah."

About the Author

SEAN B. CASEY was born and raised just south of Boston, MA. He's worked the slicer of a sub shop and been security at a courthouse for over a decade, but creating stories has always been his passion. That passion for storytelling drove his love for Dungeon Mastering a good campaign, or consuming the latest book, tv show or movie, especially *The Big Lewbowski*. If he is not doing any of that you might be able to find him streaming a video game online. *The Hollow City* is his first novel.

www.seanbcasey.com

www.ingramcontent.com/pod-product-compliance
Lightning Source LLC
Chambersburg PA
CBHW030024180626
46810CB00001B/195